Twisted Threads

Center Point
Large Print

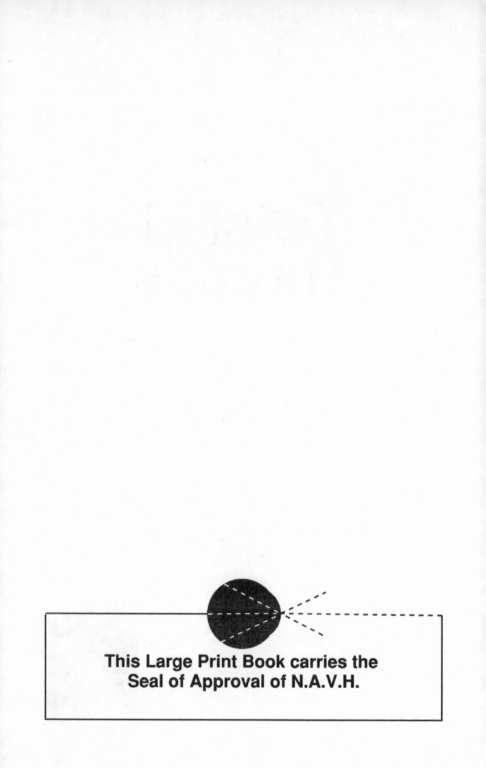

**This Large Print Book carries the
Seal of Approval of N.A.V.H.**

Twisted Threads

Lea Wait

CENTER POINT LARGE PRINT
THORNDIKE, MAINE

This Center Point Large Print edition
is published in the year 2015 by arrangement with
Kensington Publishing Corp.

The text of this Large Print edition is unabridged.
In other aspects, this book may vary
from the original edition.
Printed in the United States of America
on permanent paper.
Set in 16-point Times New Roman type.

ISBN: 978-1-62899-487-2

Library of Congress Cataloging-in-Publication Data

Wait, Lea.
Twisted threads / Lea Wait. — Center Point Large Print edition.
pages cm
Summary: "After leaving a decade ago, Angie returns to her home town
of Harbor Haven, Maine, and the grandmother who raised her following
her mother's disappearance. Her mother has been found, and now the
question of her whereabouts has become a murder mystery. When
another murder occurs, Angie discovers it may have ties to her mother's
cold case"—Provided by publisher.
  ISBN 978-1-62899-487-2 (library binding : alk. paper)
  1. Murder—Fiction. 2. Large type books. I. Title.
PS3623.A42T88 2015
813'.6—dc23
                                                              2014046995

Chapter One

Take your needle, my child, and work at your pattern; it will come out a rose by and by. Life is like that—one stitch taken patiently and the pattern will come out all right like embroidery.
—Oliver Wendell Holmes (1809–1894),
The Autocrat of the Breakfast-Table

The day had already been the sort I wanted to drown in a cold beer or a bubble bath. Preferably both. And that was before I heard Gram's voice, loud and clear as always, coming from my "missed messages."

"Angel, it's time to come home. They've found your mama."

No one in Arizona called me "Angel."

I stared across the small room I'd called home for the past ten years at the stained needlepoint cushion squashed into the corner of my couch. The couch had come from Goodwill. The cushion had come from Gram. It was her last gift before I'd lit out and left the shores of Maine and the comforts of Haven Harbor.

She'd embroidered it in the sea blues and pine greens she knew I loved. And she'd done it quickly, in simple continental stitching and petit point. But in the middle of the design, instead of the lobster or lighthouse or puffin that was usually the center of a pillow she'd designed for the tourist trade, Gram had stitched her phone number.

Large. Complete with 207 area code.

Men who'd come and gone in my life had kidded me about it. "What's that? So you won't forget to call home?"

I'd laughed. Made a joke of it. I never told them why she'd stitched the number there, even though I hadn't called home half as often as I should have.

The number was there in case I was sick, or worse, and police searching my apartment needed to find my next of kin.

Gram wanted me to be found. She hadn't wanted to lose me, as she had Mama.

I pulled my duffel out of the closet and started packing. Wally would have to find someone else to sit surveillance on young Mrs. Juanita Simpson.

Mama had been found. Gram was right. It was time to go home.

At the last minute I decided to take my gun. I wouldn't need it in Haven Harbor, but I had a case for it—and a lock. And I didn't know how long I'd be away. It would be safer to take it with me. My apartment wasn't in the classiest neighborhood. And I'd gotten used to carrying.

Nine hours, two connecting planes, and an expensive taxi ride from Portland later, I walked in the front door of the house where I'd grown up. The one my sea-roving ancestors had built, and my great-grandparents had equipped with bathrooms, a furnace, and a wide front porch. Other than that, it was pretty much the same it'd been in 1807, the year it was built. Weather-worthy and standing tall across from the village green.

"Gram! I'm home." I dropped my bags in the wide front hall and followed my nose to the kitchen, as I always had, noting along the way that the old place could use a coat of paint. There was also a new sign in the front yard, which read MAINELY NEEDLEPOINT, and a section of the living room was now arranged like an office.

Gram had gone commercial on me.

Still, despite the changes she'd made and the reason for my return, I felt my blood pressure dropping as I walked into the kitchen. At least I was calm until something unexpectedly streaked by me and headed for the stairs. My pulse rate soared. Then I realized it was a large yellow coon cat.

Gram didn't live alone now, after all.

I hadn't returned her call, but she'd known I'd come. A tin of my favorite lemon sugar cookies was on the table with a note: *Angel, welcome home. I'm over to the church, arranging her service. Get yourself unpacked. I'll be home soon. Love you.*

I took two cookies. "One for each hand," she'd always told me when I got home from school. Her words popped into my head without my knowing they were still there.

7

I remembered Mama in flashes. Smells. Touches. Laughs. The hollowness after she'd gone.

At least now we'd know where she was. What else would we know? Why she'd left? Whether she'd been dead this whole time?

I hoped Gram, or the police, had the answers.

I finished off the second cookie and headed up the stairs to my room.

Gram hadn't changed it since I'd left. I'd thought I was too smart to do anything as conventional as get married, or go to college, or enroll in beauty school down in Portland, like other girls in my graduating class. Instead, I'd taken the few hundred dollars I'd managed to save up from summers working the steamer at the lobstermen's co-op and headed west. As far as I could get from anyone who knew Angela Curtis, the girl with no dad whose wild mother had disappeared.

I'd gotten as far as Mesa, Arizona, taken a couple of classes at the university there, found class work dull, and ended up working for Wally Combs, a private investigator. Ten years ago it had sounded like exciting work. But turned out investigating meant sitting outside buildings waiting for people to come out, and then snapping pictures of them if they were with people they shouldn't be. Divorces were my boss's bread and butter, so they became mine.

First I worked in the office, deciphering Wally's expense accounts and handling the billing. Then I learned to focus a camera, take notes, be observant, and not fall asleep on overnight stakeouts. Wally liked that, and encouraged me to get a license to carry. I hadn't shot anyone, although I came close one time. In a state where a lot of folks carry—and weren't hunting moose for winter meat—having a gun was almost required when you were young, female, and had a job like mine. Came in handy off the job, too. Single women living alone in my part of town needed all the help they could get.

I never planned to stay in Arizona, though. Summers there are killers, and I missed the sea and the seasons. Whatever I hadn't found at home wasn't in Arizona, either. And a lot of what I learned there I wasn't proud of.

I kept thinking I'd come back to Maine sometime. Show Haven Harbor I'd become more than that betrayed teenager they'd watch struggle to find herself.

Now I had. At least for now. I wasn't ready to commit to more than *now.*

My old room was a time-free zone. The rocks and dried starfish and sea glass and shells I'd found on the shore, and the books I'd pored over to help me name the sea creatures and birds and stars, were still there. My roots were deep in this coast of Maine, wound in the mermaid's hair and rockweed that covers the rocks at low tide.

So deep that my toes were permanently scarred

by gashes from clam and barnacle shells. I'd always refused to wear the old sneakers Gram set aside each year for shore and rock walking, preferring the feel of the rough sands and cold waters on my feet.

Mama used to say I was born at high tide; and when the doctor lifted me up to show me the ocean, I stopped crying. The first thing she'd done when she saw me was kiss the birthmark on my shoulder. She had a matching one on hers. We were linked.

She'd always liked to party more than most, and one night, three weeks before my tenth birthday, she hadn't come home.

There were searches, of course, and police questions, but although kids whispered and pointed, no grown-up said anything directly to me. Not at first. I was too young to understand, they thought. But I knew more than they imagined. I watched people shake their heads and hold their own children closer when I came near. Gram cried at night, sometimes. I could hear her. She could probably hear me, too. But we took one day at a time, just as she said. Some days were rockier than others.

After a while the police stopped looking, so it came down to Gram and me. And we mostly did all right. At least until I was about fifteen. Folks said I took after my mama. Once, when I was wearing a bathing suit that didn't cover much, I heard someone say my birthmark was the mark of Cain. I pretended not to care.

But Haven Harbor wasn't easy on me, and I wasn't easy on Gram. She did her best, but it wasn't enough to change me.

The view out my bedroom window looked past the village and the lighthouse, out to the sea. Nothing there had changed. That's what I'd always loved about it. No matter what happened on land, the sea was always there. Always had been, always would be. Maybe life was like the tides. When I was eighteen, it was my time to go out. Now was my time to come in again.

"Angel! Angel, I know you're home! You get down here so I can see that face of yours!"

Gram. Thank goodness, Gram was still here. Steady and reliable as the sea.

I couldn't get to the staircase fast enough.

Chapter Two

Light or fancy needlework often forms a portion of the evening's recreation for the ladies of the household, although this may be varied by an occasional game at chess or backgammon.

—Mrs. Isabella Beeton,
The Book of Household Management, 1861

"Angel! You're skinny as a razor clam. Didn't you eat out there in Arizona? And you've cut your hair." Gram held me at arm's length, which wasn't far, since she was several inches shorter than I was. I grinned and looked her over, too.

"I'm not eighteen anymore, either," I agreed, laughing. "And, let's see—how have you changed?"

She brushed me off. "I'm just the same. Your old Gram. I don't change. Now set yourself down. You must be exhausted and hungry. Did you fly all night?"

"Pretty much. Slept some on the planes, though."

Gram had changed, too. Her balance of gray hair and brown now tipped toward gray; she was a bit heftier than she'd been ten years ago; a few more lines had appeared on her hands and around her eyes. Mainers' idea of skin care was wearing a

Red Sox cap if you were going to be on the water all day, and slathering on Wool Wax Creme in winter, a potion fishermen used to keep their hands from cracking in frigid salt water. Worked pretty well on dry land, too. And the only hand cream you could pick up at the same place you bought your flounder fillets or haddock pieces for chowder.

I hadn't thought about Wool Wax Creme in years.

Arizona women had permanently tanned skin, bought expensive moisturizers by the gallon, and compared Botox sources. Wearing sunblock was one of the healthier habits I'd picked up in my years away.

Gram was still talking, but had already put two bowls on the table and started ladling out chowder. "I didn't know exactly when you'd get in, so I cooked up a pot yesterday with extra bacon and a touch of sherry, just the way you like it. Figured it'd be easy to heat up when you got here."

"And better the second day," we chorused together.

The yellow cat had smelled the fish. She meowed and rubbed against Gram's ankles.

"I see you have a new friend," I said. "Scared me half out of my wits when I came in. She's a beauty. I haven't seen a Maine coon cat in years."

"Her name's Juno, because she demands that I wait on her like she was a goddess. You should have seen her when she first got here. A scrawny stray trying to keep warm in the barn." Juno meowed loudly. "All right, all right. I'll stop my talking and give you some fish."

Gram spooned a piece into a bowl on the floor, which was clearly Juno's. The fish was gone before Gram'd sat down again.

"Mmm. I've missed your chowder," I said, lowering my spoon into the bowl that was swirling with melted butter, mixed with just enough cream and broth and seasonings to turn potatoes and haddock and bacon into a feast. "And lobsters—remember when I said I never wanted to smell another lobster after steaming thousands every summer? Well, I've missed those, too. And some days I'd die for a decent fried clam. Fresh, lightly battered . . ." I took a spoonful of chowder and almost inhaled it. "Fantastic. Nobody makes chowder like yours."

Gram sat with a smaller bowl and smiled, relishing my enjoyment. "It's starting with lobster broth that makes the difference." She tasted a spoonful herself, and then passed me the bowl of oyster crackers. "Lord knows, I've missed you, Angel. It's been a quiet house all these years with you gone."

"I saw the sign outside and the living room. You haven't been sitting around mourning my absence. We need to get caught up. But, first, tell me about Mama."

14

"I figured you'd want all the details, and might as well hear them from the expert. State's reopening her case. So, after you finish your chowder, you call the trooper in charge of the investigation. He'll tell you what's happening. He wants to ask you a few questions, anyway."

I nodded. "Fine. I want to do that as soon as possible."

"Thought you would." Gram slid a business card across the table. "He knows you'll be calling. His office is up near Augusta, but he'll be in Haven Harbor today and tomorrow because of the memorial service."

"That's when the service is? Tomorrow?" Gram had sure been confident I'd come home right away.

"Late tomorrow morning. It's been a lot of years, but some folks still remember her. And when she was found, it was all over the papers and on the TV. A few will come because of that."

I shuddered. "Curiosity seekers. The service should have been private. After all these years . . ."

"The police wanted an open service. Said it might encourage someone who'd have infor- mation to come forward. You ask the trooper. He'll explain."

I reached over and read the card. Twice. "Is this . . . the same Ethan Trask who used to live here in the Harbor?"

"Same fellow. I wondered if you'd remember

15

him. He was a few years older than you, as I recall."

Four years, three months, and six days. Ethan Trask. Quite possibly the most gorgeous boy to ever walk the halls of Haven Harbor High. The year I was twelve I'd followed him around like a sick puppy until he and his friends noticed the awkward kid always finding an excuse to walk past his house or browse at his father's hardware store when he was working a shift there. Thinking back, they could have been meaner—boys my own age treated me like dirt, or lower, because of Mama—but Ethan's laughter was the first that hurt. It sent me into hiding until he and his pals left town for wider horizons. And I grew up, and a couple of years later learned more direct ways to get boys' attention.

"I remember him."

"Well, he's turned out all right. He's a detective with the Maine State Troopers, and in charge of your mama's case. Lives over to Hallowell now, he said."

Maybe he wouldn't remember me.

"You can reach him at his cell phone number. He told me to tell you that. And if you want to talk with Lauren, her number's on the wall by the phone."

"Lauren?"

"You remember Lauren? She was in your class in school, or one grade ahead? Lauren Greene she was then. She married Caleb Decker, so she's Lauren Decker now, and she waitresses over to the Harbor Haunts Café."

"Why would I want to see her? We were friends for a while in third and fourth grade, but not after that." Everything had changed after Mama left. Including who wanted to be my friend.

"Well, Lauren's been working with me, so I've gotten closer to her recently. Maybe I've forgotten what it was like when you were both girls. You took after your mama. You never talked much about your friends. But the reason I thought you might want to talk with her is, Lauren's the one found your mama's body."

Chapter Three

Women were major founders of the American abolitionist movement. One way they raised money was through antislavery fairs where they sold pen wipers embroidered with "wipe out the blot of slavery," needlework bags embroidered with a black man being lashed, and linens with the motto, "May the points of our needles prick the slaveholders' consciences."

Gram was right. Ethan Trask had sure turned out fine.

He was taller, broader, and even better-looking than I remembered him, and his pressed state trooper's uniform didn't hurt the image any. Despite our shared history and the current circumstances, I was sorely tempted to flirt a little. After all, Mama'd been gone nineteen years. I wasn't exactly in mourning. Unfortunately for me, the wide gold band on the third finger of Ethan's left hand was as clear as a stop sign. I'd promised myself I'd show Haven Harbor a new, mature Angela Curtis. Prove to them, and to me, I wasn't the same girl I'd been. I played it straight with Ethan.

"Sorry to bother you on your first day back, Angie. Is it all right if I call you 'Angie'?"

I nodded, probably looking as dumb as I felt. He'd smiled and I'd reverted to my seventh-grade self.

"Your mother's disappearance was filed as a cold case until Lauren Decker found her body, and Haven Harbor's in my district. There's a home court advantage theory at headquarters when it comes to territories. They figure a homicide detective should know his or her hometown better than anyone else, so we get assigned cases close to where we grew up."

"Guess it makes sense." I shrugged. Why he was on this case wasn't my issue, so long as he knew his stuff. He could tell his troubles to his wife. "Gram hasn't told me where Mama was found, or how. She said you'd do that. I want to know everything."

"It's a little unusual, but not complicated. You remember Lauren Decker?"

"Used to be Lauren Greene."

"Right. Her parents, Nelly and Joe Greene, ran Greene's Bakery in town here for years." He grinned and leaned a little toward me. "I'll bet you remember those great gingerbread cookies they used to have at Christmastime, and the birthday cakes they baked for parties in town."

"I remember." I leaned back. I remembered Mr. Greene, especially. And not for his gingerbread men. But this was Ethan Trask's story, and I didn't know where it was going, or how friendly I should be, considering I wasn't the same girl who'd left town. Although no one here knew that. Towns have long memories.

"Anyway, after Nelly died, a few years back, Joe closed the bakery. Retired. Sold out to a young couple from Quebec, who bake French bread and croissants and pastries and are open Sundays. Joe died—cancer, it was—last New Year's. Left every-thing to Lauren, of course, since she was his only kid. Well, she's been going through the house and barn and shed, deciding what she wants to keep and whatever. She found a key and a history of monthly bills for a self-storage unit over at Union."

I frowned. "Union? That's a distance."

"That's what she thought. And Joe'd left the barn and shed packed with old equipment from the business, and who knows what else, so she had her hands full. She didn't take the time to go to Union right away. Not till last week, actually."

I could see it coming. "And she found?"

"The storage locker was one of those climate-controlled ones, so there was electricity. An old freezer chest was in there. Plugged in." He was watching me closely, looking into my eyes, as though judging my reactions. They probably taught that in state trooper school. "There was a body in it."

I thought I was prepared. But, somehow, I hadn't been prepared for that.

20

"She was . . . frozen? All this time?"

"She had been. Off and on. But there'd been power outages, or the bills hadn't been paid some months. The medical examiner said it was hard to tell exactly when she died. But, yes, we're guessing she'd been there since shortly after she disappeared." He paused. "The ME identified her through her dental records."

I sat at the kitchen table, looking at Ethan, but part of me was floating somewhere else, watching us. "She didn't die naturally, did she? She was murdered." It seemed obvious, but I wanted to hear it, straight out.

"She was murdered."

"How?"

He shifted a little, as though he found the old kitchen chair uncomfortable. "Sure you want to know?"

"I'm sure."

"She was shot. In the back of her head. The bullet came from a handgun, not a rifle."

In the back. A coward's way. I pressed my hands together. Hard. I couldn't help the picture in my mind of the soft blond curls Mama was so proud of, soaked in blood. And brains.

"The obvious assumption would be that Joe Greene killed her and hid her body in the freezer," Ethan continued.

"And left the locker key so his daughter would find the body after he was dead?" I couldn't help being dubious about that assumption.

"Hell of an inheritance," Joe agreed. "But all we have to go on. It was nineteen years ago." He looked into my eyes, as though searching for an answer there. "Before we close the case on Joe, we'd like to have a motive."

"What about DNA? Were there traces anyone else'd been in the storage unit?"

"We're having it checked. Lauren found enough of Joe's things—hairbrush, toothbrush—for us to isolate his DNA. We expect to find his, of course. If anyone else's shows up, that will be a bonus."

I nodded.

"I'm talking to everyone who was around when your mother disappeared. According to the files, the officer on the case didn't interview you."

"Gram didn't want anyone upsetting me. She thought I was too young to be involved in the investigation." I paused and looked down at my clenched hands. I deliberately unfolded them.

"Do you remember much about that time?"

The room was silent except for the ticking of Gram's old wall clock. "I remember the day she disappeared."

Ethan pulled out his notebook. "Do you mind talking now? The sooner, the better—so far as I'm concerned."

"I don't think I know anything that will help you. I've gone over and over that day thousands of times in my mind, and I haven't made any sense of it. No clues that would lead to what happened to her."

"Your grandmother told me you've been working for a private investigator near Phoenix."

"So you think I'd know what might be important. What you might be looking for."

"Maybe. Maybe not. I'm hoping I can put something you remember together with something someone else remembers and it will all suddenly make sense."

The man was dreaming.

"Or maybe Joe Greene shot your mother and hid her body in a freezer and we'll never know why."

"I need to know what happened." I'd been waiting to know since I was nine. Wondering if Mama had run away with someone. Run away from me. Run away from Haven Harbor—and her past.

"I'm sure Lauren would like to know, too," said Joe softly. "Right now half the town thinks her father was a murderer."

"Go ahead. Ask your questions." I'd already decided I'd tell him the truth. But not the whole truth. The whole truth was mine, and, at least for now, I didn't see the use in sharing it.

"Where were you living when your mother disappeared?"

"You already know that. Here, in this house. Mama and I lived with Gram."

"Be patient with me. I have to confirm what the records show. Had you always lived here?"

"When I was two or three, Mama and I lived in Portland for about a year with one of her boyfriends, but that didn't work out, so we came back to Haven Harbor. Another time we moved in with a girlfriend of hers, across town, for a few months. Then we came home here again. I don't remember much about those times."

"What was the name of the boyfriend?"

"I don't remember. I was just a toddler, and I don't think Mama saw him again after that."

"And the woman she lived with?"

"Cynthia Raye. She moved back to Boston to get married. She sent Christmas cards every year."

"So, what was a day like in this house those last few months when your mother was still alive? You were . . . nine?"

"Almost ten. Gram made sure I woke up on time in the morning and got dressed and ready for school. Mama worked late and slept late."

"And after school?"

"I came straight home most days. Gram would be here. She always had cookies or popcorn or a sandwich waiting for me." It was all so clear in my mind. As though I'd never left.

"What about your mother?"

"She wasn't here much in the afternoons. She waitressed at different restaurants. In summer, when the tourists were here, she was busy all the time. She was either sleeping or working. But in the fall and winter, when I was in school, sometimes she worked and sometimes she didn't, depending on what days the restaurants were open, and whether she had a job. Sometimes in the afternoon she was out with friends." Others in town would be saying worse about Mama. I was reciting facts.

"Did she have a lot of friends?"

"Yes."

"Men or women friends?"

I hesitated. "Both. If you're asking if she had boyfriends, then, yes, she had boyfriends."

"Did she stay out late at night?"

"She was a waitress, and I was nine. I was usually asleep when she got home. It seemed late to me."

"Did she ever bring any of those friends home with her? Or to spend the night?"

"Not to spend the night. Gram wouldn't have allowed that."

"But you did meet some of her friends."

All those uncles: Uncle Paul, Uncle Richard, Uncle Bill, Uncle Louis. "Yes. Sometimes they'd meet her here. Or she'd take me with her when she went out, say, to Funtown, or to the Maine Wildlife Park in Gray, or to Reid State Park."

"Do you remember any of their names?"

"I never knew their last names. It was so long

ago. They all blur together. And I only met a few of them."

"And what do you remember the last day you saw her?"

I could see her, so clearly. "She was wearing a yellow dress and an orange scarf and really high heels and she smelled good. It was Sunday afternoon. Gram had taken me to Sunday school in the morning, and she and I were making oatmeal raisin cookies, right here, in the kitchen. Mama came in and picked me up and swung me around and said, 'The world is a beautiful place! No matter what happens to you, Angel, don't ever stop being strong. I'm always on your side. Remember that, Angel! Always remember that!' Then she turned and said, 'You're going to be terrific at the fly-up ceremony. I can't wait to see you.' Then she left. She didn't come home that night. Or the next morning. Or the next. Then, I think it was Wednesday, Gram called the police."

"Angie, was Joe Greene one of your mother's boyfriends?"

Whatever I said on that topic was going to sound wrong. "Mama had a lot of friends. Mr. Greene liked her. He used to give her extra cookies at the bakery when his wife wasn't looking." That was true. One hundred percent true.

Ethan smiled at me. "Your mother was a very pretty woman. I remember her. I'm not surprised he gave her extra cookies. But do you know if she ever saw him socially—late at night, or outside the bakery?"

I shook my head. "She went out with a lot of friends. She didn't tell me who they all were." I looked Ethan straight in the eye. "If I knew who shot my mother, don't you think I'd tell you?"

He paused. "Yes. I believe you would. So you don't have any memories that would confirm—or deny—that Joe Greene had any reason to kill your mother?"

"I don't have any memories of seeing them together except at the bakery." Truth. Absolute truth.

"Was your mother afraid of anything, Angie?"

I shook my head. "If she was, she didn't show it. I never saw her afraid of anything. Or anyone. How long will it take to get those DNA results?"

Ethan shrugged. "It's a cold case, so there's no rush. It could take weeks." He closed his notebook. "If you think of any other details that might help, let me know. You have my number."

I looked down at his card. "I have your number."

Chapter Four

All my scattering moments are taken up with my needle.

—Ellen Birdseye Wheaton (1816–1858), abolitionist and women's rights crusader, 1851

Dinner was more chowder, which was fine with me. Juno again demanded her share of the haddock, and Gram added a piece to her dish. Coon cats are naturally large, but Juno exceeded size expectations. No wonder she'd startled me.

I was beginning to wear down. The travel, the time change, being back in Maine, hearing about Mama . . . the past thirty hours or so included a lot to get my head around.

"Have you got any wine or beer?" I asked Gram, on the off chance she had a bottle put away somewhere. She'd added sherry to the chowder, after all.

"Wine's in a rack in the dining room. I should've thought of that earlier. You can bring me a glass of red," she said.

Gram? A glass of red? Something else had changed since I'd left.

I chose a bottle of pinot noir, noted that Gram didn't have bad taste in varietals, poured each of us a generous glass, and returned to the kitchen. Juno followed my every step, almost tripping me as she rubbed against my legs. I'd have to get used to having a cat. But I could see how she'd be company for Gram. The house was quiet.

"When was a wine rack added to the décor?" I asked as we clinked glasses.

"After you left. When you were a teenager, I didn't want to add any more temptations to your world. You were coping with enough as it was," said Gram. "But I do enjoy a glass in the afternoon, and after the day you've had, I suspect you could do with a glass or two yourself."

"And then a bath and bed," I agreed. "Especially with the service tomorrow. I want to hear a little about your business, though. I saw the Mainely Needlepoint sign when I came in, and the desk and file cabinets in the living room."

"As you assumed, I'm now a working gal." Gram shook her head. "What you can't see is that I've gotten myself in over my head. You remember those little needlepoint balsam pillows I used to make for Betty down to Harbor Lights?"

"You were always after me to learn needlepoint so I could help with the backgrounds, but I was too impatient. This house used to smell of balsam in the winter when you were putting them together."

"Right. Since they were hand stitched, they were high-end . . . a world away from those printed pine cushions tourists buy at souvenir shops to tuck in their sweater drawers. Every summer Harbor Lights sold several dozen of the ones I stitched showing our local lighthouse. Making them up kept me amused, gave me something to do each winter. Brought in a few extra dollars, and kept my fingers busy."

"As though your fingers were ever empty! You were always either knitting or doing needlepoint." The wine was beginning to relax me. I got the bottle from the dining room and refilled both my glass and Gram's. "So? You're still making balsam pillows?"

"Just you listen. You asked, so you'll hear. A few years back a bride-to-be, who summers here, saw my pillows at Harbor Lights and asked if I'd make up a special order for her. She wanted seventy-five balsam pillows needlepointed in white on dark green, with the date of her wedding and a pine tree, to give as favors at her wedding."

"Seventy-five? That's a winter's work!"

"Exactly. But she was paying well. Twice as much as Harbor Lights, and she was paying me directly, so there'd be no commission. It seemed too good a deal to pass up. So I asked around, and Ruth Hopkins and Dave Percy both agreed to do some up for me. We thought it would be fun, and it was. The three of us got her order done over the winter, along with the usual pillows I did for Harbor Lights." Gram took a deep sip of her wine. "We thought when we delivered her pillows, the project would be over. We never dreamed what would happen next."

"Which was?"

"Turned out one of the guests at the wedding was an editor at one of those magazines aimed at Maine tourists. He included a picture of one of the pillows in his column and wrote about what a unique gift idea it was. Next thing we knew, we were overwhelmed with orders from all over."

"That's fantastic!" I said. "You must have been thrilled!"

" 'Not so much,' as you young folks would say," said Gram. "I couldn't stitch near fast enough to fill all the orders, even with help from Ruth and Dave. So the three of us had a serious meeting and decided to go into business. We called ourselves 'Mainely Needlepoint,' as you saw on the sign. A little cutesy, if you ask me, but Ruth and Dave liked it, and it did say right out what we did. We started calling up friends in town who did needlepoint and asked if they'd help. And they called other folks. That second year we went from three of us to seven, all handy at needlepoint, who agreed to fill orders."

"I'm impressed! Gram, you're a needlework queen!"

She shook her head. "For the first four years I worked with the customers, taking orders, and then giving out assignments. Some people thought Mainely Needlepoint was a factory—that in a few days we could turn out forty pillows or place mats or whatever they were looking for. Took a while to make sure they understood how long it would take to fill their orders. And even then, a few of 'em changed their minds halfway through and decided they wanted green lettering on a red field for a Christmas gift, instead of blue on white for a birthday. After that happened two or three times, I learned to ask for fifty percent in advance, and have 'em sign a contract saying what we'd be doing for 'em and when the order would be delivered. That helped considerable, although some customers still needed hand-holding, as it were, even if they lived in California or Iowa or some such place. A lot of phone calls. E-mails. And that's not counting ordering supplies and billing and talking to people at gift shops. And making sure everyone's work was on schedule."

"How did you ever find the time to do the needlepoint yourself?"

"Every year I did less. I missed the stitching, but keeping the books in order and the customers happy had to be done. That's when Jacques Lattimore approached me."

"Approached you?"

"Just showed up on my doorstep, all dressed up like he was going to church, and offered to help us. I didn't know him from Adam, but he'd admired our work down in one of those fancy home-furnishing stores in Portland. The owner got to telling him about Mainely Needlepoint, and how it was run by"—Gram pursed her lips a bit—"an old woman and her friends. The way Jacques tells it, he thought we were all sitting on our graves, and he'd better buy the needlepoint piece he liked—one of Dave Percy's wall hangings, of a four-master—because work like that wasn't done much anymore. Anyway, he bought the wall hanging. But he also found out Mainely Needlepoint was in Haven Harbor, and he came calling. He told me he traveled up and down the coast of Maine, as far as Vermont and Massachusetts, and he knew a lot of decorators. That if we could do custom work for them—wall hangings or pillows that would match upholstery or paintings—he could sell our work for twice, maybe three times, as much as we were asking. He'd take a commission—forty percent, he said—to cover his salary and expenses, and he'd bring us the orders, and take care of the customers and the paper-work. I'd still figure out who had the time to do the stitching, and once a month he'd stop here to pick up the finished work and deliver our money."

"When did this happen?"

"About two years ago. It was mud season, because I remember asking him to take off his shoes afore coming into the house. The ones he had on were leather, no waterproofing at all, and looked as though he'd walked through a pigsty before he came here."

"And you agreed with his plan?"

"I told him I'd talk with the others, but they didn't much care. I was the one he'd be helping out and working with. We figured if he took forty percent, that would leave ten percent extra for me, since I'd still be fronting orders for silk or wool and canvas and whatever else was needed, and the person doing the stitching would get fifty percent. In my case, I'd get sixty, which sounded real good to me."

"So . . . you agreed." I sensed Gram was coming to the problem part of her story.

"We did. And at first it seemed to be working. We'd been doing more and more needlepoint, and getting bored with the same patterns. There's a limit to how many lobsters and lighthouses a person wants to stitch and stay sane. Jacques got us contracts for floral designs to match wallpaper, and monograms, and once even a pair of bedroom cushions to reflect the pattern in a painting. Much more challenging work than we'd been doing, and more of it. We invested in software to help design new patterns. We weren't getting paid as much as Jacques originally said we would, but he kept saying that would come as our reputation increased."

I nodded, sipping, and hoping Gram would get to the point of the story. The wine was beginning to make me drowsy.

"But, Angel, it hasn't. Truth is, he hasn't paid us

34

anything for more than three months now, and only a fraction of what he owed us for the two months before that. And my stitchers are depending on his checks. Lauren's husband is furious with her for not contributing her usual share to their budget. And Ob Winslow had stopped doing his wood carving and doesn't have another source of winter income. They need the money they're due."

I put down my wineglass. I may have been away for a while, but I hadn't forgotten how much people in Haven Harbor depended on their second or third jobs—their crafts or jams or Christmas wreaths in December or blueberry sales in July—to get through the year. Haven Harbor was based on a tourist economy. When the tourists left for warmer climes, so did their dollars.

"What have you done about it, Gram?"

"Called the man and complained, of course. But it doesn't seem to be doing any good. Now he doesn't return my calls. And when I decided to contact our customers directly, I realized I don't even know who most of them are anymore. Jacques put himself in the middle, and by doing that, we had no way of going around him."

"That doesn't sound good."

"It's not. And I'm the one who got everyone into this, so I'm feeling ten times as bad than if it were just me in trouble. If Mainely Needlepoint fails, I'll have taken my friends and neighbors down with me."

We sat for a few minutes, sipping wine, looking at each other across the kitchen table. I felt as though I should have my algebra homework in front of me and Gram should be knitting a pair of mittens, or, yes, stitching a small pillow for Harbor Lights Gifts. We'd sat in these same chairs so many nights, so many years.

"I can help." In the past those had been Gram's words. It was time they were mine.

"What can you do? Much as I tried to teach you, you were never much good at even a basic outline or continental stitch."

"And that's the truth. At needlepoint I was a disaster. But since I left home, I've learned a few other skills. I'm not a bad private investigator."

"Don't you need a license to do that sort of thing, Angie? And isn't it dangerous?"

"To be an official PI, sure, you need a license. And I promise I won't do anything dangerous. I'll just find out what this Jacques Lattimore is doing. Find out where he is, and why he hasn't paid you the money you should be getting. I've done jobs like that lots of times before. I'm here. I might as well see if I can do something to help."

"I don't want my concerns to be a trouble to you."

"Investigating Lattimore wouldn't be a trouble. Besides, after all you've done for me? That's the least I can do. You wouldn't want me to sit around here and be bored while Ethan Trask investigates

36

Mama's death." Wally would have a fit if he'd known what I'd just agreed to do. No one but a licensed investigator or the police should do what I'd promised Gram.

Gram looked at me, smiled, and shook her head. "Angel, you may have changed some when you were out in the world. But there's one thing you have never done in your entire life."

"What?"

"Never in your entire life have you sat around anyplace long enough to be bored."

For the first time in a long, long time, I laughed. Life in Haven Harbor might not be perfect, but, yes, I was home.

Chapter Five

And he made a hanging for the tabernacle door of blue, and purple, and scarlet, and fine twined linen, of needlework.

—Exodus 36:37

I gave myself the luxury of sleeping a little late the next morning, making up for what I'd missed the day (and night) before. By the time I'd gotten up and put on "something decent and respectful" for Mama's service, Gram'd been answering calls for a couple of hours and arranged that no one would come back to the house after the service. "It's been too long in the past for that sort of mourning." Instead, the Ladies' Guild would serve coffee and cake in the "family room" of the church, where receptions were held after Sunday services.

She fried me a couple of eggs, defrosted one of the blueberry lemon muffins she'd made last summer, handed me a cup of weak instant coffee, and inspected me to make sure I didn't look too "citified." After suggesting my heels were "a mite higher than necessary," and making sure my stomach was filled to her satisfaction, she handed me a large straw hat that looked more appropriate for a July picnic than a May funeral.

Then she announced, "We'll go out the back way and take my car."

I looked at her. "Why not walk?" It was only a few blocks to the Congregational Church our family, and most of those in Haven Harbor, attended, although about 150 years ago the town had graciously acknowledged the presence of Methodists and Baptists in its midst and there was even a Catholic Church in the next town down the coast. (You had to go farther to find a synagogue or mosque, but Maine had those now, too.)

"Angie, have you looked out one of our front windows this morning?"

I started toward the front of the house.

She cut me off at the hall.

"Well, if you haven't done it yet, then don't! We're hemmed in by press and media folks from Portland and Augusta and Bangor. Can't believe you didn't notice. They've been staked out for hours, trying to get a peek at the bereaved family of the woman found in the freezer. There'll be less chance of them sticking a microphone in our faces if we go out the back. There's a parking space saved for us next to the side door of the church."

I peeked around the drapes she'd closed over the hall's front windows. It wasn't the crowd there'd have been for Angelina Jolie and Brad Pitt, but at least two networks had brought trucks, and a handsome young man was broadcasting live from our front yard. Amazing. This must be a very slow news day in Maine.

For the first time in my life, I saw the wisdom of Gram's insisting I wear a hat.

"Don't look 'em in the eye," she was advising. "Walk fast, keep walking till you get in the car. Keep your hat down so they can't see your face. Don't look out the car window. Scrunch down. Me, they've already seen, but you're a novelty around these parts. Pete Lambert from the police department is out there. He'll make sure we get out the drive."

I looked at her with increasing respect. "You've done this before."

"First time was when your mother disappeared. But it wasn't as bad in those days, and I managed to keep you away from most of it. But ever since Lauren found that body, those TV folks have been all over the place. They want us to be crying or screaming or doing something else dramatic for them." She shook her head. "Harrumph. We're civilized folks. We're not putting on that kind of show here in Haven Harbor."

I'd never before credited Gram with press savvy. "Got it. Low heels on, hat pulled down, and look down or straight ahead."

She patted my arm. "Good girl. And keep your knees together in that short skirt. No reason our problems need to be carrion to be feasted on by those media maggots."

I wasn't sure whether to giggle or salute. I put on the hat.

The drive to the church went exactly as Gram planned: out the door, into the car, help from Sergeant Lambert to get through the hordes, and then a swift push on the gas pedal to get us up the hill to the side of the church, where the current minister greeted us with an open door and ushered us into his office, safe from prying eyes. I had the distinct feeling that he found aiding and abetting pseudo-celebrities pretty exciting.

"Miss Curtis?" He put out his hand. "Reverend McCully. I'm sorry we meet under such sad circumstances. May I offer you a cup of tea or coffee while you wait?"

"No, thank you," I said. "But I appreciate your help this morning." He wasn't as old as the ministers I remembered. He was about my height, about ten years younger than Gram, and not bad-looking. I wondered if he was married. I'd never dated a minister.

"No trouble—no trouble at all." He turned to Gram. "Charlotte, it's all going to be very simple, just as you wanted. No coffin or urn."

I suddenly realized: a body. Of course. Some-where there was whatever was left of Mama. I hadn't considered that fact before. If the morning's events had seemed a bit surreal before, now they were very real.

Gram nodded. This wasn't new to her. She

and the reverend had arranged the service.

"The picture of Jenny and the flowers you ordered are at the front of the church. A few other people sent flowers, too." He handed her a list. She glanced at it, nodded, and tucked it in her pocketbook. "I'll say a prayer and give a short statement, then we'll sing the hymns you requested. After that, I'll ask if anyone else wants to speak." He turned to me. "Perhaps you'd like to say a few words, Miss Curtis?"

I didn't remember the last time I'd been to anyone's funeral. I hadn't thought of speaking, and hadn't prepared any words. I shook my head. "No, I don't think so."

"Well, if you should change your mind, there'll be an opportunity. Under these circumstances, with the police present, it will be a short service."

"The police are here?" I blurted. "Inside the church?"

"Ethan Trask said he'd come, and I suspect one or more of the local force will be here, too," Gram said quietly. "It's part of the investigation. Just in case—"

"In case anyone jumps up and says they shot Mama?" I said. I looked from one of them to the other. "I thought most of the town figured Joe Greene shot her."

Neither Gram nor Reverend McCully said anything. Then the reverend volunteered, "Miss Curtis, you've been away for years. I know this is difficult for you. And, of course, you're right. But the police want to confirm that Joe Greene is the guilty party, and, if possible, find a reason for what he did. Some here in town take issue with that. They find it difficult to believe their old friend was guilty of murder. He was well liked, you know. Very well liked. Chamber of Commerce president. Active in the church." He hesitated. "And there's no proof."

"No proof? They found Mama's body in a freezer in his storage unit."

"True enough," agreed the reverend as he put on a long black robe, which had been hanging behind his office door. "But Joe's not here to defend himself. He's innocent until proven guilty. I hope Ethan Trask and his team are trying to keep open minds about the investigation, at least until they find more evidence."

I looked from Gram to Reverend McCully and back again. "But aren't they? When Ethan said he was assigned to investigate the case, he sounded as though he was treating Mama's murder as an open homicide investigation. He wasn't just going to dot the *i*'s and cross the *t*'s."

"Perhaps not that open, dear," said Gram. "But I believe he'll do the best he can. The town *is* divided. Some people are convinced Joe Greene couldn't be the murderer. Others believe there's no doubt he was. Ethan's under pressure to find more evidence that Joe killed your mother, or come up with another killer. Neither option will be easy after nineteen years."

Mama was dead. Joe Greene was dead. But, clearly, the dead weren't going to rest in peace. Not yet.

Yesterday I'd told Ethan I wanted to understand what happened to Mama. But maybe I knew enough.

Now he was going to dig everything up again. Digging unearths dirt and mud. I'd worked hard to wash away that dirt and mud, all those years ago.

Right that minute, sitting in my funeral clothes in Reverend McCully's office, all I could think about was how fast I could get out of Haven Harbor.

How fast I could get away from whatever Ethan Trask might find out. Away from reporters with television cameras and microphones. Away from memories I'd managed to repress while I was in Arizona.

I never should have come back. I'd made a mistake. Gram had been doing fine without me.

"Before we go in, Tom, let me tell you some good news," Gram was saying. "You remember I told you Mainely Needlepoint was having a problem with our agent?"

"Of course, I remember," said the reverend. "Jacques Lattimore—that scoundrel should be in jail!"

"Well, we've made a big step toward solving our

problem," she confided, reaching out proudly and touching my arm. "Angie has a lot of experience in private investigations, and she's volunteered to check him out for us. Once we know more about what we're dealing with, we'll be able to go forward."

"That's wonderful, Charlotte," said Reverend McCully, beaming. "Maybe it was fated that Jenny's body would be found now, so Angie would come home when you needed her."

"It was," said Gram. "And a blessing." She smiled at me as though I'd just been named savior of Haven Harbor.

How much could Ethan find out, anyway? It had all happened so long ago.

And I didn't have to stay in Maine forever. I'd stay just long enough to find out about that man —Jacques Lattimore—who wasn't paying up. I owed that to Gram.

Then I'd get out of town.

Chapter Six

From 1887 until 1930 American women fond of needlework of all sorts subscribed to *The Modern Priscilla*, a monthly sixteen-page magazine featuring embroidery, crochet and knitting patterns, recipes, and decorating ideas. During World War I it featured simple patterns for gloves and socks to be sent to soldiers, and ways to stretch household budgets while still supporting the war efforts. Copies of *The Modern Priscilla* may be found today on eBay, at paper and ephemera shows, and in used bookstores.

Light streamed through the tall glass windows on both sides of the church, and more floral arrangements than I'd expected lined the front. Gram's friends must have sent them. Sadly, Mama was best remembered not for her life, but for her disappearance and death.

She would have loved the attention she was getting today.

Gram and I'd been seated in the front pew, almost on top of the flowers. They smelled sickly sweet, like incense in one of those New Age stores where you can have your palm read and buy crystals and angel ornaments. The kind of place

Mama would have laughed about. Although the day I'd taken my First Communion in this church, she'd given me a small gold angel on a chain, "to keep you safe."

Even then, I'd questioned its powers, but it was my first piece of jewelry. After she'd disappeared, I'd worn it all the time. Each time the thin gold chain had broken, I'd replaced it. As the reverend went on about families and love that had no end, I reached up and held the angel for a moment before slipping it down inside the top of my dress.

Mama might not have had what others would call "religious faith," but she'd believed in herself, and in me. When times had been tough during the past ten years, I'd worn the angel, and somehow felt that wherever Mama was, she was looking out for me. Sappy, I know. But it helped.

Gram, on the other hand, had always attended services. When I'd been little she'd taken me with her. We'd sat here together at the beginning of the service, until the children would be called forward to hear a brief message and then be herded to the family room for Sunday school to draw pictures of Noah's Ark or cut out snowflakes for the church's Christmas tree.

After Mama disappeared, I'd refused to come. People stared and went out of their way to be kind to me. I'd hated that. I didn't want to be pointed out, to be known as "that poor girl whose mother deserted her. Although you know her mother . . .

so maybe it was for the best." School was bad enough, but church was worse. All their good intentions did was remind me I was known for Mama's life. Not my own.

But despite my not attending services for years, this was the church I'd always pictured when, like every little girl, I'd dreamed of walking down the aisle in a white dress, seeing at the altar a man who'd love me forever.

Had Mama ever imagined a day when she'd wear a white dress and the sun would shine through those tall, clear windows onto her life? She'd never said. And she'd disappeared before I was old enough to ask her all the questions I'd had over the years. Today the flowers at the altar were in memory, despite Reverend McCully's words about "the celebration of her life."

I hoped some of her dreams had come true. But who dreams of being pregnant when you graduate from high school, and then living with your mother and flirting for tips from men who sometimes followed you home after they'd had a few too many?

No. That couldn't be anyone's dream.

It certainly wasn't mine.

What was mine? I wasn't sure. But I knew it wasn't my mother's life. Or death.

The service was brief. Reverend McCully read a few verses, and we sang "I Would Be True" and "Amazing Grace," Mama's favorite hymns, in quavering off-key voices. That was it. No one stood up to talk about her.

After the service we walked the few steps to the family room, where I'd eaten many Saturday-night church suppers. True to Haven Harbor form, today the ladies of the church had filled a long table with cookies and cakes and small sand-7wiches. A woman I didn't know handed me a plastic glass full of sickly-sweet fruit punch.

I wasn't thirsty, but I accepted it. No one would try to hug me while I held a glass of punch.

I smiled and nodded as people came up to me and said the required words: "We're so sorry"; "Such a sad ending to the story"; "Good to see you back in town"; "You look wonderful"; "Your grandmother is so proud of you"; "You look just like your mother did at your age."

When she'd been my age, my mother had been the town slut. When she was my age, my mother had been shot and put in a freezer.

I kept smiling.

After the first dozen greetings I forced myself to pay attention to who these people actually were. No one from the media had been allowed in, thank goodness. Ethan Trask was standing in the back of the room. As our eyes met, he nodded slightly. But he wasn't munching cookies or sipping punch. He was watching everyone, taking mental notes. What did he see in this room?

I tried to place long-forgotten names with faces.

Few there were my age. People I'd gone to school with had left Maine for larger cities, higher salaries, and bigger dreams, just as I had. Those still here, like Ethan, had claimed positions in the old order.

Knowing these people was now his business. People greeted him, I noted, but then walked on. He wasn't here to socialize, and they recognized and respected his role.

I didn't remember most of their faces, even when a name was attached to the face.

One exception was Lauren Greene (now Decker).

"Oh, Angie, I'm so glad you came. For Charlotte's sake. She's missed you so much," she said, touching my hand that wasn't holding the punch. "But under such horrible circumstances. I know your work has kept you from visiting before, but I hope now you'll be staying awhile." Lauren had put on weight. It wasn't flattering. And I was glad. We'd been close friends until Mama'd disappeared, but I hadn't forgotten how she'd turned her back on me after that. At the very moment I'd needed her most, she'd found new friends. I hadn't forgotten the times she'd giggled and called me "Little Orphan Angie" behind my back, just loud enough so I'd hear it. I hadn't forgiven her cruelty.

My relationship with Gram was none of her business.

"A while," I agreed, noting she'd called Gram by

her first name, and not committing to a departure date. There was more than a hint of sarcasm in her voice. I wondered what she thought about her father's being the prime suspect in Mama's murder.

"You look great. Tan and all. That must be from living out in the desert. You know Maine. We won't be getting enough sun to make a difference until June." She smoothed her long brown hair. "I wish I had time to take better care of myself. There's just no time between keeping house and taking care of my husband and working. You're not married, so you have no idea."

Maybe I did have an idea. Maybe that's why I wasn't married.

I hated small talk. Lauren clearly excelled at it. "You haven't changed since high school," I assured her. In high school she'd been plagued with acne and curled her hair until it frizzed.

"Charlotte's such an absolutely wonderful person. You were lucky to have her to live with after your mom . . . well, you know. You didn't have to end up in foster care or anything. She talks about you all the time. Worries about you living so far from home. If she'd been my grandmother, why, I don't think I could have left her by herself for this long, in that big old house. Of course, I love working with her, and I try to stop in and check up on her a couple of times a week, but you never know what might happen to someone her age. She could fall, or have a stroke, and you wouldn't even know, being so far away."

"Gram and I stay in touch." She might be right, though. Gram was getting on, although she seemed fine to me. Right now she was at the center of a group of people, accepting their condolences. She looked calmer than I felt. After nineteen years I hadn't thought there were many tears left. I'd been wrong.

Lauren was still chattering. "You know, I wasn't sure I'd like needlepoint, but she's taught me, and it's so relaxing and creative. I'll bet I burn more calories on my needlework than I do when I'm waitressing. I work so fast now!" She giggled a little.

I forced myself to smile.

"Growing up with her, you must be good at it. I still have a lot of stitches to learn. The basic ones are simple, but the fancier ones really take concentration."

"I never learned needlepoint," I said. "Gram tried to teach me once, but I couldn't sit still long enough to focus on it."

Probably because I was missing my mother, who was in your dad's freezer. Or dreading the overheard gossip in the school corridors. Or following in my mother's footsteps, and hoping I, too, wouldn't get pregnant at seventeen.

"Well, you should try it again! It's terribly relaxing." Lauren reached out and squeezed my hand. "You look a little tense. Although, who wouldn't, under the circumstances? I know I cried my eyes out at my mother's funeral. And then later, when Dad died—"

"Where was the key to the storage unit?" I interrupted. I needed to talk about what was real. Not keep smiling at people I'd left town to escape ten years ago.

"What?" Lauren stopped in midgesture. "The key?"

"Ethan Trask told me you found the key to your father's storage unit in Union. Where you found my mother. Where was the key?"

Lauren stepped back slightly and glanced to my left, as though planning her escape. "It was in an envelope stuck at the back of one of his file cabinet drawers. What does it matter where I found it?"

"Ethan said you'd had it for a while before you went to see what was in the unit."

"Angie, this isn't the time to talk about that. My dad's gone. So's your mother. We'll never know what happened between them, and I don't care. It's over. We can't bring either of them back."

"But the case is still open," I pointed out. "That's why Ethan's here. It's not over. Not yet. Do you think your dad killed my mother?"

Her mouth closed at that. Her lips tightened. "I don't think we should be talking about that. You're right. The police are investigating. We're survivors. We have to go on."

"But don't you want to know the truth? If my mother had been accused of murdering someone, I'd want to know for sure whether or not she did it."

Lauren took another step backward. "It's over, Angie. Years over. If you need to talk about what happened, that's your problem. Talk to Ethan Trask. As I remember, you had a real crush on him. Now you have an excuse to call him. I've already told him everything I know. I'm trying to put it behind me. You need to do the same." She turned and headed for the table covered with food, where she started chatting with a young woman I didn't recognize.

"Angie!" A slim blonde ignored my cup of punch and hugged me. Luckily, not much spilled. "It's so good to see you!"

I stared. Her voice sounded familiar, but I couldn't place her face.

"You don't recognize me, do you?" she bubbled. "What fun! I'm Clementine Walker!"

I blinked and looked again. "Clem?"

"I've changed, haven't I?"

Gradually the pieces came together as she laughed at my discomfort.

"You're a blonde. And skinny!" I blurted. Clem Walker had been the one friend who'd stuck by me. Her family hadn't lived in Haven Harbor for generations. They'd moved to Maine from Boston when we were in fifth grade. She hadn't known my mother.

She'd also been pudgy, with short brown hair and glasses.

"I don't believe it! You've totally changed!"

"Just on the outside, Angie. Just on the outside. I was a disaster in high school, wasn't I?"

"Oh, Clem!" This time I hugged her. My punch glass was almost empty. "It's so good to see you. Are you still living in town?"

"In Portland. I work for one of the TV stations there."

I backed off immediately. "You were my best friend, but I'm not giving any interviews."

"No, no. I'm not a reporter or a producer. I work in the office there. For now, anyway. You look great, too!" She looked around. "I saw you talking to Lauren Greene. Lauren Decker, now. She's aged. But being married to Caleb probably hasn't helped."

"And you?" I glanced at her hand. "Married? Engaged?"

"Independent." She smiled. "You?"

"The same." I saw Gram heading in my direction. "I'd love us to get together. Talk. Catch up."

"Give me your cell," she said. I fished it out and she tapped her number into it. "Now you can reach me. And do! Promise!"

"I will." I watched her cross the room to the refreshment table. Others watched her, too. If it took looks to be on television, Clem was on the right track. And she'd always been bright. She'd headed for Orono, to the University of Maine, when I'd headed west.

How would my life have been different if I'd taken her path? But my grades weren't great, so a scholarship was out of the question, and Gram didn't have enough money to send me. Truth was, I hadn't been interested in college. Those couple of courses I'd taken in Arizona had bored me to death. Looked like higher education and serious attention to her appearance had paid off for Clem, though.

"How're you holding up?" Gram asked. "I saw you talking with Lauren and Clem."

"I was glad to see Clem," I said. "That was a surprise. But this whole memorial is a lie. All these people, pretending they were Mama's friends. Pretending they care what happened to her. They probably haven't even thought of her in years. When she was alive, most of them didn't speak to her, or only pretended to like her."

Gram's eyes filled, but she held back her tears. "It's not all that bad, Angel. I know this is hard for you. And you're right—even I don't know everyone here, and certainly some came out of curiosity. But you've been gone a long time. Many of these people are here to give us their support. We should give them the benefit of the doubt. Be pleasant."

I looked around the room. "How can you tell the difference? By the number of cookies they're eating? That woman in the purple dress hasn't spoken to anyone. She hasn't had time. She's eaten three plates of food and just filled her plate again. Does she think this is an all-you-can-eat buffet?"

"Have faith," Gram answered, not even turning to see which woman I was describing. "Can you hold it together a little longer? Before we go, I'd like you to meet the other Mainely Needlepointers. They sent most of the flowers in the church, and they've heard me talk about you, and how well you've been doing. They'd like to meet you."

I nodded. "I'm okay. Don't worry."

She gestured to three people standing near one of the windows. "After you meet them, we'll leave. We've given everyone a chance to say something to us. Some took it; some didn't. We'll let Tom handle those still here. He'll know how to deal with them." She smiled as her friends came closer. "And here are three of my fellow Needlepointers." She touched the arm of a man who looked about forty-five, although his wavy hair was gray. In his navy suit and red tie, he could have been a stockbroker or lawyer or banker who started every day at the gym. "This is Dave Percy. He teaches biology at the high school now, but he learned needlepointing when he was in the navy. Not much to do when you're off duty in a submarine."

Dave put out his hand and I shook it. His handshake was firm. "Sorry about your mother. I'm glad to finally meet you. Your grandmother got me involved with Mainely Needlepoint, and I keep busy with that, summers and winters, after school. Or I did keep busy until our problems with Lattimore."

"And you remember Katie Titicomb? Your friend Cindy's mother."

I did. "You used to win awards for your quilts at the Common Ground Country Fair every year. I remember. They were gorgeous."

She looked pleased. "I'm surprised you remember. Young folks don't pay crafts so much attention anymore."

"Cindy used to brag about you," I said. Bragged that she had a wonderful and talented mother who cared about her—and wasn't it too bad my mother had up and deserted me? And then by junior high school Cindy had left Haven Harbor for private school. Yes, I remembered Cindy and her mother.

"Well, Cindy's married and lives down to Blue Hill now. Has three little ones. Doesn't get back to Haven Harbor as often as I'd like."

"Are you still quilting?"

She shook her head. "Not much. A person can only use so many quilts. And quilting eats up time, even if you do it by machine, like most folks do now. Charlotte's talked me into going into the needlepoint business."

"Katie's one of our biggest producers," Gram put in.

"Maybe you remember my husband, Gus? Dr. Titicomb?"

I shook my head.

"Well, just as well. He's a surgeon. No one you want to meet professionally unless you have to. He learned needlepoint in medical school, to practice stitching with a needle. Taught me how to do it, too."

"Wonderful," I said, turning to the third member of the group. "And I'm pretty sure I remember you. Captain Winslow?"

"That's me. You were a cunning thing when you were little. You've grown up wicked pretty."

"Thank you." I smiled at his phrasing—high praise from a Mainer.

"Real sorry about your mother."

Ob's hands were calloused and hard and tanned like leather. The hands of a man who made a living by the sea.

"Thank you. And have you done needlepoint for years, too?"

"Not me. Lauren and I are the beginners in the group. I still run my charter fishing boat in summer, and used to carve decoys for the tourists in winter. But my back was givin' me problems about five years ago. I talked to Dr. Gus, Katie here's husband, and he recommended the needlepointing. It keeps my hands and brain busy and I can sit and relax, 'stead of standing like I do when I'm carving, and I can still make money in winter."

"At first, he put up such a fight," Katie said, giving Ob a gentle shove. "Men and embroidery, you know. He didn't see it. But my Gus kept after him, and he finally decided to give it a try."

"Have to admit, the doc was right," said Ob. "Now I'm making more money than I did with decoys. Or I was," he said, looking over at Gram, "until our problem."

"I've told Angie about Jacques. She worked with a private investigator in Arizona." Gram was beaming with pride. "She's going to find him for us, and try to get the money he owes us."

"Thank you, Angie. That would mean a lot"— Katie's hands swept to include all of them—"to all of us."

"I'll do my best," I promised. I couldn't let these people down. "And thank you for coming today."

Gram put her arm around me. "You go on to the car now, Angie. I'll let Tom know we're going home."

I started moving toward the door, watching as Gram went over to the reverend. He nodded and they both looked over at me. No doubt I was Gram's excuse for leaving a little earlier than expected.

I pulled my hat down farther as I realized other people were looking at me. Watching me. Were they waiting for me to do something crazy? I'd already heard the whispers. "Doesn't she look just like her mother?"

But I wasn't Mama. And she wasn't as sinful as some of them thought.

Others in Haven Harbor were worse. Much worse.

One of those other virtuous citizens had killed her.

Maybe Lauren's father? Maybe one of these nice churchgoing folks nibbling cookies and sipping punch?

Whoever it was, for nineteen years they'd gotten away with it.

Chapter Seven

Old Mother Twitchett had but one eye,
And a long tail which she let fly;
And every time she went through a gap
A bit of her tail she left in a trap.
What is she?
                   —Traditional nursery rhyme riddle

Our house had always been my sanctuary. The one place I could be myself, no matter what people in the outside world said or did.

But my years away had made a difference. Walking through those once-comforting rooms now felt like walking back in time. A time I wasn't proud of. I hadn't fit in, and I'd flaunted the reasons why. Seeing those people at the funeral had brought back a lot that I hadn't thought of in years.

I remembered Maine days in May as warm and smelling of freshly plowed gardens and sea breezes. I hadn't remembered the chill I felt today.

"Tea?" asked Gram. "And maybe a tuna sandwich?"

"I'll make the sandwiches," I agreed.

Neither of us had taken advantage of the funeral food.

Gram put the kettle on while I found a can of

tuna in the cabinet and got out jars of mayonnaise and pickles. "You only have whole wheat bread now," I noticed, opening the bread box. Who but Gram still used a bread box?

"Doctor says it's healthier for me. Better for the cholesterol," said Gram, putting two yellow mugs on the table.

"How are you? Seriously," I asked, mixing the tuna salad. I'd heard Lauren's message. I'd deserted my grandmother. And, much as I hated to admit it, Lauren was right. I'd left Gram to deal with what I couldn't. In the ten years I'd been away, I'd grown up. But I wasn't the only one who was ten years older. I should have asked about Gram's health earlier. She looked good, but maybe Lauren knew something I didn't.

"I'm fine. Being sixty-five isn't the end of the world. My brain still works, thank the Lord, although parts of my body aren't as limber as they used to be. I'm just supposed to pay attention to that cholesterol. I figure, whole wheat bread and oatmeal for breakfast in the winter should keep me going a few more years. So far, no complaints."

I nodded, hoping she was telling the truth.

The kettle was singing. I cut each sandwich into four triangles, as Gram had always done, while she poured hot water over our tea bags. I hadn't realized I was hungry, but my sandwich disappeared before Gram had half-finished hers. I added another teaspoon of sugar to my tea.

"There's more tuna in the cupboard," she said, looking at my plate.

"I'm okay for now," I answered. I sipped the tea. In Arizona I'd become addicted to cup after cup of coffee each day. I'd forgotten how comforting tea was.

"Your mama always added extra sugar to her tea," Gram added.

"Did she?" Usually I wanted to remember details like that. But right now, today, I'd heard enough about Mama. I pushed my mug away. "Tell me more about your business. About Jacques Lattimore. If I'm going to help you, I'll need some place to start."

Gram nodded. "I told you Jacques found us, not the other way around. Mainely Needlepoint was doing pretty well. Our biggest problem was finding people to stitch. People called or e-mailed looking for personalized pillows to commemorate events from births to birthdays and anniversaries. Family reunions. Weddings. Even a Bas Mitzvah once! And that didn't count the orders from gift and decorator shops. I'll tell you, we all had sore fingers and tired eyes trying to keep up with the orders."

"Who are 'we'? You, of course, and the others you introduced me to: Dave Percy and Katie Titicomb and Ob Winslow. And Lauren. She told me you'd taught her needlework."

"I did. Several years ago when I was at the

Harbor Haunts Café, where she waitresses, she said one of her customers had shown her our work. She asked if I could use any more help. I told her 'yes,' of course . . . but then it turned out she didn't even know how to thread a needle." Gram shook her head. "But she was a quick learner. I'll say that for Lauren. And a hard worker. She and Caleb were newly married then, and struggling financially. They were trying to pay off their lobster boat. Lauren could do needlework on her breaks at the restaurant, or at home at night. She and Caleb depended on the extra dollars she brought in from stitching. After a while she only needed to waitress when the tourists were here. She's had to go back to waitressing regular since we've had troubles. She and Caleb don't have it easy. Lobster prices have fallen in the past few years, you know. Been hard on those trying to make a living from them."

I hadn't known that. Another sign I had a lot of catching up to do. Lobster prices were critical to many Haven Harbor families' economies.

"So you taught Lauren. Who else works with the two of you? Anyone else I'd know?"

"Six of us work at it steady. Ruth Hopkins helped at the beginning, but she's getting on. When her arthritis flares, she has to stop for a while. She hasn't taken more than a couple of jobs in the past year."

I nodded. Mrs. Hopkins had seemed ancient to

my teenaged eyes ten years ago. No surprise she was "getting on."

"And one more?" I asked, counting on my fingers. The business wasn't as large as I'd thought, especially if Ruth wasn't contributing much now.

"That's Sarah Byrne. She's our newest. New to Haven Harbor, and new to the United States, actually. She's from Australia."

"Australia! How did she get to Haven Harbor?"

"I don't know her whole story. Says she was driving up the coast on vacation and got to Haven Harbor and decided to stay. She bought up that little shop on Wharf Street . . . the place where they used to sell candy. Do you remember?"

"Sure. They sold saltwater taffy—had one of those taffy-pulling machines right in the shop window—and all flavors of popcorn. Red Hots and whoopie pies. Is Sarah Byrne still selling candy and popcorn?"

"Goodness, no. It was a candy shop three owners ago. Sarah's trying to make a go of an antique shop there. She goes to auctions all over the state and picks up pieces of china and silver and small pieces of furniture—a motley collection, if you ask me—but the summer folks seem to like what she's selling. They may go in just to hear her accent! She closes the shop in winter. Does her buying then. She's really skilled with a needle. She heard I could use extra hands and came looking for a job. She likes that she can stitch at the shop, or at an

66

auction, or at home. She's got no family to be a distraction. And she's good. She's one of us now."

"That's six of you working actively, plus Ruth Hopkins."

"Right. Every one of them was at the church to pay their respects this afternoon. Sarah and Ruth left before you could meet them."

"You all seem to get along."

"Most of the time, although we're all stubborn in our own ways and don't always agree. I'm the only one who's full-time on the job. They all have other obligations—work or family or both."

The people who did the stitching were important, but I needed to know more about Lattimore. "Do you have a contract with Lattimore?"

"We do. I may not be an expert on business, but we all knew we wanted to get down in writing what Jacques agreed to do. Not notarized or anything like that, which was probably a mistake. But we have a paper we all signed."

"And it worked?"

"Worked so well we got to depend on those monthly checks. It all worked fine until last December."

"That's six months ago!"

"Close to six. And don't I just know it! December and January are big months for us. We prepared orders for the holiday season, and Jacques would pick them up in October or November, and then the checks would come in, in time for the holidays. All right as rain. Until last December. Jacques said some accounts weren't paying up as well as they should, so he only paid us needlepointers half of what each should have gotten."

"That's a major difference."

"Made for pretty sparse Christmases around here, I'll tell you. But we figured we'd all get even in January. That the checks then would make up the difference. We had no reason not to trust Jacques. Lauren told me she ran up credit card bills on his promises, and I suspect others did, too." Gram got up and poured herself another cup of tea. "But January came, and, again, our checks were far smaller than we'd expected."

"And . . . ?"

"And January's the last time I saw Jacques Lattimore. In March I sent him a letter, registered and all, telling him he owed us money, but it came back. Couldn't be forwarded. I have no idea where he is now." Gram looked down at her mug of tea. Her hands were shaking. "And it's all my fault, Angel. I'm the one agreed to work with him. And now the needlepointers are angry, and people—Ob and Lauren, especially—need the money owed them. I'd pay them myself if I had it. But I don't. I don't know what to do." She looked up. "Until you said you'd find out about Jacques, where he is, and when he's going to pay back the money that's owed."

"I promise, Gram. I'm pretty good at finding people. But this sounds like a mess. You may need a lawyer and have to do a lot of paperwork to get him to pay up."

Gram nodded. "Don't I just know it. But first things first. You'll find him for me, right, Angel? Then I'll get a lawyer. Or a gun."

I knew—at least I thought I knew—Gram was kidding about the gun. We were about the only family in town that hadn't had one. I remembered Lauren bragging after she'd shot her first deer, and even newcomer Clem had her own rifle.

Guns were taken for granted in Maine.

Chapter Eight

Home tis the name of all that sweetens life.
It speaks the warm affections of a wife.
Oh! Tis a word of more than magic spell
Whose sacred power the wanderer can tell.
He who long distant from his native land
Feels at the name of home his soul expand.
Whether as patriot husband, father, friend,
To that dear point his fondest wishes bend.
And still he owns where ere his footsteps roam
Life's choisest blessings centre still at Home.
—Sampler stitched by Martha Agnes Ramsay,
   age twenty-three, Preble County, Ohio, 1849

At that point Gram declared she needed a nap. I probably should have slowed down, too. Between Mama's funeral and feeling like an outsider in my own hometown and then hearing Gram's business woes, my mind was moving too fast. But I couldn't relax. I needed to do something.

I decided to risk running into any members of the press still remaining in Haven Harbor, and go for a walk. I left a note for Gram, went out the back door, and took a shortcut through a neighbor's yard on a path that used to be well-worn but was now nonexistent. I headed for the harbor.

I might not have missed all the people in Haven

Harbor, but, especially on Arizona's simmering-hot August days, I'd longed for harbor views and breezes.

Outside of the houses and church and police station and municipal buildings, the working waterfront and commercial district of Haven Harbor was basically two streets, both of which paralleled the small harbor. Most of the shops were on Main Street. Some catered to tourists and were full of seagull and moose and lobster T-shirts and postcards and souvenir Christmas ornaments and cheap balsam pillows with MAINE painted on them. Not at all the sort Gram made. Those shops were open only when the customers from away ("visitors," Mainers call them, to be polite, but we know what they really are) were here, from about Memorial Day to Columbus Day. Other businesses, like The Book Nook, which specialized in books set in Maine or by Maine writers, were open year-round. Both the art gallery and the shop that sold high-end crafts closed in January and February.

Stewart's still displayed gold and silver jewelry, much of it made by Maine craftsmen. During the summers they featured rings and necklaces set with tourmaline (Maine's state gem) or sea glass, or "beach pebbles," for tourists with full wallets or checkbooks to take home as souvenirs. In winter they cut their staff and focused on plainer pieces of gold and silver, with a few diamond rings available for engagements or anniversaries. I'd been very proud that my gold angel necklace had come in a Stewart's box.

Hubbel Clothing was where you bought clothes when you couldn't get to the Freeport or Kittery outlets, or to branches of discount stores like Marden's or Renys. Hubbel could fill your needs for sweatshirts and flannels and wool jackets, as well as bright yellow bib pants and slickers for fishing and blaze orange hats and vests for hunting. They carried flannel nightgowns and pajamas, too. I glanced in the window. Global warming hadn't affected Hubbel's inventory.

I kept walking. I paused at the new "patisserie," where Greene's Bakery used to be. Cookies, cakes . . . and what Mr. Greene had called "treats." There was still an alley next to it, with space to drive into the lot in back of the store, or cut through on foot to Wharf Street. Had Mr. Greene killed Mama at his bakery? Had he put her body in his bakery truck when he drove her to Union?

And if it wasn't Joe Greene, how had her body gotten into a freezer in his storage unit?

I kept walking as my head exploded with memories and possibilities. An antique shop (From Here And There), which must be Sarah Byrne's, was where the old candy shop had been. I missed the smell of toffee drifting out the door when I walked by. Sarah's windows featured an old pine children's table set with small china cups and plates for a tea party. A pot of lilies of the valley decorated the table, and an old teddy bear sat patiently in a small rocking chair. Cute. But not enough to draw me in. How had someone from Australia ended up in Haven Harbor? Was she running to something? Or running from . . . ?

I walked faster. I wasn't shopping. I wanted to see what had happened to Haven Harbor in my absence. A new women's boutique looked interesting. The consignment store around the corner from it was new, too. That had been the small grocery store where I'd been sent to pick up a quart of milk or a box of cereal. I cut through another alleyway I'd always avoided, with reason, as a child, and went down to Wharf Street, which paralleled the working waterfront of the harbor.

Two lobster boats were out in the harbor, and three were docked at the Town Pier. In summer the pier would be bustling. Today, only the lobster boats and a couple of skiffs were tied there.

I walked by the marine supply house and Harbor Haunts Café, where Gram had said Lauren worked, and where Mama had waitressed. Nice enough, and open year-round. I didn't stop. Past the café was the lobstermen's co-op, where I'd spent my summers steaming lobsters for tourists to eat at benches set along the pier. My skin, my hair, my clothes, had all smelled like lobster in those days, no matter how many showers I'd taken. I'd hated it. I hadn't tasted lobster since. The co-op hadn't opened for the summer yet.

Would lobster taste better now? I wasn't ready to check it out today.

Beyond the co-op was another pier, and a rocky beach, before the mainland circled back toward the ocean. The Haven Point Lighthouse stood above the rocks on the point of land that jutted out into the Atlantic. It had been automated for years, but still blared out fog warnings. Its beams were the constant stars in Haven Harbor's night.

I walked down to Pocket Cove Beach, one of my favorite past escapes. It was low tide. Rockweed and driftwood and mussel shells, dropped by herring gulls, mixed with used condoms and broken glass and cigarette stubs and beer cans on the wrack lines high on the shore.

When I'd lived here, the elementary school had a cleanup day at the shore in May when we'd all bring large trash bags to the beach and collect the detritus from winter's high tides. If they still did that, they hadn't yet this year. I kicked a Moxie bottle filled with seawater. It didn't break. Moxie bottles were tough.

I stared out at the ocean. The Three Sisters, three small islands just off the coast, were still there, where they'd been for hundreds, maybe thousands, of years. My great-grandparents had rowed there for lobster bakes. My grandparents had explored them in small boats equipped with outboard motors. Each summer the yacht club over on the eastern point, opposite the lighthouse, held sailing races. And each summer at least one small sailboat ended up on the rocks of First Sister, the largest island. It had the highest cliffs and the longest stretch of rocks at low tide. Even at high tide you had to navigate the reach between it and Second Sister carefully.

Children were told every seventh wave would be the big one. How many times had I stood here, counting waves, trying to make that true. But the waves obeyed their own rules, and wouldn't conform, no matter what everyone said.

I inhaled the smells of the mud flats and the ocean, then smiled.

I loved this town on the sea. Even when it hadn't loved me.

I walked the short length of the beach, looking down. Mama'd shown me where to find starfish here, and limpet shells, and sea urchins, some alive and some dead, bleached white by the waters and the sun.

I looked for a sign, something to tell me what to do now. A few feet from the ledges at the end of the beach, I saw it: a pure white stone, smoothed by the sea. And, close by, another. Smooth and black.

I picked them up, one in each hand, as I had hundreds of times before. I closed my eyes, wished, and then threw them both back to the sea.

They landed at exactly the same time, sending out circles of ripples.

I would get my wish.

But had I wished for the right thing?

I took one more look at the sea and headed home. Toward Gram. First I had to help her. Find that Jacques Lattimore, and do what I could to get the money back, which I already suspected he didn't have.

Then I'd decide what to do next. One thing was sure. I'd have to navigate carefully. The hidden rocks in this town weren't only in the harbor.

Chapter Nine

From the manner in which a woman draws her thread at every stitch of her needlework, any other woman can surmise her thoughts.
—Honoré de Balzac (1799–1850)

A state police car was parked in front of the Harbor Haunts Café when I passed it on my way home. Ethan Trask? What other cop would be in Haven Harbor this afternoon? Probably filling his stomach. Or maybe Lauren was waitressing there this afternoon and he was asking more questions.

Right now I didn't want to think about possibilities. I needed time to digest everything I'd heard—to shuffle all the pieces of the puzzle in my head and try to get some of them to link.

Or maybe, for a few hours, I didn't want to think about anything. Had I seen a bottle of cognac in Gram's dining room? Cognac sounded like a sane remedy for an increasingly raw afternoon. And memories.

The media people had apparently given up their watch, but I was still wary as I headed up the hill. I circled the block and went in the back door, which opened into the kitchen.

Where Reverend McCully was kissing Gram.

They broke apart as the door opened. "I'm . . .

sorry," I said. "I went for a walk and was just coming back. . . ."

"Nothing to be sorry about," said Gram, although she stepped away from the reverend and smoothed her hair. "I should have told you before. But with your coming home, and your mama and all . . . and we haven't exactly gone public. Tom being a minister, he has to be very careful. People talk."

People had talked about Mama. They'd talked about me. But . . . Gram? And how old was this reverend?

Reverend McCully nodded. "Your grandmother's a very special person, Angie. She was helping out at the church and we became friends. . . ."

"And then . . . more than friends," said Gram. I swear she was blushing. "We've been . . . seeing each other . . . for almost a year now."

"We were blessed to find each other," said the reverend, looking at Gram with an expression less than totally holy. "We were going to announce our news to the congregation this spring, but first there was this trouble with Jacques Lattimore, and then your mother's body was found. We didn't want people to think we were ignoring problems and only focusing on our own happiness."

"Announce?" I looked from one of them to the other. "You mean—"

"Charlotte said 'yes.' She's agreed to marry

me," he continued, reaching for Gram's hand. He actually raised it to his lips and kissed it.

"Gram? Is that so?"

She nodded.

"But you never said anything. You never hinted." I looked from one of them to the other. "Well! Congratulations." I hoped I was making sense.

Gram? My Gram? Getting married?

She'd been married to my grandfather, but he'd died long before I was even born. I'd never pictured Gram married. She was just . . . Gram. I'd figured she would be forever.

"I knew you'd be happy for me, Angel. And I was going to tell you, as soon as we'd finished up with the memorial service. I was. There just hasn't been time."

But they'd been . . . dating? Did you call it dating when you were over sixty?

"I'm happy for you. Both of you. Really. I'm just surprised."

"We'd wanted to have a tiny, quiet ceremony, but with Tom's job, he's expected to invite everyone in the congregation. So we're going to do it all. Church wedding, reception. The whole traditional event." They were both grinning. They were serious about this.

"I never thought you'd be married before I was, Gram," I blurted, and immediately knew that was the wrong thing to have said. Besides, marriage was definitely not on my immediate horizon. If ever! I'd dated a guy named Jeff for a while in Mesa. It had felt pretty serious, but it hadn't worked out, and I'd almost been relieved. Marriage was a long-term decision. I was more the day-to-day type. Maybe like Mama, although I hated to admit it.

"Most grandmothers get married before their granddaughters, you know," she said, laughing. "Tom and my timing is just a little different." She looked at Tom, and I could see excitement and happiness on her face, which I'd never seen before. How had I not even considered that she might want someone in her life? She turned back to me. "We don't want to make it public for a few more weeks. But I'd love for you to be my maid of honor, Angel. Maybe a late June wedding?"

Late June! I hadn't planned to stay that long. Maybe I could leave and then come back. But I couldn't turn her down, weird as it felt. "I'd . . . be honored. You know, I've never been anyone's maid of honor."

"I'm glad you're here." Gram looked from Reverend Tom to me and then back again. "How could my life be better? Angel is home again, and we're planning our wedding. Remember though, Angel, for now it's our secret. Only the three of us know."

"Got it. Do you have any champagne? I feel as though we should celebrate!" I said. It wasn't the cognac I'd been thinking of, but champagne would do. Now I really did need a drink.

"I've been keeping one handy," Gram answered. She pulled a bottle of Moët from the back of the refrigerator. "This is just the time to open it. Tom, would you do the honors?"

A few minutes later we were raising glasses. "To a new beginning," I said.

"To forgetting the past, and getting on with the future," added Gram.

"And to the woman I love, and her understanding granddaughter, whom I'm grateful to finally meet," said Reverend Tom.

We clinked our glasses together and drank.

"Now everything would be perfect if I could get Mainely Needlepoint back on track," said Gram. "And you're helping me do that, Angel."

I nodded. I hoped she hadn't put too much faith in me. "And I want to know who killed Mama," I added.

Reverend Tom shook his head slightly. "Joe Greene killed your mother, Angie. I don't think there's much question about that."

"Maybe. Maybe he did. But I want to be certain," I answered.

"Why don't you let those questions go," said Gram. "Now you know your mama didn't leave you intentionally. She was taken from you. It's time to move on."

Maybe it was time for Gram to move on. But I

81

wanted that last *t* crossed. "First job: finding Jacques Lattimore," I said, raising my glass again. Then I'd see what I could uncover about Mama's killer. If it was Joe Greene, and I found out why, I'd accept that. I just wanted to know.

Chapter Ten

I hate a woman who offers herself because she ought to do so, and, cold and dry, thinks of her sewing when she's making love.

> —Publius Ovidius Naso,
> known as Ovid (43 BC–17 or 18 AD),
> *Ars Amatoria (The Art of Love)*, 2 AD

I couldn't slow my mind down that night. Sleep finally came, but it brought confused images so real they might not have been dreams. Each time I woke, trying to escape them, I thought about what I should do. What was most important? And I made some decisions.

As soon as the sun was up in Arizona, I called Wally, my boss in Mesa. I was relieved when he didn't pick up and I could leave a message. I knew he wouldn't be happy with me, and I didn't want to argue. I told him I wouldn't be back for a while. A couple of months, at least. I had family issues to deal with. (A murder and a wedding? They certainly counted as issues.)

I rummaged through Gram's kitchen to find her ancient jar of instant coffee and made myself a strong cup. Tea was all well and good, but I couldn't sit around being cozy anymore. I had to get to work. I added to my mental list, *Buy coffeepot.*

Despite the lack of sleep I felt good. I knew what I had to do. Gram had taken care of me for years. Now she needed me to help her. I owed her at least the time it would take to do that.

And I'd keep my eyes open about Mama's murder. That was important to me, even if Gram had put it behind her. She wanted to focus on her future.

I'd worry about mine later.

The coffee was stale, but strong; and for the first time since I'd been back in Haven Harbor, I began to feel in control of my life.

A knock on the front door interrupted my self-congratulations. "Yes?" I said to the young blond woman with pink-and-blue-streaked hair who was standing on the porch holding a large bag. "May I help you?"

She hesitated a moment. "You're Angel, right? I saw you at the church yesterday."

I hadn't remembered anyone as distinctive. But her accent gave me a clue. "You're . . . Sarah? Sarah Byrne?"

"Right. That would be me. Only Australian in town, and likely to remain so."

I couldn't help smiling. "Gram—Charlotte— isn't home right now, but she'll be back anytime. Come on in."

She headed for the kitchen, not the Mainely Needlepoint office.

"Can I offer you a cup of tea? Or, I found stale

instant coffee in the cabinet. You could have some of that."

"Tea would be lovely. Thank you."

I put the kettle on to boil. Maybe I could get Gram a microwave, too.

"Thank you for coming to the service yesterday. Although I'm afraid I don't remember meeting you." I wouldn't have forgotten that hair.

"I didn't go to the little gathering afterward. I had to get back to my shop. I've just opened it for the summer, and I didn't want to miss any customers. I slipped into the back of the church for the service and then slipped out. I hope the press left you alone. They can be so horrible. 'How dreary—to be—Somebody! How public—like a Frog—' And so forth."

"What?" The woman wasn't making sense.

"A line from one of my favorite Emily Dickinson poems. I've loved her work since I was little. They're one of the reasons I came to New England."

"I don't know much about poetry," I admitted. I gave Sarah a selection of tea bags to choose from. Did Australians drink a lot of tea? Would she have expected a teapot and loose tea? I had no idea.

"This is lovely," she said, selecting a bag of English Breakfast. "I don't know if your grand-mother told you, but I've been doing needlepoint for her. For that Jacques Lattimore, I guess would be more correct. That's how I've come to know her."

"She did tell me about you. She said you were really talented. And that you had the antique shop down on Main Street."

"That's me. I'm glad she likes my work. It's relaxing, and reminds me of home. I learned the stitches from my grandmum when I was little. Working with floss takes me out of where I am, back to a place I was happy."

"If you were happy there, why did you leave?"

She shrugged. "I grew up. Wanted to see the world. Had questions to answer. You left here, didn't you?"

"Yes." I looked at her. She was about my age, maybe a year or two older. It was hard to tell. "Why Haven Harbor? Of all the places from here to Australia?"

"I like it here. People are friendly, but not all over you, if you know what I mean. And I love the sea. I lived near the sea in Australia, and I'd missed it. I'd seen your West Coast, and wanted to see New England. Went to visit Emily Dickinson's home first, of course, but then drove up Route 1 on holiday. Stayed in Merry Chase's bed-and-breakfast, up on the hill. And the next morning I went walking and saw the Harbor and the Three Sisters and the lighthouse. I thought I'd woken up inside a picture postcard. There was a 'for rent' sign posted on that little store, and I decided it was for me. This was where I should be. Have you ever felt that way? 'I learned—at least—what Home could be—How ignorant I had been.' "

I shook my head, assuming she was quoting Emily Dickinson again. Haven Harbor was home. But was it where I was supposed to be? I didn't know.

"Well, it's a great feeling. I signed the lease that day, and then had to figure out what I'd do with the store! I ended up with antiques. Life in Haven Harbor has been good. The building came with a small apartment on the second floor, so I don't have far to go for work. And my bedroom window looks out to the sea." I poured hot water over Sarah's tea bag. "I can keep the store open even in bad weather and don't even have to think about putting my boots or heavy coat on, although for now I'm only open from the middle of April through Christmas." She dunked her tea bag a few times. "It suits me."

Gram pushed the back door open. "Oh, hi, Sarah! Let me put these groceries down."

I took the bags from her and put them on the counter. "Are there more in the car?"

"No. That's it."

"Shall I pour you a cup of tea? Water's hot."

"Sounds wonderful." She took off her jacket and sat at the table opposite Sarah while I got out another mug and tea bag. "How have you been,

Sarah? I got a peek of you at the back of the church yesterday. Thank you for coming."

"I wanted to be there. I couldn't leave the store for longer. And I'm not much for churchgoing. 'Some keep the Sabbath going to church—I keep it, staying at Home—' I didn't have a chance to say how sorry I was about your daughter. Jenny, it was, right?"

"Yes. Jenny." Gram hesitated. "I'm afraid I haven't got any new information about the business. I haven't been able to get in touch with Jacques, so I have no money for you, and no new orders."

"Don't worry about me. I've cut back on my expenses—and while we're waiting, I've made up extras of the little pillows we sell in the summer." She opened her bag. Inside were small needle-pointed cushions in dark red with green trees on them. "I felt Christmassy. They could be for a regular gift shop or a Christmas shop. Stocking stuffers."

I picked one up. "These are beautiful. You could put a ribbon on one and hang it in a closet, or on a doorknob, to bring the pine woods smell to a room."

"Excellent idea," agreed Gram. "Let's do the next lot like that, shall we, Sarah?"

Sarah nodded. "That'd be simple, and might give customers another idea of how to use them. A little marketing built in! I'll leave these with you, if that's all right."

"I'll make out a receipt for you right now," said Gram. She went over to the counter, picked up a receipt book, and started to write. "How many have you got in there, Sarah?"

"Ten," she answered. "But I came to show you something else. I bought it at a flea market in Waterville last weekend. I wanted to come right over and see what you thought, but, of course, you've been busy, and I didn't want to disturb you."

Sarah reached into the bag, pushed aside the balsam pillows, pulled out an old frame wrapped in tissue paper, and handed it to Gram. "Tell me what you think. I've never bought samplers or other needlework before. The good pieces go for high prices. But . . . you'll see."

Gram carefully removed the tissue paper.

The frame was old and damaged, and held an old piece of needlework. The glass in the frame had disappeared long ago. The stained linen inside was embroidered in faded red silk floss: *Just as the twig is bent, the tree's inclined.* Around the saying were two borders, one of small pine trees, not very different from the pine tree Sarah had embroidered on the balsam pillows, and another of concentric diamonds.

"I loved it," said Sarah. "But you can see it's stained, and some of the silk threads have rotted out. I looked up the quotation. Alexander Pope wrote it, in 1734."

"It's lovely. Or was lovely, once," said Gram, holding it close to her eyes so she could examine it better. "Some of the letters are gone, and some are so faded they're hard to make out. It must have hung on a wall, and sunlight bleached the colors of the threads. I don't know exactly how old it would be, but it certainly is at least nineteenth century. And American. I've never seen European embroidery that included pine trees like these." She touched it gently. "The concentric diamonds are typical of mid-nineteenth-century rural Maine work. I wonder who did this. It was probably saved because someone treasured it."

"I wondered if it might be a sampler. Needle-work a young girl would have done to demonstrate her skills. But the only samplers I've ever seen had the name of the girl, and often the date and place it was done, stitched right in. This piece has no identification."

"No. And it's very simple, compared to others I've seen. But that makes it even more charming," added Gram. "I love it, too, Sarah. I'm sorry it's stained, though. I don't think you should bleach it. That might take the stains away, but it would also take the little color left of the silk, and the silk could disintegrate further. Luckily, the stitching was on linen. It's held up better than the silk threads."

"I haven't decided what I'll do with it," said Sarah.

"We shouldn't be touching it, I suspect," said Gram, holding on to the frame alone. "The oils from our hands might damage it. I've never thought of what could be done to save a piece of history like this. It should come out of the frame. The wood has probably stained the edges we can't see."

"At first I thought of stitching in the missing parts, where the silk has broken. But I know with early furniture you're not supposed to take off the paint and refinish it. People did that in the past, but now it's thought preserving the look of the piece is important. And I don't want to do anything until I know what's best," said Sarah. "I thought I'd ask you first. I saw an ad in *Antiques and Fine Art Magazine* for a dealer who specializes in samplers and old needlepoint. I'll call there and ask for advice."

"Let us know," said Gram, carefully handing the framed cloth back to Sarah. "No matter what it's worth, that's a treasure. I'm glad you shared it with us."

I looked down at the old handmade frame, off-kilter and cracked, and the embroidery. Needlepoint had been part of my life as long as I remembered. I'd never had any great interest in it. It was just something Gram did.

But that scrap of old linen spoke to me. Whose needle had painstakingly embroidered that slogan and those pine trees? Perhaps it had been a young girl. The work was neither complicated nor did it illustrate different stitches. Was it done as a gift? But, then, why was there no personalization?

Sarah was looking closely at the frame. "I think once there was paper backing the piece. Perhaps the person who did this had written on the paper who she was and what the date was."

Perhaps. But the paper was gone.

Just as the twig is bent, the tree's inclined.

And why had she chosen that verse?

"Take care of that, Sarah," said Gram. "And if you solve its mystery, let us know."

Chapter Eleven

The Unicorn Tapestries in the National Museum of the Middle Ages (the Cluny Museum) in Paris are some of the most famous examples of medieval weaving. Using a combination of research and imagination, Tracy Chevalier's historical novel *The Lady and the Unicorn* takes the reader back to the fifteenth century, and weaves its own tale of how the tapestries might have been created. Another famous series of Unicorn Tapestries is at the Cloisters Museum, a branch of the Metropolitan Museum of Art in northern Manhattan.

"Gram, you need to tell me more about Jacques Lattimore if I'm going to find him."

Sarah had left, we'd put the groceries away, and Gram and I were sitting in the room I remembered as a living room. Gram had made it her office. It was where she stored completed work and supplies needed by the needlepointers, but there was still space for her old couch and comfortable chairs.

"I have his address in Brunswick. Or at least I have *an* address. The last letter I sent there came back marked as 'moved, no forwarding address.' "

"Did he ever talk about his family?"

Gram shook her head. "He never mentioned one."

"Friends?"

"When he left here once, about a year ago, he said he was going to have dinner down in Portland with 'Billy.' I don't remember him ever mentioning anyone else."

"How about a picture of him?"

She thought for a moment. "I do have one of those somewhere." She turned to her computer and talked as she searched. "We had a meeting here, with all the needlepointers, the day we hired Jacques as our agent. He took a picture of all of us—said it would help in sales to show customers we were real, down-to-earth, Maine home crafts-people. Someone, I think it was Ruth, didn't want her picture taken. Said she always looked ten years older in photographs. Finally she agreed, if we could take a picture of him, too. A couple of people took pictures with their cell phones. Everyone was laughing and kidding around. We were real happy, then, thinking he'd be an asset to the business." She shook her head. "Were we wrong! But I took a picture of him with my little camera. Hold on." She clicked a few keys. Gram clearly knew how to use a computer. That was a skill she'd learned since I was last home.

"Here he is," she said finally. "I should organize my picture file. But it never seemed that impor-tant. I take pictures of needlepoint patterns and completed work and scan in ideas I find in home-decorating or art magazines. Let me print this out for you."

As the printer hummed, she turned back to me. "Remember, Angel, I don't want you to do anything dangerous, or anything that would get you in trouble. And I want you to tell me where you're going. No big surprises or disappearances."

I could have told her I wasn't sixteen anymore. That I'd done this before. That finding people was something I'd been trained to do. But I understood the importance of that word "disappearances."

"I promise, Gram. I'll let you know what I'm doing. First I have to find this guy for you. You don't even know if he's in Maine now, right?"

She sighed. "I have no idea." She plucked the photo off her printer and handed it to me.

The color picture was a three-quarter shot of a man leaning against the mantel in our living room. Good! I could measure the fireplace and get a close estimate of his height. He was older than I'd imagined—maybe older than Gram. Definitely good-looking, and probably had been more so when he'd been younger. White, wavy hair. Slim. Maybe too slim. He was wearing black jeans and a high turtleneck, both of which accentuated his pale skin and his height.

"He looks awfully skinny, Gram. Do you know if he'd been sick?"

"He never mentioned being sick. He always looked that way. His appearance didn't change in the two years we worked with him."

"What other companies did he represent?"

"He told me he was the agent for several crafters in Maine and New Hampshire. But I don't remember any of their names." She paused, clearly embarrassed. "I guess I should have asked, and called them to check him out."

She should have. But it was too late for that now.

"Did he ever tell you about his background? Was he a Mainer?" That question usually came up early in Down East conversations.

"He'd been born in Lewiston. His grandparents came down from Quebec to work in the mills there, and his grandmother raised him after his parents died. He said he trusted me because I'd raised you. Just like his *mémé* had raised him."

"You chatted a bit." Didn't all sound like business chatting, either.

"He was very friendly. Polite. Bought me lunch a couple of times. He told me he loved our work, and although he hadn't planned to take on any more clients, he felt we could work well together."

"So he was doing you a favor?" He sounded too charming to me. Who was this guy who just arrived out of nowhere? "Could I see a copy of the contract you have with him?"

She pulled a green file folder from her bottom desk drawer and handed it to me.

"Do you have the original?" I asked, looking behind the one page for another copy.

"No. Jacques took that. I made copies of it for each of us."

I wished she'd had a lawyer look it over. There were no terms relating to anyone not fulfilling his or her part of the bargain, for example. Or who could terminate the relationship and when. I didn't say anything. She was Gram. She'd been too trusting. She'd never had a business before. But, boy, would this Lattimore character get a talking-to when I found him! Did he have "contracts" like this with other craftsmen in Maine?

"How much does he owe you for the needlework that you did for clients, gave to him, and haven't been paid for?"

Gram opened the top drawer of her desk. She might be able to use a computer, but she wasn't using it for her accounts. She handed me a ledger.

She'd divided it into sections, one for each member of the Mainely Needlepoint group. The date work was assigned to each person. The cost of the supplies she'd given them. When the work had been returned to Gram, and, for the past couple of years, when that work was given to "JL." At the end of each project its net and gross were neatly quantified.

I skipped through the sections, adding in my head.

"Gram? Am I right? Could he owe all of you

together about thirty-three thousand dollars?"

She nodded. "Plus, we've gone ahead and completed almost all the work he'd ordered. That's another fifteen thousand dollars worth of completed items we don't know what to do with."

"Can't you go directly to the people who ordered them? Do what you did before Lattimore was involved. Cut him out of the middle."

Gram hesitated. "Jacques took over all the paperwork, except the final accounting, which I did. He didn't tell us who'd commissioned our work. He just described what he'd been asked to supply, or provided a picture for us to work from."

Incredible. This was worse than I'd thought. They'd lost control of their customer base. "You don't have a clue? What about customers you had before Jacques came along. You're in touch with them, right?"

"With Betty at the gift shop here in Haven Harbor, yes, of course. But Jacques was the contact for all the others. He said it would save me time."

This was bad. Really bad.

"Now you understand why I've been worried. Sarah seems to be surviving financially, and so am I. Luckily, I own this house, and still have your grandfather's pension and some of his life insurance money, which I invested. Ruth hasn't done much work for us during the past year, since she's been more disabled. I've made sure she's gotten what she should. But Dave and Ob depend on that needlework money. Lauren too. Caleb keeps track of every penny in that family. With lobster prices down and shrimp quotas they have to abide by, the past few years haven't been easy for our men trying to make a living from the sea."

"Thirty-three thousand dollars is a lot of money to be owed, Gram. More than I suspected."

"And I'm responsible. Jacques came to me and I believed him. If I had it, I'd pay everyone what they should have gotten. We could forget Jacques and start over. But I don't have that kind of money. The first month I paid everyone a little—you can see that under the records for December. But after that, I couldn't. I didn't even have enough money to order new supplies. We'll need floss and canvas and so forth if we're lucky enough to get more orders."

I nodded. Thirty-three thousand dollars was a lot of money in Maine. Or any other place. No wonder Gram was worried.

"I'll do the best I can for you, Gram. First we have to find this Lattimore. Then we'll see what his story is."

"Angel, I trust you. But have you ever done anything like this before?"

"I've found people. Usually, husbands or wives. Sometimes a teenager who's disappeared." That word again: "disappeared." A word we tried to avoid in this house. "Most people I looked for left of their own volition. They didn't want to meet whatever their obligations were, to their family, or to a job. Or to the law. They're listed as 'missing' because they don't tell anyone where they're going."

"I know not everyone who's missing is murdered, Angel. And I'm not as ignorant now as I was when I agreed to work with Jacques. I know you may not be able to find him and, even if you do, he may not have our money."

"True. But we have to try."

"When will you start?"

"Tomorrow. May I use your car? I'd like to drive down to Brunswick, to where he said he lived, and see if anyone there knows him." I looked at the picture. "Unless he's changed his appearance—dyed his hair or something—he looks like some-one people might remember."

Gram nodded. "Handsome devil. You'd think after everything that happened with your mama that I'd be smarter. But I believed his promises. Tom knows how foolish I was. That's one reason I want this all settled before Tom and I are married. I don't want him to think I'm as harebrained as I was when I got into this situation." She paused. "Tom and I haven't talked a lot about it, but I know he expects me to live at the rectory with him after we're married. I was considering renting out this house. Or selling it. I thought maybe that way I could pay the others for the work they'd done."

I flinched. Sell our home? Mama and I and Gram had all grown up here. Gram's parents and grandparents had lived here. It was part of our family history. Always had been. Always should be.

"I'll do my best, Gram. I promise." Now I had another reason to find Lattimore. I had to save our home.

Chapter Twelve

Any little bride who expects to stay at home and keep the home fires burning will find her days less lonely, while her good man is at the front, if she has cheerful surroundings in which to ply her housewifely arts, and a touch of embroidery on kitchen linens is well worth considering.

—*The Modern Priscilla*, May 1918

Gram's blue Subaru wasn't as old as the wreck I'd left in Arizona, but it wasn't exactly state-of-the-art, either. I didn't push the speedometer as I headed for Brunswick the next morning.

As Route 1 wound its way through riverfront village communities, I could see changes from the Maine I remembered. Several towns now had bypasses around their business districts. Old 1950s-era cabin motels had been deserted or replaced by more modern buildings. Restaurants had changed names. Bridges had been rebuilt.

Time had not stopped.

When I'd been growing up, Brunswick had been an upscale community known as the home of a large Naval Air Force base, Bowdoin College, an artsy downtown within walking distance of the college, and, historically, the home of Civil War general and hero Joshua Chamberlain and the place Harriet Beecher Stowe wrote *Uncle Tom's Cabin.*

All I'd heard about Brunswick since then was that the base had closed, and, more recently, that Brunswick resident Angus King, whom I'd remembered as Maine's governor, was now one of Maine's U.S. senators. Gram hadn't told me that closing the base had emptied the upscale stores, and that the parking lot at Walmart was now full. I took advantage of the Walmart and bought a small coffee percolator and two bags of French Roast ground coffee—a selfish contribution to Gram's kitchen.

Jacques Lattimore's address was on a street close to the center of town. I parked and put my gun in the holster under my jacket. I probably wouldn't need it. I hoped I wouldn't need it. I'd checked online, using Gram's computer. My Arizona concealed carry permit wasn't valid in Maine. I'd have to apply for a new one if I stayed.

But right now, I was working; and when I worked, I carried. I hadn't told Gram I'd brought my gun with me. It would only have made her nervous. She'd never even let me have a water pistol.

I got out of the car and started looking at street numbers.

The number Gram had written down, 37, was a brick building with a dry cleaner's business on the first floor. I walked in, hoping to get some answers.

"Excuse me?" I asked the middle-aged man behind the counter. "I'm looking for someone."

"Aren't we all?" he answered. "I've been looking for someone I can trust to show up on time for his job in this place. So far, no luck. What's your guy done? Stood you up for dinner? Got you pregnant?"

"None of the above." I tried smiling. "He's actually a friend of my grandmother's." I showed him the picture. "Do you recognize him?"

He picked up the picture, looked at it, and then dropped it on the counter. "You a cop?"

"Nope. Just someone interested in finding him."

"Well, if you find him, you tell him he owes Gil Pridoux three months' back rent. He rented a room from me, upstairs. For a couple of years he paid every month, on time—no noise, no problems. Then he stopped paying. Said he'd get it to me, but it would be a little late. I told him, 'It's late, you pay interest.' He said he understood. Then, about a month later, I realized I hadn't heard him or seen him in a while. I checked upstairs. He was gone. Didn't have much stuff, but what he had, he took. Must have moved out one night after the store closed."

"He didn't leave a forwarding address."

"No way. I told the postmaster his mail was

piling up and he was gone. They didn't know he'd left. They stopped the mail from coming here."

"Did he have guests? Friends? Someone who might know where he'd be?"

"Not that I ever saw. He was always alone. Nice fellow, I thought. Until he ripped me off."

"Did you happen to notice what kind of mail he got?"

The man shrugged. "I didn't look real close. A couple of magazines. A lot of catalogs. He must've bought a lot of gifts, 'cause he got letters or bills from a bunch of gift shops. Wasn't my business to know what his business was. I'm no snoop."

"Of course not. Did he ever mention any hobbies? Hunting, fishing, golfing, collecting anything? Any clubs he belonged to? Church?"

"Nah. None of that. He wasn't my friend, you know, he was my tenant. We didn't chat a lot. All he said to me was I'd be getting the rent soon. That his luck was changing." He paused and looked at me. "That's it. Guess his luck didn't change. Or maybe it did, and he's living in Paris now. You said he knew your granny. You tell her to find another boyfriend. One who pays his rent."

"I will. Thank you for your time." I turned and walked toward the door.

"Hey, you wouldn't be looking for a job, would you? Regular hours. Right here in Brunswick."

"No, thanks! Good luck in finding someone," I called back over my shoulder as I headed out.

What next? Jacques Lattimore was alone. He'd rented a room, not a house or apartment. I walked down the block, toward Maine Street. He'd probably eaten near here pretty regularly. Men living alone usually had a favorite bar or diner. Somewhere inexpensive. I immediately ruled out the couple of upscale restaurants on Maine Street. The rest specialized in seafood or Thai or Indian cuisine. I was looking for someplace more downscale. More accessible. Less ethnic.

Then I remembered the diner I'd passed just outside of downtown. It would be walkable from the dry cleaner in good weather, and was open twenty-four hours a day.

A few minutes later I was sitting at the counter, ordering a coffee, black, and a bowl of clam chowder.

When the matronly waitress had a moment, I gestured to her.

"You want anything else, dear? You look like you could use a piece of pie. Apple and blueberry are fresh."

"Tempting. But not today." Before she could move away, I pulled out the picture. "Do you recognize this man?"

"Sure," she said. "That's Jack. But he ain't been around in a while now. Too bad, too. When he was on a streak, he was a good tipper."

"A streak?"

"When he came home from Cambridge, with

money burning a hole in his wallet. Those were sweet days." She patted her pocket.

"Cambridge?" I shook my head, confused. "In England?"

The laughter almost erupted from her. "England? No, honey. The Cambridge Casino. You from away or something?"

The ultimate Maine put-down. "You're right. I didn't think."

"Yeah, Jack was a player. You looking for him?"

I nodded.

"Then you better check the Cambridge. There's a good chance you'll find him there. And you can tell him anytime he wants to come back here, Carol knows what he likes."

I didn't ask what Jacques liked. I was afraid it wasn't pie. "Where's the Cambridge?" I asked.

"Up near Rome. You know . . . the Rome in Maine? Not that place where the pope lives. You got it?"

I got it. I'd been away. But I wasn't *from* away. In Maine those were two very different things.

Chapter Thirteen

I am obnoxious to each carping tongue
Who says my hand a needle better fits,
A poet's pen all scorn I should thus wrong,
For such despite they cast on Female wits:
If what I do prove well, it won't advance,
They'll say it's stol'n, or else it was by chance.
—Anne Bradstreet, Stanza 5,
"The Prologue," *The Tenth Muse
Lately Sprung Up in America*, 1650

I hesitated: Should I drive to the Cambridge Casino today? It was still late morning.

How far was Rome from Brunswick, anyway? I checked the GPS in Gram's car. About an hour away. Easy driving: the turnpike to Augusta, and then northwest on Route 27. I had time. If this new casino was of any size, there'd be signs. All roads in Maine did not lead to Rome. For a reason. Rome, Maine, was a pretty small place, in the Belgrade Lakes region. I suspected it was one of the many small towns in Maine struggling to make their budgets. Tax revenues from a casino would help a lot.

I was right. Signs advertising the casino started in the middle of a stretch of car dealerships still within the borders of Augusta, then continued through the farmlands between Augusta and the lakes.

The casino itself wasn't exactly Las Vegas. I'd been to Nevada once with Wally on a case; and unless I had a heavy bankroll, I wouldn't be going again. I have vices. Most people do. But gambling wasn't one of mine. I didn't see the use of wasting my dollars on a slim chance.

Mainers who drove a distance to the Cambridge Casino were either desperate for a bit of fun, or just plain desperate. And maybe lonely. If I were a gambling woman, I'd bet on which one Jacques Lattimore was.

The outside of the building was long and low and white and garnished with several architecturally unnecessary columns. Inside, the WELCOME TO THE CAMBRIDGE CASINO! sign kept up the "Rome" theme, with a map of Italy in the background and cheap plaster casts of Roman figures scattered about the floor.

The slot machines weren't far from the casino's restaurant. I checked the menu. Not much different from the menu at the diner I'd visited in Brunswick, but the prices were low, and the selections were described as *Wicked Good*. Definitely not Las Vegas.

Nickel slots. Quarters. Half-dollars. Dollars. If Susan B. Anthony only knew where her face had ended up.

About a third of the slot machines were

occupied. For early afternoon on a weekday, that augured well for the casino owners' coffers. I tried to look as though I was choosing a way to lose money. I kept looking for an elegant-looking man about six feet tall who walked out on commitments.

He wasn't at the poker tables or the roulette wheel. The place even had baccarat. Craps. I'd walked in a full circle around the floor. The only area I'd skipped was the center. Bull's-eye. Jacques Lattimore was seated at a blackjack table, with a glass of whiskey in his hand. He wasn't playing high stakes, and he seemed to be losing. When he'd finished the hand, I went over to him.

"Jacques Lattimore?"

He turned, clearly annoyed that someone was disturbing him. "Who wants to know?"

I could have played it a half-dozen ways. I decided to play it straight. "I'm Charlotte Curtis's granddaughter. I need to talk with you."

The dealer was watching, and wanting to start another hand. Lattimore hesitated, but then stood up. "I'm out for now. Keep my seat warm."

We walked far enough away from the slots so we could hear each other. Lattimore was a little unsteady and he held on to his glass. For support, I assumed. He was even thinner than he'd looked in Gram's picture.

"You're the granddaughter she raised up after her daughter disappeared."

I nodded.

"You live in the Southwest somewhere."

"Right now, I'm home. And I'm not happy. You owe Charlotte and her needlepointers serious money. They trusted you. You took advantage."

"Hey, Charlotte just has to give me a chance." He finished whatever was in his glass. I moved closer. It, and he, smelled like scotch. "I had a little problem a few months ago. I know I owe 'em. I'm working on getting that money. I am. You tell her that."

"You can tell Charlotte yourself. Even if you don't have all their money." I glanced around the casino. "But you owe her and those other people who worked for you an explanation, even if it's a rotten one. And you need to give them the names of all the customers who've ordered their products through you in the past couple of years."

"But I'll get her the money . . . I already have some of it," he started.

"Good. That's a beginning. You're guilty of fraud. But I think I can convince Charlotte not to sue you for breaking your contract and spending their money if you come back, talk to the stitchers, and give them as much money as you can. You owe them about thirty-three thousand dollars. How much can you pay back?"

Lattimore's shoulders slumped. "Maybe three thousand?"

I stared pointedly at the chips he was carrying.

111

"Okay. Maybe seven thousand. I had a good run last night."

"Then give the seven thousand to me. Now."

"But I need that to try to win the rest of the money back!"

I shook my head. "You give me the money, or I get a lawyer. If you're accused of a felony, casinos won't be happy to see you."

"You're tough, young lady," he said. "Not bad-looking. But tough."

I was gambling. Gambling where I held the high cards. I didn't know if Gram could sue him based on the simple contract she'd shown me, or even if she'd want to. But I hoped he was desperate enough to go along with me. I had to get that money now. Two hours from now, he might have gambled it away.

I followed him to the cashier, where he handed in his tokens. He counted the dollars out in my hand. It came closer to six thousand than seven thousand, but I took it.

"Now you'll come back with me to Haven Harbor," I said. "Where are your papers and records for Mainely Needlepoint?"

"I have a room. Not far from here. I didn't mean to hurt Charlotte."

"I'll drive you to your room. We'll get those papers. Then I'll take you to Haven Harbor. After you've talked to Charlotte, I'll bring you back."

He looked longingly at the table he'd left.

"You should be back here in four hours."

"But I've got no money left to play."

I hesitated. But if I needed to . . . "I'll give you two hundred and fifty dollars when we get back here. Just to get you started again. But that's it. I won't see you again, and you won't bother Charlotte again. Deal?"

"It's not a great deal for me."

"Losing twenty-seven thousand dollars isn't a great deal for the Mainely Needlepointers, either."

He looked at me. "How did such a pretty girl get so hard you could talk like that?"

"I've had experience," I said.

I put my arm through his and headed us toward my car. My gun was there, under my seat. I'd assumed, correctly, that there'd be a metal detector at the casino. I opened the passenger door for Lattimore. He didn't know that so far he'd been seeing the nice version of Angela Curtis.

Chapter Fourteen

Chains do not hold a marriage together. It is threads, hundreds of tiny threads, which sew people together through the years. That is what makes a marriage last—more than passion or sex.

—Simone Signoret,
Daily Mail interview, 1978

I called Gram from Route 27. "Hi, it's me. I'm bringing Jacques Lattimore home with me. We'll be in Haven Harbor in about ninety minutes. Get any questions you have ready, and maybe heat water." If we needed coffee, I was bringing it with me. Gram would choose tea over coffee any day. "See you then."

"It's illegal to talk on the phone while you're driving," Lattimore pointed out.

"Right," I agreed.

"I wouldn't want us to get into an accident."

"That's the only call I needed to make, and it's over. You don't have to worry. Not about that, anyway."

"Charlotte's really mad at me, isn't she?"

"How would you feel if your friends were struggling financially because they weren't paid for work they'd done?"

"I'm sorry. I'll tell her I'm sorry. I made a few mistakes. We all make mistakes."

Sure, we all make mistakes. But we don't all steal from our colleagues.

"Charlotte never told me you were so pretty. She told me a lot about you, you know. She's proud of you, making your own way in the world."

I let him talk.

"She must be happy you're back in Maine. You staying, or just visiting?"

He hadn't listened to the local news recently. "I came home for my mother's funeral."

"Funeral? Then they found Charlotte's daughter. I'm sorry. This must be a hard time for you."

"What you did hasn't made it easier."

"I understand. You're upset about your mother. It's hard to lose someone you love. I know. I lost my parents when I was six. A car accident. I've never stopped missing them, though. Are your mother's services over?"

I nodded. "Yesterday."

"So it's all still fresh in your mind. No wonder you're upset with me. You poor girl. You're grieving."

"I'm not grieving for Mama. I got over that one a long time ago. I'm angry with you for betraying Gram. And that's the last I'm going to say about it until we get to Haven Harbor."

Thankfully, he shut up.

There was more traffic than I'd imagined, but I

parked in front of our house right on time. I couldn't pull into the driveway. Three cars were already there. Looked like we weren't the only ones coming to see Gram. Jacques picked up the order forms and reached for the door handle. I reached for my gun.

"Before you go into that house," I said, carefully aiming the gun at him, "I want you to know I'll be watching and listening to everything that goes on. And I can use this. I don't want you to lie or give excuses. Just say what you have to say, give those orders to Gram, and then I'll take you back to Rome."

"You'd shoot me?" he asked incredulously.

"I'd shoot you," I confirmed. "So get going."

He got out and walked unsteadily up the path to our front door. I followed him closely. My gun was back in my holster. But both of us knew it was there.

Chapter Fifteen

Every little thread must take its place as warp or woof, and keep in it steadily. Left to itself, it would be only a loose, useless filament. . . . Yet each little thread must be as firmly spun as if it were the only one, or the result would be a worthless fabric.

—Lucy Larcom,
A New England Girlhood, 1889

The cars in the driveway had been a clue. Gram's living room/office was full. Clearly, she'd gotten on the phone after I'd called and summoned the Mainely Needlepointers. Haven Harbor was a small town. It hadn't taken long.

Some had even brought refreshments. I saw a teapot, two plates of cookies, a box of doughnut holes from Dunkin' Donuts, and a platter of scones.

I grinned as I saw the looks on their faces. Jacques stopped at the door. I might be the only one with a gun, but this was a tough crowd. If looks could have killed, he wouldn't have gotten past the threshold.

In case Lattimore didn't remember them, I made the introductions: Sarah Byrne. Dave Percy. Katie Titicomb. Lauren Decker. Ob Winslow.

Even Ruth Hopkins was there, stroking Juno, who'd found a cozy place on her lap.

"I found Jacques at the Cambridge Casino. The bad news is, you haven't been paid because he doesn't have your money. He lost it."

I had a rapt audience. Like a wolf pack, ready to spring. You don't fool with Mainers.

"But there is some good news. He had a bit over six thousand dollars." I handed the money to Gram, minus the two-fifty I'd promised to give back to Jacques. "He's also agreed to give you the sales slips and records from the sales you've made through him." I looked at Jacques. "Give the lady the paperwork." He handed it to Gram. "Now you should have the names of the customers you were working for. You'll be able to deliver any completed needlework and, I hope, get paid for that, without Jacques' commission. He's agreed he's out of the needlepoint business." I shot a look at him. "Permanently. So, Jacques, you tell these good people you're sorry, and answer any questions they have. I'll be in the next room." I picked up a molasses cookie and headed for the kitchen. I wasn't a needlepointer. The rest was up to them.

Jacques wouldn't get far without a car, even if he ran. I felt safe leaving him to the wolves.

I made a bathroom stop and then poured myself a cup of tea. Tonight I'd bring in the new coffee-maker and get it humming. Tea would be fine for now. I took a few deep breaths and tried to relax.

I couldn't understand every word coming from the living room, but the tones weren't calm. Then the hum of conversation continued, but lower. I wondered how long to leave them there. It was their business, not mine. But I'd need to rescue Jacques and get on the road to return him to the casino or to his room. It had been a long day, and it wasn't over. I glanced at the kitchen clock. They'd been together about half an hour. That should be enough time.

I heard the front door close. Jacques? I got up to check. Nope. Ruth Hopkins. She was using a walker, but was making good time down the walk.

All seemed calm. I took off my gun and slipped it into a drawer in the hall sideboard under a stack of woolen gloves. I'd know where it was, and Gram wouldn't be looking for winter gloves in May. It didn't seem I'd need protection today.

Lauren Decker was laughing and Katie Titicomb was pulling on her jacket. The party was breaking up. Everyone seemed considerably more relaxed than they had earlier. Even Jacques now had a teacup in his hand and was eating. Ob Winslow was telling a story about a woodworking customer.

It appeared Jacques' charm had worked again. Either that, or these people had chosen to see a little immediate cash and the promise of more work and money in the future as a glass—or teacup—half full.

I was about to collect Jacques for the return trip when he stood up. His teacup waved dangerously in the air. I hoped there wasn't much tea left in it. Maybe he was more upset about giving back his winnings than he showed.

"Ready to leave?" I said, entering the room. He handed me his cup. Everyone else was still. "Does anyone have any more questions for Jacques before I return him to Rome?"

A couple of people shook their heads.

"He's made a fair accounting of himself, Angel. He hasn't been forgiven, but we understand what happened, and we're ready to take the business on without him. Our agreement with him is over. Mainely Needlepoint and Jacques Lattimore are going separate ways. Isn't that right, Jacques?"

Jacques started to answer, but then suddenly bent over, as though he was having severe cramps. "Bathroom?" he managed to blurt.

I took his shaking arm. The poor guy clearly had a problem. Luckily, we had a half bath off the front hallway.

Back in the living room Lauren was standing up. "I need to go home and get dinner on," she said.

Dave Percy and Ob were also getting up. "Thank you, Angie, for helping out," said Dave, passing me in the hallway on his way to the front door. "Look forward to working with you in the future."

"With Gram, you mean," I said as the door was closing. Gram was handing Sarah a thick book from the shelf of books on historical needlepoint. They were probably talking about Sarah's quest for information about that piece of old needlework she'd found.

The situation looked under control. Until I walked past the bathroom, and clearly heard the sound of vomiting. Maybe Jacques Lattimore had had more to drink than I'd realized.

"Jacques? This is Angie," I said through the door. "Do you need help?"

"Leave me alone!" he managed to say.

I shrugged. I hoped he'd be all right to leave soon. If he'd drunk too much, that was his issue. If he had the flu, I'd already spent too much time with him. Plus, for obvious reasons, I wanted to make sure he'd finished throwing up before we got back in the car.

Gram was saying her good-byes to Sarah in the front hall.

Then she came over to me. "Thank you . . ." and then realized what the problem was. "Jacques? Can I get you a glass of water? A towel? Anything?"

"Go away," he muttered.

I shrugged and went to the living room to gather the cups and plates left there. Gram stayed in the hall, clearly concerned.

Jacques was still retching and we could hear the toilet flushing every minute or two. I washed up the few cups and plates and put away the food that was left.

"You can't drive the man home when he's in that condition," Gram whispered to me. "We have an extra room. We could make that up for him. Likely it's that twenty-four-hour bug people have had. Makes you sick as anything, but doesn't last forever."

If it was drink, he'd be better in hours. And if it was the flu and he was contagious . . . I'll admit, the idea of spending ninety minutes in the car with the man under the current circumstances was not appealing.

"You tell him he's our guest for the night. I'll go make up a bed." The only vacant bed was Mama's. Gram and I exchanged looks, and she nodded. "Clean sheets are in the upstairs hall closet, where they've always been."

At first, Gram had left Mama's room exactly as it had been, in case she came back. I'd gone in there to feel closer to Mama; to open her closet door and smell her perfume on the clothes hanging there. To wrap myself in the comforter on her bed. It had provided warmth, but little closure.

After a while I'd stopped going into the room. She'd said she loved us, but she'd left. And when we'd stopped believing she would come home, there was too much inside the room to remind me of what used to be.

Her door had been closed when I arrived home.

I went and got the sheets.

The room hadn't been touched. The same pictures

of Mama and me and Gram were on the walls. The same framed kindergarten picture I'd given Mama for Mother's Day. The same flowered comforter. The same hooked rug Gram's mother had made long before I'd been born.

I pulled down the bedspread and started putting a sheet over the mattress.

I'd half-finished when I heard Gram call, "Angel! Angel! Come down here!"

What is Jacques doing now?

I dropped the pillow I was holding and ran. The bathroom door was open. Jacques was lying on the floor, his body jerking up and down. I'd never seen anyone having a seizure, but it couldn't be anything else.

Gram had grabbed a towel and was trying to put it under Jacques' head so he wouldn't bang it on the tile floor. "Call 911! Something's really wrong!"

I was back in a minute and tried to help Gram. In movies seizures only lasted a minute or two. This one seemed to go on forever.

The EMTs got there in what seemed like an hour. It was probably seven or eight minutes. By then, the seizure was milder. Gram and I moved out of the bathroom, which reeked, and let the responders take over.

"He'd been drinking earlier, but he seemed fine. Then he started vomiting."

The responder in charge nodded. "We'll take

him to the emergency room at Haven Harbor Hospital." They got him on a stretcher and took him out.

It all happened fast.

"We should go after him," Gram said. "No one at the hospital there knows him, and he doesn't know them. He may be a fraud and a thief, but he doesn't deserve to be alone when he's sick."

"Are you sure?" I asked. This was the man Gram had been ready to kill a day or two ago.

"I'm sure, Angel. Let's go."

At the hospital, outside the emergency room, we waited for any word.

It was over two hours before a doctor came out to see us.

"You're here for Jacques Lattimore?"

Gram nodded.

"Are you related to him?"

"No. We were business associates."

I noted the word "were." Gram might be concerned about the man, but she wasn't going back in business with him.

"I'm sorry. I'm afraid we've lost him. Do you know of a relative we could notify?"

"He's dead?" I blurted. I could hardly believe it.

The doctor nodded. "He had a series of seizures. We couldn't control them. And then his lungs gave out."

"His lungs?" asked Gram. "He once told me he used to smoke. Maybe his lungs weren't the best.

But it was his stomach and intestines that were bothering him before the seizure."

"We don't know any of his relatives," I added.

"I'm not sure what happened," admitted the doctor. "I have no history on him. It could be a number of different things. We'll find out for sure in the autopsy. Thank you for bringing him here. I'll call the police and let them track down his next of kin." She turned and went back into the emergency room.

Gram and I looked at each other. Gram was clearly shaken. "What happened, Angel? What could have happened to him? He seemed fine, and then . . ."

I didn't know. I didn't wish death on the man. I'd only threatened him with my gun. But I was glad he wouldn't be able to bother anyone in Haven Harbor anymore.

I put my arm around Gram's shoulders. "Let's go home," I said.

She nodded. "And when we get there, there's something else we have to talk about."

Chapter Sixteen

Loara Standish is my name
Lorde guide my hart that
I may doe thy will also
My hands with such
Convenient skill as may
Conduce to virtue void of
Shame and I will give
The glory to thy name
          —Words stitched on possibly the
      first sampler made in the New World,
done by the daughter of Miles Standish in the
    Plymouth Colony, 1640 (now displayed in
    Pilgrim Hall, Plymouth, Massachusetts)

What else did Gram want to talk about? She'd asked me to find Jacques Lattimore for her. I'd done that . . . and just in time, since it seemed he'd been fated to leave the world rather abruptly.

I'd only eaten one cookie since late morning. I was starving. I unwrapped the leftover goodies people had brought to the meeting and nibbled while Gram called Reverend Tom to tell him what had happened. I heated the bean soup she'd made and frozen in February.

I loved her bean soup, made with every kind of bean imaginable, and carrots and peas and onions and garlic thrown in for good measure. She'd baked a loaf of bread while I'd been following Jacques Lattimore's trail, so I sliced that to go with the soup. No talking. No attempts to clean up the downstairs bathroom, which certainly could use a scrub. It could wait.

After the soup disappeared, and more of the bread than I'd like to admit, she sat back and looked at me.

"Angel, today you did what I thought was impossible. You not only found Lattimore, God rest his soul, but you even got him to pay back at least a little of the money he owed us. I consider that a small miracle. So do the other needle-pointers."

It felt good to be thanked. "We got lucky. If Jacques had stayed at the casino this afternoon and died there, I wouldn't have been able to do those things."

"True enough. But you did. And before you got home, the other stitchers and I were talking. We liked having an agent. For the first year and a half, Jacques did a good job. He got us more interesting jobs, for more money. We didn't mind giving him his forty percent. We were still doing better than we were when we were only making pillows for the Harbor Lights Gift Shop."

Fine. But that was the past. They'd have to find another way if Mainely Needlepoint was to continue. "Now that you have the names of at least some of your customers, you can contact those people. You could put up a Web site and a Facebook page. And *not* have to give anyone forty percent."

"That's just it, Angel. We agreed that's what needs to be done. But none of us—including me, and I started this business—none of us have the skills or time or inclination to pick up where Jacques stopped. Do public relations and marketing and sales. Maybe even consider advertising."

"If you don't want to do that, then Mainely Needlepoint will die," I pointed out bluntly. "When you were only making a few pillows for one or two customers, that was one thing. But, as you've said, you and the others have grown to depend on income from the business. Plus, you all enjoy creating beautiful needlepoint. Are you ready to give that up?"

Gram looked very serious. "You're right, Angel. We learned a lot from Jacques. We learned we have to do business only with those we can trust. We need a better legal contract. But if we had someone—not Jacques Lattimore—but someone else, to do what he did, maybe even do it better because we're that person's only interest—then it would be good for all of us."

"You could learn to do it, Gram. I believe you could do anything you set your mind to!"

"Except that I'm getting married, Angie. Because of Tom's job, I'll have obligations to the church, as well as to him. I can't commit to the hours Mainely Needlepoint deserves." She hesitated. "But Sarah suggested a solution, and the rest of us agreed." Gram put her hands flat on the table. "Angel, how would you like to be the chief operating officer—that's what Sarah said it's called—of Mainely Needlepoint?"

"Me!" That was a possibility I'd never dreamed of. I started shaking my head. I knew nothing about needlepoint. I was just visiting here. How could they even ask me?

"Don't say no until you think about it. You've lived away. You know how to deal with people. You know what to watch out for. I know you're not real creative"—I smiled. Gram was laying it on the line, and she knew me well—"but the rest of us can take care of that part of the business. What we need is a person who understands marketing, and accounts, and billing, and talking to customers. And you've done all of that, Angie. The rest of us don't have the practical experience you have."

"But—"

"No *buts!* You're young and you can dress up good and you understand computers and social media and all the other things people do today to drum up business. If you were the public face of Mainely Needlepoint, the business wouldn't look like just a group of old broads sitting on their front porches with their needles and floss, talking to their cats."

Juno rubbed against my legs, reminding me she was there, and I'd been ignoring her.

"Gram, you're no old broad."

"I certainly am. And proud of it. Now Sarah and Lauren and you—you're not. And, for sure, Dave and Ob aren't! But that's what people think of when they think about needlepoint."

"They're wrong, I know. Lots of younger people do needlepoint." I grinned. "Although, Gram, you have to admit it might be a challenge to get many teenagers today to stop texting and pick up an embroidery needle."

"True enough. But don't change the subject. If anyone can make this business work, it's you." She raised her eyebrows a bit. "Plus, you've got a place to live, here. You're home." She paused a moment. "And you'd get thirty-five percent of the profits."

"Wait a minute! You gave Lattimore forty percent!" I suddenly realized I was negotiating. I might really do this.

"He didn't get a free roof over his head. Course, I might ask you to chip in for your board once in a while, until I get married. After I move out of here, you'll have to walk a couple of blocks down the street to get my good cooking, or you're on your own."

I stared at her and began to smile. "Then you wouldn't sell this house?"

"Not if the new COO of Mainely Needlepoint

could get us clear of the money owed the needle-pointers."

"Gram, you're bribing me. I take over the operation of the business, and I get the house? Plus the commissions?"

"Not right away. First you have to pay off the money owed. It wouldn't be easy. Nothing comes without sweat. The accounts are a mess—who knows who these customers are—and you'd have to learn a new business."

"You're a piece of work, Gram. You and the others figured all this out while I was driving back from Rome?"

"Actually, Sarah and I came up with the plan earlier today. That's why, when you called, she and I decided to get all of us together to see if they agreed, and to greet Lattimore and have a little talk." Her eyes sparkled. "Even he thought it was a good idea. He was impressed with you."

I'll bet he was. How many times did someone hold a gun on him?

"I know it wouldn't be as exciting as that private investigating you were doing in Arizona."

I thought of my loaded gun, still in the hall sideboard. So far, this needlepoint business had been livelier than Gram thought.

For a few minutes I didn't say anything. I looked around the kitchen I'd grown up in, and then at Gram. I thought of the house that I still thought of as home staying in the family instead of being sold to people from away who wanted to telecommute to New York City. I thought of summers with cool breezes, instead of hundred-degree temperatures. And I thought of Mama's open murder case. I wanted to ensure it stayed open until I was sure who was responsible for her death.

My head wasn't convinced, but my heart was calling me home. "Gram, I've been away a long time. Can I first commit to a six-month trial, for both Mainely Needlepointers and me? It would give us both time to make sure this is right for everyone."

Gram clapped her hand in delight. "Of course. And I'm thrilled and happy to meet Mainely Needlepoint's new chief operating officer."

"But I already have one request," I put in before she got too excited. " 'Chief operating officer' sounds a little fancy, considering the size of the business. How about 'director'? That would look serious enough on business cards."

My life had just made a major turn. At least for six months.

I touched my angel for luck. I had the feeling I'd need all I could get.

Chapter Seventeen

Curly Locks, curly locks, wilt thou be mine?
Thou shall't not wash dishes, nor yet feed the
swine,
But sit on a cushion and sew a fine seam,
And feed upon strawberries, sugar, and cream!
—Classic nursery rhyme, unknown origin

The next morning, as soon as I figured people in Arizona would be awake, I called the woman who had the apartment next to mine. She and I had exchanged keys, in case of emergencies. I asked her to go into my apartment and pack and send the rest of my clothes and photos and a painting of a desert sunset, which I'd loved and saved for.

She seemed pleased when I told her she could take or sell anything else there, especially when I sweetened the deal by promising to send her a check for her trouble and the shipping costs. And did she know anyone who'd like my old car? It'd been nine years old when I'd bought it, six years ago. It wouldn't survive a trip to Maine.

I'd have to change my address. I'd cancel my lease in Arizona as soon as my stuff was out. My apartment hadn't exactly been a penthouse. I'd always thought of it as temporary. If I went back . . . when I went back . . . I'd find another one.

Now I had a job to do.

Gram and I started looking through her account books and Lattimore's, trying to reconcile the differences. Our first task—or my first task, as Gram kept saying—was to decide how much of the money we'd gotten from Jacques was due each needlepointer, and how much was still owed them. That done, I could contact all the former customers we could identify, explain the change in management, and ask what we could do for them.

I had a lot to learn. Gram had two bookcases full of books on needlepoint. She picked out two for me to start with: Jo Ippolito Christensen's *The Needlepoint Book* and Hope Hanley's *101 Needlepoint Stitches*. "After you're familiar with those, you can move on to more advanced books."

My new Mainely Needlepoint job would be more than keeping accounts. I had to understand what could and could not be done in needlepoint (upholstery, yes; clothing, except for perhaps a heavy vest or jacket, no) and learn at least a few stitches, so I could sound knowledgeable.

I also needed to take up where I'd left off when I was about ten. I needed to learn to do at least simple needlepoint. That way I'd better understand the challenges for those filling orders. Gram tried not to smile too much as she picked out a piece of marked canvas and colors for me. I'd start with a simple pine tree on a small cushion: one of the core Mainely Needlepoint products.

We were interrupted by Sarah's knock. She took one look at Gram and me going through a notebook of pictures and patterns that had been done by the group and grinned. "She said yes, then?"

I held up my hand. "Not to a total commitment. Six months, to get the company back on its feet. Then we can decide whether it's going to be a long-term relationship."

"It's a cinch. You'll love it," she declared. "Why wouldn't you? We're charming, you won't be stuck in an office, you'll get to meet people all over New England, and we'll even bake you goodies if you get us a good commission!"

"Don't make promises you can't keep," I answered. Sarah's effervescence was contagious. "But were those your scones yesterday? Because if they were, then you've got a deal. They were fantastic. I finished the last one for breakfast—"

"Sarah, we have some sad news," Gram interrupted. "After everyone else left yesterday, Jacques Lattimore had a series of seizures. He died at the hospital."

"Oh, no!" she said. "What a coincidence. I mean, for him to pay us back part of the money he owed, and then to die, so suddenly. He seemed fine until he had those stomach pains."

"Pretty awful way to begin a new job, I'll admit," I put in. "Having your predecessor die."

"I'll call the others and tell them later this

morning," said Gram. "Although I hated what he was doing to the business, he was charming and good company."

Right, Gram. When he wasn't cheating you!

"Is there going to be a funeral? Should we send flowers?" Sarah asked. Then she put her hand over her mouth. "Oh, I shouldn't have mentioned funerals. Not when I've just been to one for your daughter. And mother," she added, turning toward me.

"It's all right. Mama had been gone a long time before her service," I said. "Although that reminds me, I want to call Ethan Trask and nudge him. Find out whether his investigation has turned up anything." I headed for the kitchen phone. I'd left my cell upstairs.

Ethan answered on the first ring. "Trask. Maine State Police."

"Ethan? It's Angie Curtis. I wondered if you had any new leads about my mother's murder."

"I haven't. No. Although I do have a few things I'd like to talk over with you." He paused. "And I'd like to ask your grandmother about Jacques Lattimore."

"Lattimore? Why do you need to know about him?"

"He's dead."

"I know. And he was a thief. He cheated Gram's business out of thousands of dollars. That's all you need to know about him."

"He was at your home yesterday afternoon."

"He was. He collapsed here and we followed the ambulance to the hospital. We were there when he died."

"Then I need to talk with you both. Will you be at home in about an hour?"

"We could be." When state police called, it was good to be available. Plus, I wouldn't mind seeing Ethan again.

"Make sure you are. I'll see you then."

I walked back to the living room. "Ethan Trask is coming here. He wants to talk to both of us, Gram."

She sighed. "I wish he'd close that investigation into your mother's death. It was nineteen years ago. We may never know why, but Joe Greene certainly looks like the guilty party."

"Ethan doesn't just want to talk to us about Mama. He wants to talk about Jacques Lattimore."

"Jacques? Why would the Maine State Police care about Jacques?"

"Ethan didn't say. Maybe they have information about him," I said. "If he cheated Mainely Needlepoint, chances are he cheated other small crafting companies, too."

Sarah got up. "I'll leave you two, then. I need to open my store. I actually came to find out if you'd agreed to stay and help us, Angie. And to tell you both I've been doing investigating of my own." She glanced from one of us to the other. "Oh, no.

Not about a murder or anything like that. Sorry! I've been checking into cleaning that sampler I brought over the other day. Finding out whether or not it should be repaired. After I removed it from its frame, I looked at it carefully, and talked to several people knowledgeable about such things. I think I'll be able to clean the fabric if I do it carefully, but I won't touch the stitching. Then I'll line the back with a thin support fabric to stabilize it and keep it from deteriorating anymore."

"You know," I thought out loud. "Helping people identify and protect old needlepoint might be a sideline for Mainely Needlepoint. I suspect a lot of old samplers are in Maine homes. Probably other types of needlework, too, that people inherited and have treasured, but don't know how to conserve."

" 'Conserving.' That's exactly the right word," Sarah agreed. "And if we could provide any information about the piece—provenance, if possible—the needlework would be a lot more valuable. We might even be able to learn a little about the person who stitched it. I've been reading about the schools that wealthy New England girls went to, where they learned needlepoint, in the first half of the nineteenth century. Samplers done by students at the same school have similarities. I found books that picture many of them and include information about the schools."

"So there's source information available?" I said. "That's good news."

"See, Charlotte?" said Sarah. "Your clever grand-daughter is already coming up with new angles for Mainely Needlepoint. I knew she'd be perfect for the job!" She turned toward the door. "In the meantime I should get back to my store, and my stitching. 'Till then—dreaming I am sewing.'" She winked at me. "Emily wrote that."

"Wait and see," I put in. "I haven't even been on the job twenty-four hours. It's a little early to rush to judgment." But the idea of researching—investigating—the heritage of old needlepoint pieces and conserving them appealed to me. I doubted I'd ever become a master needlepointer myself. But I knew how to do research. Investigating the history of a piece of needlepoint couldn't be as complicated as finding a missing person.

And it shouldn't require a gun. . . .

Which I needed to get a Maine permit for. It looked as though, at least for the next six months, I'd be a Maine resident.

Was I really ready to come back to, literally, the scene of the crime?

I looked up at a framed picture Gram had stood on the mantelpiece. A photograph of Mama and me taken a few months before she'd disappeared.

People who'd stopped me at the funeral were right. We did look alike. And we had those identical birthmarks few people had known about.

Were we alike in other ways? I shook my head, chasing the thought away.

I wasn't like Mama. Not in the important ways.

A friend of Mama's had taken that picture, down on Pocket Cove Beach.

Mama had woken me up early and announced it was too beautiful a spring day for me to go to school. She was declaring a holiday.

We'd spent the whole day together, climbing on the rocks by the lighthouse. Searching for starfish and baby sea urchins in tide pools. Making patterns in the sand with our toes. The water had been frigid, but Mama hadn't cared. She'd waded out with my pail to bring back clear water for the turreted sand castle we'd built and decorated with tiny mussel shells and salty rockweed and sparkling sea glass. I'd cried when the tide turned and the waves lapped at our walls, but she'd helped me collect the shells and glass we'd used so we could take them home. "They're all memories, Angie. You don't lose memories."

I smiled, remembering. I hadn't lost them. That day seemed as clear to me now as it had then. By lunchtime we'd both been wet and sandy. We'd sat in the sun on benches overlooking the harbor and shared a pint of fried clams. We'd been happy.

I'd begged for a strawberry ice-cream cone, my favorite flavor. She'd ordered one with chocolate chips for herself. We were eating our ice-cream cones and laughing, ice cream dripping down our hands, when a friend of hers I hadn't known stopped to talk. He'd taken that picture before we'd headed home, where Gram had shaken her head, and headed me toward the bathtub. Mama had stayed on the porch, sitting in our hammock, swinging her bare sandy feet, talking to her friend.

That day we were like two children, playing together. *I grew up, Mama,* I said silently to her. *And I promise I'm going to find out what happened to you.*

Sure, Mama'd been in a lot of relationships. Some good, I hoped. Some probably not. The question was: Did she slam the door behind her when they were over, or did she leave the door ajar? Had someone from her past walked back in?

I wished I could ask her.

Meanwhile, Gram was calling the other needle-pointers to tell them Jacques Lattimore had died. And I'd agreed to be the director of Mainely Needlepoint.

Chapter Eighteen

Useful and ornamental needlework, knitting, and netting are capable of being made not only sources of personal gratification, but of high moral benefit, and the means of developing in surpassing loveliness and grace some of the highest and noblest feelings of the soul.

—*The Ladies' Work-Table Book*, 1845

Ethan Trask sat at the head of our kitchen table. He looked serious, even for a Maine State Trooper.

"Coffee?" The new electric coffeemaker I'd bought was now plugged in on the kitchen counter. It was the shiniest appliance in the room.

He shook his head. "I had an early lunch. With caffeine."

"You wanted to talk with us," I said. "With both of us." Gram reached down to scratch Juno behind her left ear.

"That's right." Ethan looked from one of us to the other. "I'm sorry, ladies. I realize this has been a rough week for you."

"Life's hard, young man. Whatever you've got to say, get on with it." Gram and I both sensed that whatever Ethan had to say wouldn't be good.

His eyes were sea blue. But today they were shrouded. Looking at them was like looking into cold, dark waters. He wasn't smiling as he checked his notes. "According to Haven Harbor Hospital, Jacques Lattimore was brought by ambulance to their emergency room last night from your home."

"That's no secret. The man was sick. He started throwing up and then he had a seizure. We weren't going to let him lie on the floor of our bathroom. Of course, we called for help," Gram said.

"I understand that, ma'am. You did the right thing. And you know Mr. Lattimore is now deceased?"

"He's dead. Yes. We went to the hospital last night and finally one of the doctors there told us."

Ethan nodded, referring to his notes. "And you don't know who his next of kin might be."

"No clue. That scoundrel was no relative of ours." Gram was playing this a little heavy. I wondered if she'd acted this way with the police after Mama had disappeared.

"How had you known him?"

"He was the agent for Mainely Needlepoint. But he hadn't been paying up the money he owed us. Last night he paid us some, and we fired him." Gram looked over at me and nodded.

"That's why he was here yesterday afternoon? To pay you money he owed?"

"That's right." Gram didn't mention how he'd gotten here. I had the feeling that question was coming next.

Sure enough: "Did Mr. Lattimore have a car? How did he get here?"

My turn. I smiled sweetly, hoping to get Ethan to lighten up a bit. "I drove him here."

"From his home?"

"No. I heard he might be at the Cambridge Casino, so that's where I went. I found him there. A little the worse for scotch, but at the blackjack table. I drove him to a room he'd rented, so he could pick up his records of Mainely Needlepoint accounts, and then I brought him back here." I thought for a moment. "He left his car at the casino."

"Can you give me his address?" He passed me a small notebook and I wrote it down. "I'll check with the casino about his car. And I'll try to find any relatives he might have, to let them know of his death."

"All I know was, once he told me he was born in Lewiston," said Gram.

Ethan wrote that down. "Lewiston. That might be helpful."

"If you don't mind my asking, why is a Maine State Trooper concerned with the death of a needlepoint business agent? Seems to me you should be working on cases a little more serious. Like my daughter's murder." Gram had laid out what I'd been thinking.

"Well, it appears we have a couple of issues with Mr. Lattimore. First, as I've mentioned, we need to find his next of kin to notify them of his death. And, then, there's the possibility he didn't die of natural causes."

Ethan was sitting as though he was at attention, showing no emotion. What had happened to the friendly Ethan I'd talked to on my first day home?

"What?" I said, practically jumping out of my chair. "The man wasn't young. He looked almost emaciated. He drank, and he hung out at a casino. All that happened was he started throwing up, like he had the flu. Anyone could have the flu. Then he had a seizure. I don't know what you're thinking, but just because a man gets sick in this house doesn't mean we had anything to do with it!"

"I didn't say you did," Ethan said, still not smiling. "And until we get the autopsy results, we won't know more. But the doctor at the hospital said vomiting and seizures don't usually come together. And Lattimore's pupils were dilated. You said he'd been drinking. He also could have been using drugs—maybe amphetamines." Ethan looked from one of us to the other. "Or he could have been poisoned."

I'd had enough. "You're accusing my grand-mother of poisoning him?"

"You told me he cheated her and her friends. That's motive. But"—he raised his eyebrows and looked at me—"you were the one who brought him here to Haven Harbor. You were with him the longest period of time. Did he eat or drink anything while he was with you?"

I shook my head. "He drank scotch at the casino. After that, nothing, until he got here."

"And what did he have to eat or drink here?"

You got me there.

"I don't know. I was in the kitchen."

"Where was Lattimore?"

"He was in the living room with me, and with the others who do needlepoint for hire. He seemed perfectly fine. I remember he had at least two cups of tea. He may have had a cookie or two, or a scone. We were all eating," Gram said.

"Who else was here?"

"Lauren Decker, Dave Percy, Ob Winslow, Ruth Hopkins, Katie Titicomb, and Sarah Byrne. All fine people," Gram said decisively. "Not a murderer among 'em."

"And all people he cheated."

"True enough. But he'd come to apologize and pay back part of the money he owed. Heavens, Ethan, none of us would have killed him!"

He nodded. "Maybe not. We'll wait to see what the autopsy says. In the meantime I'll find out what I can about the man. Maybe he had a seizure disorder, and the combination of the liquor and his own meds interacted. I hope that's what they find. Neither of us wants another murder connected to your family. But that's up to the medical examiner to decide."

146

"You're still working on my mother's case," I reminded him.

"I am," said Ethan. "So no one will be surprised to see me in Haven Harbor if I stick around for a few more days. I shouldn't even have told you ladies Lattimore's cause of death is being questioned. But I thought maybe you'd have seen or heard something that would help explain what happened."

Gram's tone was calm, but she was clearly furious. "The man was here. The man died. Not every death has to be someone's fault. People do up and die sometimes. No one else who was here yesterday got sick or died. He wasn't a young man, you know."

"According to the driver's license in his wallet, he was seventy-one. And people do die of natural causes. That may be what happened. But in the meantime, until we're sure about that, would you make a list of any food he might have eaten while he was here? And who prepared it. And served it."

Gram grudgingly took the pencil he handed her and started writing. When she'd finished, she handed the pad back to him. "So, Ethan Trask, you're going to spend more time with us in Haven Harbor."

"I'll bunk in with my mom and dad. They keep a bed made for me." He finally smiled.

"Won't your wife miss you?" I said, looking at the gold ring on his left hand.

"My wife's serving in Afghanistan," he answered. "My little girl, Emmie, and I—we're living with her parents for the time being. They help out with her when I'm on duty. If I work down here, I bring Emmie along and my parents have a turn making a fuss over her. That little girl has four devoted grandparents, for sure."

"I'm sorry. I didn't know about your wife," I said, embarrassed. He was not only married, but he was a father. Why did he have to be so darn good-looking? Probably honest and trustworthy, too. What people always say about all the good men being taken . . .

"You've been away, like you told me last time we talked. There's a lot you don't know about Haven Harbor today," he pointed out.

And a lot none of us knew about in Haven Harbor's past. And now Lattimore might have been murdered.

It was time to revisit what was happening in Haven Harbor nineteen years ago.

Chapter Nineteen

Methinks it is a token of healthy and gentle characteristics when women of high thoughts and accomplishments love to sew; especially as they are never more at home with their own hearts while so occupied.
—Nathaniel Hawthorne (1804–1864),
The Marble Faun, 1860

Ethan opened another file and turned to Gram. "Mrs. Curtis, you reported your daughter missing on a Wednesday morning. You told the police officer you hadn't seen her since Sunday afternoon."

"That's right," Gram said.

"That was two and a half days later. Why did you wait to go to the police?"

"I've been over this so many times, Ethan. Isn't that in your records?"

"It is. But a lot of time has passed since this case was active. I'd like to hear what you think now." When talking about his little girl, he'd relaxed some. Now he was definitely back in law enforce-ment mode.

"I think exactly what I thought then. You've heard my daughter wasn't the most reliable person. She sometimes stayed out all night, or even left for a couple of days, without letting me know." Gram's lips tightened. "I loved my daughter, but she wasn't an easy person to live with."

"Knowing that, what made you call the police Wednesday to report her missing? Why not wait another day or two?"

"Because for all her faults, and I'm sure you have pages of notes on those, my daughter loved Angie, here, very much. Jenny might be late to a job, or call in sick when she'd partied too much, but she kept her commitments to her daughter."

"Is that so, Angie?"

I'd never thought about it that way, but Gram was right. Mama didn't tell us where she was going or with whom. But if I were in a school play or she'd promised to take me fishing, she'd be there. Not always dressed like the other parents, and sometimes with an attitude that annoyed other adults, especially other women, but always there for me.

"Yes. Mama kept her promises to me. Always."

"And she'd made a promise to you that week?"

"Before she left Sunday afternoon, she'd said she was looking forward to seeing me fly up. I told you that the other day."

Ethan frowned. " 'Fly up'?"

"It's a Girl Scout tradition. A ceremony when you graduate from being a Brownie and become a Junior Scout." I smiled, remembering. "I was really excited about it. We had to recite the Girl

Scout Laws and Promise. Mama had been helping me memorize them."

"I guess I have to look forward to that with Emmie." Ethan's soft spot was clearly his little girl.

I nodded. "Our troop made a big deal of it. A junior troop was going to be there to greet us as we crossed over a little bridge we'd built. We'd each make a wish and then get our Girl Scout pins and sash. Our parents were invited. Mama hadn't usually helped with our Brownie troop, but she'd promised to come to the ceremony and bring a contribution for the refreshment table."

"And she didn't show."

I shook my head slowly. "No. You were there, Gram. I remember that. But I kept looking for Mama. And she never came."

"If Jenny'd been able to come, she would have been there," said Gram firmly. "No question about it."

"This ceremony was Tuesday afternoon?" said Ethan, going back to his notes.

"Brownies met after school. I don't remember the day of the week."

"It was Tuesday afternoon," Gram confirmed. "When I hadn't seen or heard from my daughter in forty-eight hours, I was certain something was wrong. But I didn't want to disappoint Angie. I left a note, in case her mother came home. I baked cookies and went." She looked at me. "Angie did real well, too." She reached over and patted my hand, as though I was still in the fourth grade.

I shook my head. That was all long ago. I was surprised Gram remembered all the details.

"But she was so upset that her mama hadn't come. She held it together during the ceremony and the reception afterward, but I could tell she was disappointed. She kept looking at the door, hoping her mama would appear. By the time we got home, she was in tears." Gram's expression was strained. "It was a hard evening. I was worried, too, but I kept assuring her that her mama would be home soon, that she'd gotten stuck in traffic or had to work late."

"You didn't call the police then?"

"I didn't. I didn't see how that would help. My daughter would come home when she was ready to come home. She always had. And I had a child to console. I didn't want her overhearing me calling the police."

"But you did, the next morning."

"After I'd gotten Angel off to school. I was afraid there'd been an accident and Jenny was in a hospital somewhere. That was what I was most worried about. I thought if she'd had an accident or gotten in trouble, the police would know, or have ways to find out."

He nodded and made a note.

"I don't see how going over these details so many years later is going to help," I interrupted the questioning. "Mama left home Sunday afternoon and didn't come back. What's important is where she went."

Ethan turned to me. "We know she left here and walked toward Main Street. The last confirmed information we have about her is from one of your neighbors at the time. Mrs. Lydian Colby said she saw Jenny walking down the hill toward Main Street. Mrs. Colby is deceased now, but then she was an elderly lady who spent a lot of time looking out her window. She particularly remembered your mother because of the bright yellow dress she was wearing."

"She walked down the hill and disappeared?" I said. "That's all you know after all these years? Lots of people in town knew her. Someone else must have seen her!"

"No one else ever came forward and said so. Of course, she could have met a friend who gave her a ride. That's what the officer in charge of her case then thought, since no one remembered seeing her on Main Street. He assumed she'd left town. But now, knowing where her body was found, I'm thinking maybe she did get to Main Street. Maybe she was heading for Greene's Bakery. It was Sunday, and the bakery was closed, but maybe she was meeting Joe there. But Joe's gone, and his wife's gone. The only one left in the family is Lauren, and she says she doesn't remember that day."

"Lauren and I were in the same Brownie troop.

Mrs. Greene was one of our leaders. She would have been with us Tuesday afternoon," I said, trying to remember.

"Tuesday afternoon was forty-eight hours after your mother left home."

Mama didn't come to the ceremony because she was already dead. That's what Ethan was saying. "When did Joe Greene rent that storage unit in Union?"

"Good question." Ethan looked through his notes. "Looks like he rented it about a year before your mother's death."

Just because Mama didn't come to my Girl Scout meeting didn't mean she was dead. She could have been in a place she couldn't leave. Someone could have tied her up, or locked her in a room some-where.

"How often did he visit the unit? What else was in there?"

"Not much," Ethan answered. "Lauren said her father had a great-uncle who used to live in Union. She guessed he might have left her dad a few pieces of old furniture and a couple of appliances, and her dad rented a storage unit to hold them. She doesn't know why."

"Instead of throwing them away or selling them?"

Ethan shrugged. "Your guess is as good as mine. Besides the freezer, there were a couple of cartons of old books, two bureaus in pretty bad condition, a washing machine, and an old couch in the unit. That was it."

"Have you got any other suspects?"

"That's one of the points I wanted to check with you both. At the time, Mrs. Curtis, you said you didn't know where your daughter was planning to go when she left on Sunday. But she was dressed up, in a new dress."

"She was. Looked real pretty that day."

"Yes," I said quietly. "I remember. And happy. She was very happy."

"That sounds to me as though she was going to meet someone. A boyfriend, maybe?"

"All I know," said Gram, "is that she didn't tell me where she was going or what she planned to do."

"She had a lot of friends in town. And in other towns, too," I added. "We didn't always know where she was going, or with whom. That was her way."

"Part of it was her trying to keep that part of her life separate from you, Angie," Gram pointed out. "She didn't want you getting ideas about any of her . . . friends . . . or getting fond of them, if she didn't think they'd be in her life for long."

"What about Angie's father," Ethan asked. "Who was he?"

"Even I don't know," said Gram. "She'd never say. Didn't put anyone's name on the birth certificate."

"She had Angie when she was seventeen. She was living here. Who was she dating at the time? As her mother, you must have known."

Gram sighed. "There were boys . . . but I don't know if any of them were Angie's father. I wondered, of course, but I always had the feeling that if he'd been a Haven Harbor boy, she would have said." Gram looked at me, her eyes clearly hoping I'd understand. "She got pregnant during the summer. That time of year folks in town are from all over. The father could have been anyone. Could be . . . ," Gram said sadly, "It could be she didn't know who he was."

"Did you ever ask her about your father?" He turned to me.

"Once. All she said was that he was handsome, and tall, and that I would probably be tall, too." She was wrong about that. I was taller than Mama'd been, but five feet seven wasn't tall. "Ethan, I was only nine when she left. I knew I didn't have a dad like other kids did, and I was old enough to know that was embarrassing. Somehow wrong. But I wasn't old enough to press Mama about it."

"Mrs. Curtis, your daughter never received child support? Or ever had more money than you would have thought?"

"No child support. She never mentioned the possibility. Jenny never had much money. Her salaries and tips came in, and went out. That's why she and Angie lived here most of the time. She didn't have the money to live anywhere else, or the money to pay a babysitter when she was working. I did that for her. And I made sure we had food on the table and Angie had clean clothes that fit her. Jenny loved Angie. But when it came to money, she spent on herself first. She knew I'd make up the slack if Angie didn't have what she needed. I should have pushed more—maybe she would have taken more responsibility. I wasn't a perfect mother, Ethan. I tried. But I couldn't change Jenny. I had hopes for my granddaughter."

She turned to me and smiled.

I knew Gram had supported us after Mama disappeared. I'd always figured Mama contributed to my upkeep when she was still at home.

"You did a great job, Gram. If I'm not perfect, it isn't your fault."

She reached over and covered my hand with one of her worn ones. "Thank you for that, Angel. I did my best. But I couldn't replace your mama."

"Okay," said Ethan. "Then neither of you has any ideas about who Jenny would have been meeting that Sunday afternoon. Even after all these years of thinking, you haven't come up with any possibilities."

Gram shook her head. "She was working at the Harbor Haunts then. You probably have that in your file. Maybe someone at the café would remember. Maybe she met someone there. At the time everyone kept quiet. No one had any ideas about who she'd met. At least, none they shared with me. Or with the police."

"Did she have any enemies? Anyone she'd argued with? Anyone who'd threatened her?"

I shook my head.

"If she did, she didn't tell us," Gram said. "But she always kept her troubles to herself."

"Ken Bisson owned Harbor Haunts then. I'll talk to him." Ethan closed his notebook. "If either of you think of anything else that might help, you'll let me know, right?"

"What if you don't find anything new?"

"Then we'll have to assume that, intentionally or by accident, Joe Greene killed her. Since Joe's gone, we'll close the case."

Shot in the back of the head by accident? It might have been Joe Greene. I knew that. But no way was it an accident.

The question was: Why? The answer to that would point to the killer.

Chapter Twenty

Woman has relied heretofore too entirely for her support on the needle—that one-eyed demon of destruction that slays thousands annually; that evil genius of our sex, which, in spite of all our devotion, will never make us healthy, wealthy, or wise.

—Elizabeth Cady Stanton,
in open letter to women,
Seneca Falls, New York, May 1851

Ethan Trask had left. Gram had gone grocery shopping. All was quiet, except in my head. I started in on the accounts for Mainely Needlepoint. They were tedious and confusing, and I couldn't concentrate. Not a good sign for my first day on the job.

I kept going back to Ethan's questions that morning. They were all so obvious, and covered the same ground police in the past had put under microscopes. There were two directions to take in Mama's murder. One was to start with her body, and figure how long it had been in the freezer, and who put it there. . . . Basically, work backward. Find out when Joe Greene, or anyone else, had visited that storage unit.

I was more intrigued by working forward. Where

was Mama going when she left the house in her new yellow dress that Sunday afternoon? And, thinking of that day, that year, who would have had any reason to kill her?

I pulled a clean sheet of paper out of Gram's printer and labeled it, *People to check.* Ethan had asked if Mama had any enemies. Gram and I had said no, but we didn't know everything about her.

"Enemies" was a strong word. The sheet stayed blank.

Okay. Who might have been angry with her?

That was an easier question. I didn't know specifics, but I knew enough about her life to be able to imagine.

Had she rejected any of her male friends recently? Her reputation to the contrary, Mama sometimes said, "No."

Did she have problems with those she worked with at Harbor Haunts? More than once, she'd "forgotten" her hours or gone in late. That didn't endear her to others who worked there. She'd been fired from that job, and other waitressing jobs like it, more than once or twice. Fortunately for her, there weren't many attractive young women who wanted to work twelve months of the year at a small café. She often got her job back. But maybe this time . . .

Gram was sometimes impatient with her. But . . . no. Gram would never hurt Mama. She might have been frustrated with her, and worried about her, but she wouldn't have harmed her. And she didn't have a gun.

Gun. Handgun. Lots of people in town hunted for deer or moose in the fall, and birds of various sorts in season. Hunting and fishing and Maine went together. Most hunters aimed at filling their freezers. A few just liked the sport or the camaraderie of other men (and women) who hunted. A hunter who didn't want to be bothered with the meat could take his kill to one of several processors in the state who'd prepare and freeze the venison or moose meat and deliver it to a food pantry or soup kitchen.

Some kids I'd grown up with had learned to shoot before their First Communions. By the time they were twelve, some had entered their names in the annual state moose lottery, hoping for a chance to kill one of Maine's most famous animals.

But Mama'd been killed by a handgun. Who in Haven Harbor had a handgun nineteen years ago? Mama was scared of guns. A childhood friend of hers had been playing in her backyard during hunting season. Despite wearing an orange scarf, she'd been shot and killed by a hunter. It was ruled an accident. Mama had told me that story many times. She'd never forgotten her friend, or forgiven the hunter for shooting close to posted land, to her friend's home. She'd made sure I wore blaze orange during hunting season, even though I was here in town, or walking along the beach, where no one hunted.

But I'd seen handguns. I knew I had. I thought hard, back to before Mama disappeared. Back to when I was just a little girl, like other little girls, and played at my friends' homes.

Was it at Lauren's house? No . . . the bakery! Yes, Joe Greene kept a handgun at his business.

"So he can protect himself from bad people," Lauren had told me. She'd showed me the gun once, although she wasn't supposed to touch it. I shuddered, thinking about that day. Children didn't always do as they were told, and something forbidden was often a temptation. Joe had owned a gun. But who knew where it was now? Or if the medical examiner could identify it based on what had been left of Mama.

But the Greenes weren't the only ones. Captain Winslow, Ob, who'd retired from the navy and carved wooden decoys and deer and chipmunks before he became a Mainely Needlepointer, had a handgun. I'd seen it once when his wife had been ill and Gram sent me over with a bowl of turkey barley soup for her. The gun had been right on their kitchen counter. I hadn't known why, and I hadn't asked. The Winslows had a son younger than I was. Josh was the kid who wriggled so much he kept falling off his chair in class, and drove neighbors crazy with his loud voice and nonstop activity. I remembered hearing a neighbor complain Josh was sinking baskets in his driveway in the middle of the night. Where was Josh now?

But, no matter Josh's issues, his dad—the captain—had had a gun.

I thought carefully of all the other places in town. I couldn't remember seeing any other handguns myself, but I was sure other store-keepers had them. And a lot of homeowners.

Even today you didn't need a license in Maine to buy a handgun, you just needed a permit to conceal the one you carried. Nineteen years ago you probably hadn't even needed that. There was no way the state police would be able to find out who had a handgun then. It could have been half the people in town, not counting people outside Haven Harbor.

The more I thought about guns, the more I knew I had to apply for that concealed carry permit. I checked to see if I had my passport for identifi-cation, wrote a note for Gram, and headed across town.

Sergeant Pete Lambert, who'd helped us get to Mama's service without being bothered by the media, was on duty. He pulled out a form and handed it to me. "Fill this out and I'll send it to the state for you. We need to take your picture to go with it. Stacy, over there," he said, pointing at a young woman sitting at a desk in the corner, "has a camera to do that. But you'll need to have been a resident for six months."

163

"That long? But I already have a permit from Arizona." I pulled that out to show him.

He nodded. "I see. And I know you've moved home. But six months is the law. You can have your gun, of course. Just don't conceal it, and you'll be within the law. I know you. I'll hold your application here and file it for you in six months. You should get your permit pretty soon after that."

Six months! I might not stay in Maine longer than that.

He stared at my Arizona permit before handing it back to me. "You be careful, though. A handgun isn't a toy."

"I know." I didn't tell him I'd once had to use mine, not counting when I'd threatened Jacques Lattimore. Wally'd insisted I go with him to the gun range once or twice a week until he was sure I knew what I was doing. Carrying wasn't something he, or I, took lightly.

Having made an attempt to establish that I was once again a citizen of Maine, I walked down the hill to the commercial part of town. Seasonal businesses started opening in early May, and those open year-round changed their inventories to appeal to summer folks—those people with more money. Flannel shirts, wool socks, and rain and hunting gear were replaced by sweatshirts emblazoned with pictures of lighthouses or moose or sayings such as *I found my Haven in Haven Harbor, Maine.* Goods no local would ever wear.

Mama had walked down from our house toward Main Street. Had she gotten all the way there? Joe Greene's bakery, now the French patisserie, was a couple of blocks west of where she would have crossed Main if she'd come straight down the hill.

I waved at Sarah Byrne, who was watering the lilies of the valley in the window of her antique shop. Nothing of interest there. That shop hadn't been there nineteen years ago.

The hardware store Ethan's family owned was still open. Mama never went into the gift shops. They were for people from away. And she didn't buy her clothes in Haven Harbor; she shopped in Freeport. She only wore heavy coats or sweaters on the bitter-cold days when she'd walk to work in below-zero temperatures and snowdrifts blocked cars from seeing around street corners.

When I reached the Harbor Haunts Café, I decided to stop in and have a cup of coffee.

I sat at the old red Formica counter. Lauren was waiting on tables. A young woman I didn't know took my order.

Mama was working here when she left. Had she been on her way here that day? She wasn't dressed for work, but maybe she was planning to meet someone later, after the café closed. In May the customers would have been a combination of people who lived or worked in town and snowbirds, back from winters in the south. Snowbirds,

165

who wintered in North Carolina or Florida, or even Vermont for the skiing, returned as early as April.

I spun around on my stool, looking at the tables. The place hadn't changed much, although Ethan had mentioned it had changed hands.

Once in a while Mama had brought me here as a special treat. We'd always sat on the end of the counter, right by the kitchen, and she'd order me hot chocolate with marshmallows or a peppermint stick in the winter, or a one-scoop hot-fudge sundae in summer. Lemonade too. I remembered drinking lemonade here and adding sugar because it wasn't as sweet as Gram's.

In high school I'd come here with friends. We'd order Pepsis or Moxies or, if we had a little more money, root beer floats. In the winter we could sit here for an hour or two with our sodas, sharing an order of french fries. In the summer we knew better. Tables then were for folks ordering lobster rolls or fried clams. But we didn't need the shelter of the café in the summer. We had the beach, and the piers, and were too busy with jobs, helping in family businesses or restaurants or keeping the beach clean, to idle time away. It took a lot of hands to keep a small town spruced up for the tourists.

I watched Lauren smiling and talking with a couple whose toddler was in a high chair.

I'd finished my coffee and was pulling out my wallet when she stepped behind the counter.

"Glad you were able to squeeze a few dollars out of that Jacques Lattimore. And congratulations. I heard you've agreed to replace him at Mainely Needlepoint."

"On a trial basis. We'll see how it works out."

She leaned toward me and lowered her voice. "How soon will I be getting my share of the money you got from Lattimore? I really need it."

"Soon. One day, maybe two."

"I sure hope so," Lauren answered as the waitress who'd taken my order moved back behind the counter. She raised her voice a little. "You're not going back to . . . Arizona? That's where you were, right? Before you decided to come home."

I'd come home because she'd found my mother's body. Because, maybe, her father had killed my mother. Not totally my own decision. "I lived outside of Phoenix. I worked for an investigator there."

"So you're giving up your job to stay here?"

"I want to take care of some business here. And I hope I can be a help at Mainely Needlepoint."

"You don't even do needlepoint."

"True. I'm not good at crafts." I looked down at my hands. "I'm not good with my hands." Unless there's a gun in them. "But Gram asked me. And Lattimore didn't do needlepoint, either. I'll be working with the accounts and orders, and talking to customers. I won't be creating the products."

"The 'products'?" She looked at me disdainfully. "Needlepoint is a highly skilled craft. An art. One that deserves more respect than it gets."

"I have a lot to learn, but I admire beautiful needlepoint. It connects us to all the women in the past who did it to add beauty to their lives. It's part of our heritage."

"Maybe. You make it sound romantic. Remember, our needlepoint is a way of paying bills—if we get enough orders."

"Gram said you're talented. She's going to try to teach me, too, so I'll understand more about it."

Lauren picked up my empty coffee cup and swept the counter with a damp rag. As she stretched, I noticed a large purple bruise on the back of her right arm. "That's a nasty bruise. A fall?"

"Right. I was clumsy." She turned to go back into the kitchen. "Well, I'll be waiting for my share of Jacques' money, and for the chance to get new orders to fill. I can make as much doing that as I can breaking my back carrying trays of dirty dishes here."

"If you have a few minutes, I'd like to talk with you. About . . . the storage locker. About Mama. And your father."

"There's nothing to tell. My father's dead. His locker had some junk in it, and one of those big white freezers most folks have in their barns for venison and tomato sauce and blueberries. The kind you open from the top." She paused. "You know what was in there. That's all. There's nothing more to say. I'm sorry about your mother. Now I have to get my orders."

Lauren went back into the kitchen and picked up two plates. I could see the thick cheeseburgers and onion rings from a distance. She put them in front of an older couple sitting in the far corner. Then she went back to the kitchen. She didn't look at me again.

I paid my check and left a decent tip.

I'd have to start over here. People knew who I was, but they also knew I'd had baggage when I left, and they didn't know whether that load had increased when I'd been away, or whether I was ready to settle into Maine ways.

Truth to tell, I didn't blame them. I wasn't sure myself.

Chapter Twenty-one

Since every man is born in Sin
O lord renew my Soul within
Prepare me in my youthful day.
Humbly to walk in wisdom's ways
In all requirements of Thy Laws
And from Thy word my comforts
May thy good Spirit guide my youth
And lead me in the way of truth
Disclose the evils of my heart
Direct me how with sin to part
O let me not Thy spirit grieve
Come Let me now thy grace receive
Kindly Thy pardoning love bestow
So That I may my savior know.

> —An acrostic sampler stitched by
> Sophia Maddocks, Cape Newagen,
> Boothbay, Maine, 1821

Lauren wasn't going to help me. I couldn't blame her. If her father had killed Mama, that didn't augur well for a solid family history. She'd have to live with being the daughter of a murderer.

That had to be even harder than being the daughter of a victim.

I turned toward home. The wind had shifted. It was now brisk, and coming from the northeast. I hoped a storm wasn't brewing. I pulled my jacket closer.

I hadn't liked the heat of Arizona summers, but I'd gotten used to them. I'd forgotten the chill of afternoon sea breezes.

I wasn't convinced Ethan was taking Mama's cold case seriously. Especially since now he'd been distracted by the possible situation with Jacques Lattimore.

Why couldn't I feel like Gram, and get on with my life, whether that life was going to be here in Haven Harbor, or back in Mesa, or somewhere else? Why did I feel such an obligation to the past?

I'd held Mama's hand and skipped along this sidewalk, knowing that people sometimes looked at us and whispered. I'd thought it was because Mama was pretty. It wasn't until the years just before she disappeared that I'd begun to notice she was different from other Haven Harbor mothers. Her clothes were tighter, and lower in front, and she wore bright colors when others favored more subtle hues. Women in Haven Harbor considered themselves dressed up when they combed their hair and put on lipstick. Mama wore bright eye shadow and curled her long, layered hair until it looked like a movie star's.

She was beautiful. I'd wished I looked like her.

Everything about her sparkled: her blond hair, the bright colors she wore, her shiny fingernails, the gold jewelry she wore.

"With my coloring, silver looks dull," she'd told me once. "Gold jewelry goes with my hair."

I'd nodded, seriously taking in her lesson.

Then she'd whispered, "Someday maybe my jewelry will be real gold, not just gold-colored. Gold colors wear off. Real gold stays forever."

"What color jewelry should I wear?" I'd asked her, looking in her dressing-room mirror at the two of us. My straight brown hair was a fashion world away from her curls.

She'd tilted her head a bit, considering. Then, "Silver is your color, Angel. Bright silver. It doesn't cost as much as gold, so you'll be able to buy the real thing. Make sure you do. Don't waste your money on imitations. You're worth the real thing."

And then she'd laughed and hugged me.

Silver might have been my color, but the angel necklace she'd given me was gold. Real gold. Fourteen karat.

But on the rare occasions when I bought jewelry for myself now, I always bought silver. Mama had said it was my color.

Hugging myself in my light jacket as I walked, I wondered whether her clothes were still in her closet. Would any of them fit me? I didn't want to wear them, but I was curious. I was pretty sure I was an inch or two taller than she'd been. Maybe trying on her clothes would bring me closer to her.

I looked in the window of what had been Joe

Greene's Bakery. The wind grew even brisker. Or maybe I just noticed it more.

How many times had I been in that store? Hundreds? Likely. Mama'd bought me cookies there, or cupcakes, when I was little. When I was older I'd be sent on errands there: "Pick up a loaf of bread and a sweet for dessert."

Sometimes I'd refused, but then Gram would get angry.

What little girl wouldn't want to go to the bakery? It was only three blocks from home. Nothing bad could happen in three blocks.

I stood outside the window. They were right. Nothing bad had happened in those three blocks. At least nothing I knew about.

I took a deep breath and went in. The little bell on the back of the door, which announced customers, was still there. Its sound stopped me.

But I was grown up now. This was a patisserie. Whatever had happened in the past was over. Gone.

I walked to the familiar display case, now filled with fancier pastries than the Greenes had ever sold.

"May I help you?" said the young woman in back of the counter.

"Two éclairs," I said, pointing at a tray behind the glass.

"I'll put them in a box for you," she replied, reaching into the cabinet.

I pulled out my money.

Who else could I talk to? Did anyone else remember what this town was like?

"Thank you," I said, accepting the white box tied with red string. "They look delicious. I've been away for a few years. I didn't know you were here."

"My husband and I bought the building from the Greenes," she said, smiling. "You probably knew them. We love Haven Harbor. I'm glad you stopped in. I hope you'll be back."

"Most likely," I said. "The éclairs look delicious."

"They're one of our top sellers," she confirmed. "Nice to meet you. And have a good day!" I'd almost gotten to the door when she added, "Welcome home!"

Chapter Twenty-two

Work is inspiring where there is not too much of it, and sewing is a restful occupation if taken up and put down when the inspiration is upon one. It becomes a cross when the tyranny of fashion demands too much of nervous fingers, and when the hours spent at it are taken from nobler pursuits.

—Laura C. Holloway, *The Hearthstone, or Life At Home: A Household Manual*, 1888

"Those look delicious," said Gram, peeking into the bakery box at the éclairs I'd bought. "But we'll save them for tomorrow. Tom's invited us to his home for dinner tonight."

"I don't have to go," I answered. "I'm sure he's just asking me because I'm your granddaughter. You go. I'll make my own dinner here at home."

"Nonsense! He invited you specifically. And I'd like you to get to know him, Angel. After all, soon he'll be your stepgrandfather!"

I hadn't thought of that.

"He's an excellent cook, and a kind and interesting man," she continued. "I know what people think when they hear he's a minister, but that's only part of his life. He doesn't spend every hour of the day reading the Bible or ministering to the poor and indigent."

Or to older women, I thought.

"How old is he, Gram? He's good-looking, but he doesn't—"

"Doesn't look my age? Heavens, no. Tom's ten years younger than I am. He's fifty-two." Since Gram was sixty-five, she seemed to have a little problem with subtraction.

"Gram! You're a cougar!"

"What?"

It wasn't the moment to mention I'd once dated a man who was fifty-two. Jonathan had been bright and interesting, but he'd been in love with me because I was twenty-five. He'd left when I couldn't promise never to change.

"A cougar, Gram. What people call a woman who dates a man much younger than she is."

"People can call me what they want. I call myself 'smart.' Everyone knows men don't live as long as women. Smarter to pick one who's younger. We'll have more years together, and he might be around to take care of me someday, instead of the other way around. Have you noticed how many widows there are, compared to widowers?"

What could I say?

"You're thinking I'm a little crazy in the head and I shouldn't be thinking of getting sick and dying. But at my age it's natural that those thoughts pop up more often than they do for you,"

Gram said. She looked at the kitchen clock. "We'll leave about five-thirty. Did you have much time to go over those accounts?"

"I started. The records you've kept are clear. The problem is merging what you've been recording with what Lattimore did. You focused on each person contributing to the business, what they'd been assigned, and how long it took them. He focused on the people who'd ordered the work. It's hard to get it all to match up. Like, Mrs. Sam Bailey ordered needlepoint seats for her dining-room set. Eight straight chairs, which had smaller seats, and two armchairs for the ends of the table. All that's clear. And I found the floral pattern to be used. Your binders keep those in order, but I couldn't figure out who was working on the actual pieces. According to Lattimore, they haven't been completed."

"They hadn't been finished when he vanished a few months ago, but they're done now. Let me show you," said Gram, and she and I headed into the living-room office.

Heavy knocking at the front door interrupted us.

The man standing outside was huge. My first impression was that he was in his thirties, but life hadn't been kind to him. His hair needed a cut, his arms and neck were covered with tattoos, and his skin was the permanent tan of a man who'd spent his life on the water. Most important, he was furious.

Furious enough that I wished I had my gun close at hand. I moved closer to the sideboard, where I'd left it. But then I was afraid he'd think I was backing away from him. I didn't want him to know how afraid I was.

"I suppose you're the granddaughter. Angela."

"I'm Angela. Who are you?"

"Caleb Decker. I'm here to get the money due my wife."

Caleb Decker. Lauren's husband. "We haven't gone through all the accounts yet. Lauren will get her money as soon as we finish."

He pushed the door open wider and strode past me into the living room. "Charlotte, we've been owed that money for months now. I want it now."

Gram stood up. "Caleb, Angie's told you the truth. We've just started to go over the accounts."

"Lauren said that agent of yours gave you a fistful of dollars yesterday. How long's it take? Just give me the cash."

The money was in the desk drawer of the living room. I hoped Gram wouldn't mention that. I put my hand on the drawer holding my gun.

"Probably tomorrow, Caleb. Take it easy. Lauren'll get her share of the money when everyone else does. Not before."

He took a step toward her. She didn't move. "Tomorrow, Caleb. No later than the day after. I promise you."

He looked at me, my hand on the sideboard

178

drawer, and at Gram. "It had better be soon. Or I'll be back." He stomped past me, slamming the front door in back of him.

"Wow," I said, relieved that the situation seemed to have resolved itself. "That's Lauren's husband? He's off the wall. I'm proud of you, Gram. You stood up to him."

"That's the only way to deal with bullies," she said. "Call their bluff."

"How can Lauren live with someone like that?" I wondered out loud.

"She hasn't had an easy life," Gram confirmed. "And, for the record, make sure the money she's owed goes to her. Not to Caleb. Keep that in mind for the future, too."

I nodded. "Absolutely." I didn't have to ask her why.

We spent what was left of the afternoon going over the pattern books and correlating the work done with the work delivered and the work paid for. Some work had been completed, but not delivered. A few pieces had been delivered, but were not paid for. I'd have my hands full getting it all sorted out, without even beginning to try to find new work.

"We have a lot of repeat customers and referrals," Gram assured me. "We can all work on gift shop items for now. We'll be getting calls for those any day now, and shops will ask for backup items later in the summer if sales have been good.

Those orders don't pay as much as the special ones, but they'll keep people in soup and hamburger for the moment."

There was no more time to think about Mama's murder before Gram and I left for the rectory.

"Glad you could both come," Reverend Tom said, greeting Gram with a hug and a kiss and me with a touch on the arm. "Dinner is cooking. I decided to make something simple." I sniffed. Whatever it was smelled fantastic. *"Boeuf Bourguignon."*

"I'm impressed," I said. The reverend was wearing close-cut jeans and a beige sweater. He didn't look like my idea of a minister.

"Don't be. It's not complicated. Just beef stew with mushrooms and red wine."

"I told you he could cook," Gram said, nodding. "Wait until you taste it."

"Come and have a glass of wine while it's cooking," said the reverend.

I didn't remember ever having been in the rectory before. But I was pretty sure no other minister who'd lived there had decorated like Reverend Tom.

"What?" I spun around. "But . . . you're a minister!"

He and Gram both laughed. "You didn't tell Angie about my collection, then," he said.

"I thought it would be more fun for her to discover it herself," Gram answered.

I walked slowly around the living room. The walls were covered with shelves too shallow for books, but the perfect size to display an amazing collection of Ouija boards. Most were rectangular and made of wood, but Reverend Tom also had circular boards (one labeled an *Angel Guidance Board*, with pictures of angels surrounding it) and one that was triangular. Many were plain, just listing the alphabet and numbers and *yes* or *no* in corners, and *good-bye* in English, French, or Spanish. Still, others, like the angel board, were decorated with stars or eyes, turbaned sorcerers or witches. There were boards large enough to cover a tabletop, and miniature boards complete with miniature planchettes, the moving pieces that would spell out users' fortunes. Maybe the tiny boards were for New Age dolls? I was fascinated. "How many do you have?" I asked. "And why?"

"I started collecting when I was in high school. One of my uncles had a board, and I was fascinated by the possibility that spirits could speak through it. I tried it out every time I visited him, and eventually my uncle gave it to me." Tom pointed at the board over the mantel. "It's one of my least valuable boards, but it was my first, so I put it in a place of honor. I have about a hundred boards now."

"Do many people collect things like this?" I'd never collected anything but sea glass. Maybe I didn't fully appreciate the passion of a serious antique collector. But this wasn't just an unusual collection. It was weird. And fascinating. Especially because it belonged to a minister.

And Gram was going to move into this house? It gave me the willies.

"Lots of people are collectors. Christmas collectibles have been popular for years, but today Halloween collectibles are catching up with them. Ouija boards aren't only for Halloween, of course, but, like tarot cards, they're categorized by collectors and dealers as related to Halloween because sometimes people use them at Halloween parties. They became more popular a few years back when 'New Age' people began collecting angels and crystals and scented candles, along with other 'mystical' decorations and jewelry."

I touched the angel pendant I was wearing under my sweater. "Do you believe people can contact spirits through the boards?"

"No," Reverend Tom answered. "But I still like to try once in a while, if someone is visiting and promises not to take any answers the spirits give us too seriously."

"I've never used one," I admitted. "I don't know much about them, but it sounds like fun." I turned to Gram. "Can we? Can we try to contact spirits tonight?"

"I don't know if this is the right time," she said.

"Tom, we have another problem. When I talked to you yesterday, I told you Jacques Lattimore had collapsed at our house."

"Yes. You clearly did the right thing, getting him to the hospital. But from what you said, no one could have saved him."

"Turns out that was only the beginning," said Gram. "Ethan Trask stopped in today. It appears there's a possibility Jacques was murdered."

"Murdered?" said Tom. "But that's impossible! He was right there in your house!"

"That," Gram answered, nodding, "is the problem. He might have been poisoned by something he ate while he was with us."

"I'm sure Ethan's mistaken," said Tom, handing us each a glass of burgundy. "Who was with you yesterday?"

"Just the needlepointers. And Angie and me."

"And Ethan thinks one of you poisoned Lattimore?"

"He said he wouldn't know for sure until the final autopsy results are in, particularly the toxicology reports. But the doctor who treated Lattimore was suspicious."

"I'm surprised Ethan mentioned it to you if he doesn't know for sure."

"I suspect he wanted to warn us," I said. "To give us a chance to confess if we'd been involved, or to think through who else at the house might have done it."

Reverend Tom shook his head. "And I thought, after the service for your daughter, that your life might be simpler. Easier."

"It will be in some ways. Angel's decided to stay with me for a while. . . ."

"Six months. A trial of six months," I put in.

"And be the director of Mainely Needlepoint. She's going to get us straightened out and contact the customers. Do what Jacques Lattimore should have been doing." Gram looked at me proudly. "She's already had an idea of how we might expand the business. She suggested we learn about heritage needlepoint—the sort people buy in antique shops or at auctions or inherit. Learn how to conserve it, or perhaps do minor repairs, and be able to tell people a little about the history of their piece."

"Good for you, Angie. That sounds like a good sideline for the business. And you have Sarah Byrne already, who's an antique dealer."

"She's the one who got us thinking in that direction," Gram admitted. "She showed us an old piece of embroidery and wanted to know what she should do about it."

"Angie, I'm glad you're here and going to help with the business. Charlotte doesn't realize how much a minister's wife is expected to do. She's a special woman, for sure"—he looked over at her and they both smiled—"but I was afraid she might be taking on too much with both the needlepoint business and what will be her new church responsibilities."

"I refused to close the business, even when that Lattimore was making it difficult," said Gram. "I enjoy the work, and so do the others I've gotten involved."

"I hope I'll be able to live up to everyone's expectations," I said, sipping my wine. "I've kept books before, but it was for a company that did private investigations. Not exactly needlepoint."

"I'm sure you'll do fine," Reverend Tom said, adding a little to each of our glasses. "And dinner won't be ready for an hour. How would you like to try out one of the Ouija boards now, Angie?"

"Could we? I'm sure I don't believe, either, but they look like fun!"

"Are you sure that's a good idea, Tom? With everything else that's been happening. Maybe this isn't a week to disturb the spirits."

Gram was smiling, but I sensed real concern behind her words.

"Don't worry, Charlotte. It'll be harmless. Which board, Angie, for your virgin attempt to contact the spirits?"

I was game. "The older boards are intimidating. Why don't we use your first board? The one your uncle gave you."

"Done," he said, taking it down. "I'll check the dinner and then we'll begin."

I held the board. I'd never thought much about

spiritualism. I'd visited Sedona a couple of times, and I once had my fortune told there. It had been fun, but the woman reading my cards said things that could have applied to any young woman. Definitely a waste of twenty-five dollars. Could a Ouija board be different?

And yet people had consulted boards and cards for years. They must have delivered messages that meant something, or no one would be manufacturing them. From the modern look of the ones in this room, most had been made in the twentieth century. "It's too bad the spirits can't speak out in courts," I said as Reverend Tom came back in the room. "We could forget forensics if departed souls could come back and tell us what happened."

"I've often imagined a prosecutor in court cross-examining a spirit through a Ouija board," Reverend Tom agreed, nodding. "We'd have to come up with a whole new set of laws regarding the testimony of non-corporeal beings."

"Ghosts, you mean," put in Gram. "This isn't a good idea, Angel. Spirits can't come back and talk to us." She shook her head. "The whole idea gives me shivers."

"You mean, with all these boards available, you've never tried to contact Mama?"

"Never have. Never will." She poured herself another half glass of wine from the bottle Reverend Tom had left on the coffee table. "When you're dead, you're dead. I don't know if you're in Heaven or just in the ground, but I don't believe you can come back again."

"It's a game," said Reverend Tom. "Charlotte, if it upsets you, we don't have to do this."

"I'm not going to do it myself," she said. "But if Angel wants to try, you two go ahead. You need two people, don't you?"

"Two people," he agreed. "People who feel extraordinarily attuned to the spirit world do it alone, but usually it requires two people. We'll try it once." He glanced over at Gram. I had the feeling he was sorry he'd suggested we use the board, if only because she was upset. "People have been trying to contact spirits for thousands of years. The Ouija board was invented in the late nineteenth century when spiritualism was popular in the United States. Today scientists say there may be truth in them . . . perhaps a way of contacting the users' subconscious. Not spirits. Angie, you sit on that side of the card table." He sat on the other side.

I put the board in the middle of the table. He added the planchette.

"When we start," Tom explained seriously, "you and I will put the tips of our fingers on the planchette, very lightly, on different sides. We'll concentrate. If you don't believe, then the spirits won't come. Sometimes even then, they don't. If a spirit wants to communicate with us, he or she will move the planchette to answer our questions."

187

"Do you do this often?" I asked.

"I assure you, not as often as I read my Bible," he replied.

That wasn't a direct answer.

"I'll start, and then, if we get an answer, you ask the second question," he said. "We'll alternate."

I nodded. We were silent for a minute or two, and then Reverend Tom put his fingers on the planchette. I followed his lead.

He spoke softly. "Is there a spirit nearby tonight who would like to speak with us?"

I focused on the planchette and on my fingers. It all felt a little scary, and a little stupid. Not a good combination. I forced myself to focus on the planchette. Might as well give the spirits a chance. Then, without warning, the planchette started moving. It circled for a few seconds, and then went directly to *yes*.

Reverend Tom nodded at me. It was my turn. "Will you answer our questions?"

More circles, and then the planchette quickly went to *yes* again. And then to *no*. And then back again.

"Do you mean that maybe you'll answer our questions?" asked Reverend Tom.

Incredibly, the board answered. *Yes*.

I asked what I'd been worrying about all day. "Did someone kill Jacques Lattimore?"

The board answered. *Yes*.

I shivered. This was too easy. I looked at

Reverend Tom. He was pale. I suspected he didn't usually ask the spirits questions like that.

He asked, "Why was Lattimore killed?"

The planchette spelled out, *C-H-A-N-C-E.*

Whoa. What does that mean?

My turn. "Who killed Jacques Lattimore?"

The planchette circled for what seemed a long time before it speeded up. And went to *good-bye.*

Maybe Reverend Tom's collection illustrated one answer to the larger questions of life. Like prayer, Ouija boards offered ways to express desire, hopes, needs . . . whether for forgiveness or love or, eventually, eternal life in another world. They offered hope that there was a place, an abyss, where souls drifted until they were called back to aid someone still on earth. Called back by a memory. Or by a simple board.

I was certain I hadn't moved the planchette. Why had the board been so sure Lattimore had been murdered?

Chapter Twenty-three

Catherine, meanwhile, in the parlour, picking up her morsel of fancy work, had seated herself with it again—for life, as it were.

—Henry James (1843–1916),
Washington Square, 1880

The rest of the evening in the rectory was considerably less exciting than the first hour. Reverend Tom's interest in the occult seemed the most unusual thing about him. I would have liked to have asked him more questions about his boards, but Gram was clearly not comfortable heading off into the unknowns of spiritualism.

She and I went home early. Gram went to bed. I was restless.

First, I called my old friend Clem. Of all the people I'd seen since I'd returned to Haven Harbor, she was the one I most wanted to see again. Except, of course, for Ethan Trask. But seeing him wasn't a good thing, for an increasing number of reasons.

Not only was he married and a father, but every time I saw him, he was questioning me about a murder. Not exactly the conversations my fantasies had dreamed up on a regular basis since I was twelve. I didn't need a Ouija board to tell me I needed a new fantasy.

I left Clem a message suggesting we meet for lunch tomorrow if she could get away from her job. I even volunteered to drive to Portland. I loved being with Gram, but what I really needed— I decided after an inch of cognac—was a little distance from Haven Harbor.

Time to get my bearings . . . and a friend. Someone who remembered me as a decent person. Possibly misguided. Possibly unfocused. But, still, someone who could be trusted to keep your secrets and might share a few of her own. A female friend, so there wouldn't be romantic complications or misunderstandings.

In the meantime I wandered through the house. It didn't take long before I decided to deal with Mama's bedroom. At lunch Gram had mentioned that maybe it was time to dispose of her clothes. I'd volunteered to go through them, and Gram had looked relieved.

I gathered boxes and bags from the cellar and tackled Mama's closet.

She may have been my age, but she'd been smaller than I was. I sorted her clothes either into garbage bags to throw away or boxes for Goodwill. Decisions were easy: stained blouses, out-of-date or wild patterns, went into the garbage bags. A couple of sweaters I held out. I might be able to wear those, and I could use extra sweaters. I hesitated when I came to the dress Mama had always worn when Gram shamed her into going to church. I held it for a few minutes before letting it go. Someone else could wear it now.

Dresses that would be too short for me, and too young for Gram; shoes, leather now cracked; T-shirts advertising places and events in the past—all gone.

I held up a pair of black wool slacks that looked practically new. Had moths gotten to them? They were too short for my legs in any case. I was about to drop them in the "donate" pile when I heard paper crackling. I looked again. This time I checked the pockets.

A folded scrap of paper was tucked deep inside one. On it was a scribbled telephone number, in Mama's handwriting.

It probably meant nothing. But right then, after the evening with the Ouija board and my second glass of brandy, it felt like a message from her grave.

Whose telephone number was it? It had the same first three digits as numbers in Haven Harbor. A local number.

I put the note on Mama's bedside table as I quickly checked through the piles of clothes I'd already sorted. Nothing was in any other pocket.

Mama would have worn wool pants in the winter and as late as April or early May. And she hadn't had these cleaned for the summer. Chances were she'd worn them in the month before she'd died.

I finished going through the closet, ending up

with two cartons for Goodwill and several sweaters I could try on. Everything else I threw away.

I still had the bureau to go through, but suddenly I was exhausted.

I took the scrap of paper I'd found and went to my room. It was close to midnight. Too late to call anyone.

Clem hadn't called back.

The rest of the night my head swirled with numbers and faces. I didn't recognize any of them.

Chapter Twenty-four

How frail is life! It is like a fading flow'r,
That flourishes and withers in an hour.
Now we're in health but ere the day is fled,
We may be numbered with the silent dead.
          —Words on a sampler, "wrought by
             Hannah G. Sevey," at age thirteen,
                      Machias, Maine, 1818

The next morning I dialed the number Mama'd written down. The woman who answered had never heard of Mama. "Excuse me, but can you tell me how long you've had this number?" I asked.

"About six years now," she answered.

I thanked her, then tucked the paper in my jeans pocket. I'd borrow Gram's computer and run a search on it later.

A few minutes later, Clem returned my last night's call. She'd love to have lunch, but she wasn't free until Monday. And why didn't we include Cindy (Titicomb, now Bowers)? They'd been planning to get together, and it would be fun for the three of us to see each other. I agreed. Cindy and I had had our issues back in school, but that was a long time ago. She'd left Haven Harbor to attend a private high school. I hadn't seen her since elementary school. And Cindy's mom was a needlepointer. If Clem liked Cindy, maybe I could too.

Clem hesitated a bit before asking, "And what about including Lauren? She's still in Haven Harbor."

I thought for a moment. No, there were too many issues between Lauren and me. "Maybe after a little more time has passed. Right now, I'd like the three of us to have a relaxed lunch."

"Monday, then? And is meeting in Bath okay? I've been longing for Beale Street Barbeque."

I smiled to myself. Barbeque wasn't exactly typical Maine, but Clem was right. Beale's had always done a great job with it. It was one of the places we'd loved when we were teenagers and one of us could get a car. And some cash.

"I'll call Cindy," Clem promised. "She left me a message last night, too. She's visiting her folks in Haven Harbor now. When she does that, she can usually escape from her kids for a few hours because her mom loves to babysit. I'm really looking forward to this!"

Gram approved the plan at breakfast. "You need to reconnect with your old friends. It'll help you feel more comfortable here."

How did she know I didn't feel "at home" here yet? But I was excited about seeing Clem again, and even Cindy again. Her mom had said Cindy had three kids! How did she cope?

"In the meantime," Gram started to say, when

there was a knock on the front door. Ethan Trask and a man and a woman I didn't recognize were standing on our porch. A large once-white van identified as belonging to the State of Maine Crime Unit was parked in front of our house. It was official enough to be marked with the state seal. It was intimidating, and no doubt meant to be.

A van like that had visited here after Mama'd been gone a couple of weeks. I'd come home from school and found people going through her room. Gram and I had sat in the kitchen, watched by a policeman. They hadn't found any clues that day to help their investigation. After they'd left, Gram and I had stayed up half the night putting Mama's clothes and papers and pictures back in their places. I was convinced that if we messed with her room, she'd never come back to it. *To us.* Gram'd listened to me. Here it was, close to twenty years later, and I'd just started cleaning out Mama's closet and drawers.

But this morning's visit couldn't be about Mama. It had to be about Jacques Lattimore.

"May we come in?" asked Ethan.

"Do we have a choice?" asked Gram. She knew what it was about, too.

"This will be a lot easier if you cooperate," he said, almost apologetically.

Gram nodded and moved aside.

"Angie, you need to hear this," he called down the hall to where I was standing in the kitchen.

"Don't touch anything. Put down your coffee and come here."

"What's happened?" I asked. I could have guessed. But I knew from my own investigating that it was best to let the other person volunteer information. Even if that other person was a state trooper.

"Autopsy results for Jacques Lattimore determined his cause of death was poisoning."

Bingo! But not a total surprise. I hadn't thought they'd come here looking for wild turkeys. "And?"

"Nothing, so far. He didn't test positive for any of the usual drugs, legal or illegal. The ME's office has sent blood and tissue samples out to a federal lab to test for other substances."

"Do they have any clues?"

Jacques shook his head. "I shouldn't even be telling you about the poison. But because Lattimore's death is now considered a possible homicide, and he collapsed here, your home has to be considered a crime scene. I'll need to talk to you while the crime scene technicians work."

Gram sighed. "Angie and I were planning to finish going through Mainely Needlepoint's books this morning to divide the money she got from Jacques. I don't want anyone to think we're holding on to it. That money belongs to the needlepointers, who earned it."

"We'll be as fast as we can. Do we have your

permission to search the house for anything that might be relevant?"

"Do you have a search warrant?" I asked.

"Not yet. But we could get one. I hoped you'd let us search without one."

Gram threw up her hands. "We have nothing to hide. Go ahead. But, please, don't mess the place up."

She, too, was thinking of that earlier visit by the police.

"We'll try," Ethan answered. He didn't sound terribly reassuring. "Can we sit on the porch while the team is working?" he asked.

Our wide front porch overlooked Haven Harbor's Green. In the nineteenth century, sheep had grazed on the green. Now it was crisscrossed by sidewalks and used for occasional church fairs and bridal portraits. Once I'd tried to fly a kite there, but my string had gotten caught in the branches of a large maple tree. My kite was up there for weeks, a spot of red and yellow among the green leaves, until finally a nor'easter tore it down.

We sat on the wicker chairs Gram had gotten out of the barn in anticipation of summer breezes.

"Lattimore was only in the living room, which we also use as an office, and in the hall and bathroom," Gram said. "The needlepointers and I were meeting in the living room when Angel and Jacques came in. He sat down. We chatted. He apologized. He had a cup of tea or two, as I remember. And a couple of cookies. Then he looked as though he was having bad cramps, or stomach pains. I showed him where the bathroom was." She paused. "Just as I told you yesterday."

"He vomited in the bathroom?"

"That's what it sounded like," I said. "And smelled like. We asked him if he needed any help. He said, 'no,' so we left him alone."

"When did you call 911?"

"I opened the bathroom door when he stopped answering me," said Gram "He was having spasms. Fits. Seizures. His head was hitting the floor. I tried to hold him to keep him from hurting himself. I called to Angel and she called 911 for help."

"Let's go back a little. Angie, earlier that afternoon you went to find Lattimore and bring him back here."

I nodded.

"Where was he?"

I explained again about going to the address Gram had for him in Brunswick, and then following his trail up to the Cambridge Casino. We'd gone over this before. I suspected he was testing us to see if we'd give the same answers we had the last time he'd asked.

"Was he eating at the casino?"

"He might have eaten earlier. It was the middle

of the afternoon when I got there. He did have a drink with him at the blackjack table."

"Do you think it was his first?"

"I didn't give him a Breathalyzer test. But I'm pretty sure he'd had more than one."

"And where did you go next?"

"To the room he'd rented, where he was living."

"In his car?"

"In the one I was driving. Gram's." I hadn't wanted Lattimore to head off in another direction. By driving, I was in control. I didn't say that to Ethan.

"And when you were at his room, did he eat or drink anything?"

"No."

"And then you drove him here."

I nodded.

"Did he eat or drink in the car? Did you?"

"Neither of us did."

"And then you got here and joined the needle-pointers in the living room."

"He did," I corrected slightly. "After I gave Gram the money I'd gotten from Lattimore, I went into the kitchen and had a cup of tea there. I wasn't one of the needlepointers." I hesitated. "Then."

"The last time I was here, you gave me the names of those who were at the meeting. Have you thought of any other details since then?" He directed that question to Gram.

200

"There's no way anyone could have poisoned him here, in our house," I insisted. "He didn't leave the room. No one else left the room. Everyone was drinking from the same teapot and the same plates. If he was poisoned, it must have been slow acting. Something he'd eaten or drunk before I saw him at the casino."

"That's what we're trying to figure out," said Ethan. "But since we don't know what caused his convulsions and, ultimately, his death, we have to go backward from his time of death. I'm sure you understand that."

I sighed and nodded.

"I'll be talking with everyone who was here, of course, to confirm your stories," Ethan added. "Is there anything else you'd like to mention?"

Both Gram and I shook our heads.

"I assume you'll both be staying in the area?" He looked straight at me. "Angie?"

"I'm not going anywhere."

"Angie's now the director of Mainely Needlepoint," Gram added. "She's going to get our books in order and contact our customers. Try to put the company back together."

"Angie's taking over Lattimore's job?"

"Partially," Gram agreed. "But he wasn't our director. He was our agent. Angie will have broader responsibilities."

"And when was that decided? That Angie would take on that job?"

"At the end of the meeting that afternoon. Right before Lattimore got sick."

"So you got the information you needed from him, and some of your money back. And Angie replaced him in your business. You both benefited."

"From his coming here. Not from his death. And Angel didn't ask for the job. We all thought she'd be good at it, and she agreed."

Ethan paused. "I've known both of you ladies many years. You've had your troubles. Big troubles. But you understand that the circumstances under which Jacques Lattimore died makes both of you persons of interest in his death."

"We're suspects?" Gram asked.

"Not yet," said Ethan. "Not until we know exactly how he died."

Chapter Twenty-five

My mother considered it indispensable that every girl should be taught the expert use of her needle. I have to thank her for excelling in an accomplishment which it is oftentimes a pleasure for me to exercise.

—"The Partners," by Miss E.A. Duffy, *Godey's Magazine and Lady's Book*, 1846

Great. Gram and I were possible suspects in the murder of someone I'd only known for a couple of hours, and who'd cheated Gram and her friends out of over twenty-seven thousand dollars.

And right now I couldn't think of anything to do about it. Why wasn't Ethan working on Mama's case? "What about Mama's death? Is there any new information in that investigation?" I asked, trying desperately to change the subject. I glanced over at Gram. She was a tough lady, not a violent one. But right now she looked ready to kill.

"We've had a preliminary report back from the lab looking at DNA in the storage facility where your mother's body was found," said Ethan, turning to me. "Joe Greene's the only person we can connect to that space. That matches the records the facility has. Joe rented the place, and went there about once a year for a while. For the last ten years of his life, he just sent rent checks in. That's not surprising. During that period his wife was ill, and then he had cancer. Lauren, of course, went there this spring to empty it."

"No one else's name was on the record for the room?"

Ethan shook his head. "Just Joe's. There's no way of knowing whether anyone was with him when he first rented the facility. Or any other time." Ethan paused. "He did visit it the day before your mother was reported missing."

"So she was killed right away. She probably died before we called the police," said Gram quietly.

"That's what we're thinking," said Ethan. "Of course, there's no proof. But it seems too great a coincidence that Jenny disappeared and then, only two days later, Joe Greene visited the place her body was found."

"Was there a freezer in the unit before then?" I asked.

"No way of knowing. A lot of folks put freezers in those facilities when they don't have space at their homes. No one would have taken any note of Joe moving a freezer in there."

"But a freezer big enough to hold . . . a person . . . had to be heavy. Joe Greene couldn't have moved it there himself. He had to have help," I thought out loud.

"True. But without surveillance footage, or anyone signing in with Joe, or coming to the police, we don't know who that might be. And," Ethan reminded me, "no third-party DNA has been identified. Plus, the freezer could have been there before your mother was. Again, there's no way of knowing. Joe can't tell us. His wife's gone now, too, although I doubt she would have known."

"Who worked for Joe at the bakery back then?" Gram asked. "If he'd needed help moving a freezer, seems to me he'd go to someone who worked for him."

"I thought of that," said Ethan. "I'm asking around, to see if anyone remembers. Lauren has copies of his old tax filings, and we did look at those. But Joe and Nelly worked that bakery themselves most of the time. If they had extra help, Joe paid them off the books. There's no record he had any employees then."

"But you are asking around," I repeated. Someone, somewhere, must know what happened.

"I'm talking to Joe's friends in the Rotary and the Chamber of Commerce. Everyone I've talked to is convinced Joe didn't do it—that somehow he was framed. They can't think of any reason Joe would have killed anyone. They'd like to put the focus on someone else, but no one's come up with any other suspects."

"Maybe Joe did it," I admitted. "But, like those people you're talking to, I can't understand why. That's what bothers me. There has to be a motive."

"We haven't uncovered one," Ethan said. "I wish

we had. Now, with this Lattimore guy, finding a motive doesn't seem to be an issue. He'd cheated everyone at Mainely Needlepoint out of money, and they were all in the room with him right before he showed signs of poisoning. And you," Ethan's voice lowered as he said, "you ended up with his job. It looks pretty obvious that someone connected to Mainely Needlepoint didn't want Lattimore going back to Rome that night. The only question is, who?"

Gram and I looked at each other. Besides us, there was elderly Ruth Hopkins. Dave Percy, the navy retiree who now taught biology at Haven Harbor High. Katie Titicomb, the grandmother and quilter. Her husband was a doctor. Money wasn't as much of an issue with her as with the others. Lauren Decker, Joe's daughter, whose husband was struggling to make a living from the sea. Ob Winslow, whose back gave him problems and who did wood carvings. Sarah Byrne, the antique dealer.

None of them acted like killers. Although, who knew? Joe Greene hadn't been perfect, but even years later, no one was saying, "Oh, of course. Joe Greene. He would have shot that young woman in the head."

Homicide was not logical.

And yet . . .

"When did you call the needlepointers and ask them to come to the house?" I asked Gram.

"Right after you called me. I decided Jacques Lattimore should face all of us. Apologize to all of us. I wanted everyone to hear what he had to say. I wanted him to understand he'd hurt people."

"You told them he'd be here," I confirmed.

"I did. I told them I wanted them here to confront him."

"But none of them knew before your call that he'd be in Haven Harbor that afternoon?" I knew the answer, but I wanted to make sure Ethan understood what I was getting at.

"Of course not. We didn't even know where he was living. That's why I asked you to find out. You did that faster than I thought you would." Gram gave me an admiring glance.

Ethan was listening. "What you're getting at, Angie, is that no one—not your grandmother, and none of the others—would have had time to figure out how to poison Lattimore on that short notice."

I nodded. "The food they shared had to have been made ahead of time. People picked up what they had in their kitchens and brought it with them. There was no time to prepare anything special. And if there'd been poison in the doughnuts Lauren brought, we'd certainly have heard on the news."

"Of course, we all have poisons in our homes. Antifreeze. Medications. But until we know what caused Lattimore's seizures and death, it's hard to narrow down the suspect list," Ethan admitted.

"I'd say it's almost impossible," I said. "Unless someone in that room was seen adding something to Lattimore's tea. Since everyone ate the food, it seems unlikely that the poison was in that."

Ethan nodded. "I agree it sounds as though the poison was in Lattimore's tea. And I assume you cleaned up after the meeting? Washed the dishes and such?"

Gram and I exchanged glances. "We did. We didn't think he'd been poisoned. We just thought he'd gotten very sick all of a sudden."

"That he did," Ethan said. "But unless the crime scene team's able to find a lead to help us in your house, your cleaning up destroyed the only evidence we might have had." He looked from one of us to the other. "It might even be seen as covering up evidence."

Chapter Twenty-six

Of female arts in usefulness
The needle far exceeds the rest
In ornament there's no device
Affords adorning half so nice.
> —Verse on 1821 sampler made by
> fourteen-year-old Louisa Otis,
> who probably lived in Gorham, Maine

Ethan was through with his questions before the crime scene technicians had finished. Since we weren't wanted in the house, Gram and I took a walk and stopped for a light lunch on our way back.

During lunch I asked her if she recognized the telephone number I'd found in Mama's slacks. She'd just shaken her head. When we got back home, we found the police had taken her computer. I was pretty sure they wouldn't find she'd been searching the Internet for poisons, but in the meantime she was upset that some of her business files were now out of reach. And I wasn't going to do any computer searches today.

The police had been looking for evidence of poison, not wrongdoing. For now at least, the Mainely Needlepoint files not in the computer hadn't been touched.

"You're going to Bath on Monday?" Gram confirmed.

"Meeting Clem and Cindy for lunch."

"Bath isn't far from Brunswick. There's a Goodwill drop-off there, where you can leave the clothes you've packed up."

"I think I'll buy a laptop, too," I said. "I've been meaning to do that for a while, anyway. I can load the software I'm comfortable using to set up the Mainely Needlepoint accounts." Both Gram's accounting records and the information we'd gotten from Lattimore were in old-fashioned paper files. I'd have to start from scratch to put them into the computer.

I wasn't looking forward to that, but it had to be done.

We spent the afternoon cleaning up after the crime scene people. They'd been as careful as they could, but they'd emptied the kitchen and bath-room cabinets, and moved all the old cans of paint and turpentine in the barn off Gram's neat shelves.

It was logical to take advantage of the mess to sort through the cans and bottles that had found their way into Gram's house, from cellar to attic, and into her barn. By the time we'd finished, I had more bags and boxes to take to the town dump. And a major headache.

Gram and I worked silently. The mess that was left reminded both of us that if I wasn't able to get the money owed the needlepointers, she might have to sell the house. If that happened, we'd have to do a lot of cleanup. The house had been in our family more than two hundred years. I'd never sat and counted how many people had been born, lived, and died here. But I was pretty sure they'd each left something behind: Ghosts? Maybe. For sure, there were old trunks of fabrics saved to be used in quilts. Toys that hadn't been played with since I'd been a child . . . or even a hundred years before. Garden tools that dated back to at least the 1920s or 1930s. ("They work perfectly well. Why replace them?") Shelves of empty mason jars that once were filled with tomato sauce and canned vegetables.

Old houses held stories. And secrets. And although there might be treasures, more likely there was junk. Or, I smiled to myself as I filled cartons for Goodwill with generations of Easter baskets that had been stacked in the barn before the crime scene investigators had thrown them on the ground, *Vintage Junque.*

While I loaded cartons for Goodwill into her car, Gram finished going through all her papers. "I'll have this done today," she assured me. "Then you can deliver the money. After that, the accounts will be yours to put on your computer, or arrange however you think best. I'll be here to answer any questions, but I'll be happy to hand over that part of the business and get back to stitching."

I didn't see any vacations in my near future.

Chapter Twenty-seven

[Lady Bertram] was a woman who spent her days in sitting nicely dressed on a sofa, doing some long piece of needlework, of little use and no beauty.

—Jane Austen (1775–1817), *Mansfield Park*, 1814

The next morning I picked up the envelopes of cash Gram had divided and marked for each of the needlepointers. But before I made my first delivery, I decided to take care of other unfinished business. I went to the Haven Harbor police station.

"Could I speak with Sergeant Pete Lambert?"

I smiled sweetly.

My charm was not appreciated. "Sergeant Lambert's out of the office right now." Stacy, the clerk who'd taken the photo for my permit application a few days before, didn't even look at me. But she did hand me a minuscule pad of paper and a pencil. "You're welcome to leave him a note."

I wrote, *Pete. This is Angie Curtis. Sorry I missed you! Have an idea about my mother's case. Call me.* I added my cell phone number, folded the little paper into something an elf would have been able to carry, and handed it back.

Stacy unfolded it in front of me, clearly demonstrating that nothing she handled was private.

"I'll give it to him when he comes in. But I don't know when that will be." Finally she looked at me. "He has a girlfriend, in case you were wondering." She said it more like a threat than a "between us girls" piece of gossip.

"Good for him," I answered. Were so many Haven Harbor women longing for Pete's attention that she was warning me? Or maybe she was the girlfriend, and hoping to eliminate any potential competition.

Until that moment I hadn't thought about Pete Lambert other than he'd done a good job keeping the media away from Gram and me on the day of Mama's funeral. Now she'd made me curious.

"Make sure he gets the note. It's important."

I decided to stop at Lauren's house first. From all accounts she needed the money.

No one answered the door. A gray-haired woman kneeling on the grass in the next yard called out, "You looking for the Deckers?"

She wore garden gloves caked with mud and was digging deep holes to plant the bulbs lying next to her on the grass. I knew nothing about gardening except that Gram planted daffodil and crocus bulbs every fall. Thanks to naturalizing, our lawn was a field of purple and white, and then yellow, every spring. I'd missed the flowers this year. Now we had a small field of withering leaves. Our only other gardening attempts I remembered had been a few tomato plants and a row of Black-Seeded Simpson lettuce each year.

"Looking for Lauren," I said.

"She and Caleb left real early this morning. I'd guess they went up to their camp for the weekend," she said. "They do that pretty regular. Anything I can help with?"

I shook my head. "I didn't know they had a camp." If they were in such bad financial shape, how could they afford a second home?

"It's on a lake, north of here. Inherited it from her parents, same way they got this house." She looked at me. "You're the daughter of that woman Lauren found in the freezer, right? The one they had the funeral for this past week."

"That's right. Angela Curtis."

"Sue Warden. Pleased to meet you." She started to put her hand out to shake mine; but then she realized she was covered with dirt, so she shrugged. "Sorry about your mother."

I nodded in thanks. "What are you planting?"

"Lilies. They'll bloom in August, if I'm lucky. This dirt's rocky, and the season's short. A lot of lilies don't make it here. But I keep trying. Day-lilies, those big yellow ones, they do fine. But I'm hoping to grow a few of the more exotic Asian ones."

She stood up and dusted herself off, which got

more dirt on her clothes, as I stared at the house where Lauren and Caleb now lived. I knew it well. I'd visited it many times as a child. Too many times. Brownie meetings had been held there, and I'd often walked home with Lauren when we'd been in the second or third grade. I didn't remember this neighbor. I turned back to her. "Have you lived here long?"

"About five years. Seems a good stretch to me, but around here someone who's only lived in Haven Harbor five years is still considered a new-comer. My husband and I moved up here from Boston after he retired. Beautiful place, the coast of Maine."

"It is," I agreed. "So you were here when Lauren's parents still owned the house."

"Mrs. Greene, her mother, was in pretty bad shape when we got here. Seemed like a nice lady, but you could tell she didn't have long. After she died, Mr. Greene seemed lost. Guess that happens when a couple has been together for years. He used to come over and talk to me while I was gardening, like you just did. We'd invite him to dinner with us once in a while."

"So you've known Lauren all this time."

"Actually, no. She used to be in and out when her mother was ill. But after that, I didn't see her. Of course, she had her baby to look after then. Robin was a charmer. And maybe I'm telling tales out of school, but I always thought her dad was lonely and Lauren should have visited him more often. She and Caleb lived in a trailer west of town then, not far away. But maybe she was mourning her mother and her daughter." She sighed. "That young woman's had a lot of sadness in her life. But you'd understand that."

Lauren had lost a child? I made a mental note to ask Gram about that.

"I'm surprised Mr. Greene was alone so much. I thought he was active in a lot of town organizations."

She shrugged. "Maybe when he was younger. When I knew him, he just puttered around his house. Went to church Sundays, but that was it. Ate down at Harbor Haunts, or picked up fast food at one of those places outside of town. A sad existence, if you ask me. When he told my husband and me he'd taken sick, we wondered if it might have come on because he had nothing left to live for."

"Sad," I said, because that's what she thought. I didn't feel much sympathy for a man who might have shot Mama in the back of her head.

She looked at me. "After Lauren found your mother's body—awful for her!—there's been talk around town that Joe Greene did it. I don't know how that body got into his freezer, but the Joe Greene I knew wouldn't have killed anyone. He was a lonely old man."

"It was almost twenty years ago," I pointed out. "People change."

"True. Our bodies wear out." She smiled ruefully. "I won't be able to garden on my hands and knees many more years. But if we're lucky, our minds keep going. I think the same way I did twenty years ago, more or less. I suspect Joe Greene was like that. He'd only changed on the outside. And he didn't seem like a killer to me."

"You never know."

"Just saying my piece. We'll probably never know what really happened to your mother. But it's sad for Lauren that her dad is blamed when he isn't here to defend himself."

I thanked her for her time and headed back to my car. I didn't feel like hearing good things about Joe Greene, even if I was one of those questioning his guilt. I hadn't liked the man. But had he been a murderer?

I glanced at the addresses I'd jotted down at home and then at the time on my cell. It was getting toward lunchtime. I decided to head down to Harbor Haunts for a clam roll and then stop to see Sarah Byrne.

I was halfway there when my phone rang. It was Pete Lambert.

"You stopped in today and said you needed to see me?" he asked.

"Yes. I have an idea you might find helpful," I answered.

"I'm in my office now," he answered.

"It's almost time for lunch. I'm on my way to

Harbor Haunts. Why don't you join me there?"

He was silent for a moment. Then, "Save me a seat."

The sought-after Peter Lambert was going to join me. I hoped Stacy, the police department clerk, choked on her words. Politely, of course.

It wasn't yet noon, but Harbor Haunts was half full. When you're the only place in town that serves food year-round, locals love you. And summer people like to eat "where the locals" eat. They didn't know most of those locals are too busy working at fancier places and at places like the co-op, where I used to work, to eat out during the summer. They didn't know the menu changed in summer. Just try to find a crabmeat roll or lobster club sandwich from November through April. Locals wanted a good burger, or maybe a haddock sandwich, with fries. If they craved lobster, they got one from a friend who had a license. Or one who didn't, which was rare. Lobstermen knew whose pots shouldn't be there. Anyone who tried to drop a few for private use would find their lines cut before the state was notified.

Not all of Maine is as pretty as the postcards would have people think.

"Someone's meeting me," I said to the very young hostess. I looked in. "Could we have a table near the window?"

"Sure thing," she answered, looking me over.

She would have been too young to remember me as Jenny Curtis's daughter who left.

She handed me a menu. "We've got specials. You care?"

Charming. Charming.

She looked at my short sleeves and V-necked pale green T-shirt. From her angle she could probably see most of what I'd squeezed into my bra that morning. "Sure you want to sit by the window? There's a draft there. It's warmer in the corner."

"This will be fine." I smiled back. I looked around the room. No one else was wearing a short-sleeved T-shirt. Or one that was light green. There were definitely no deep V-necks. People in Haven Harbor dressed differently than those in Mesa, a town caught between downtown Phoenix and Arizona State. Lots of students there; lots of heat. In Mesa my outfit would have fit right in. Today, at home, not so much.

I ordered a pint of Shipyard and waited.

My beer arrived before my luncheon date.

He stood in the door and looked around. I waved.

"I didn't recognize you at first," he said, sliding his long body into the chair across from me. "At the funeral you had on that big hat."

I smiled. "I didn't wear the hat today."

"That's fine. Fine."

He was looking at my cleavage, not my head.

The waitress was back. "Would you like to order now?"

"I'll have a clam roll and spicy fries," I said. "Toasted bun, please."

"Cheeseburger and fries," Pete said. "Burger well done. And a cup of coffee." He looked at my beer apologetically. "I'm on duty."

"Luckily, I'm not," I said.

"I figured you'd stopped in to ask about your carry permit. I told you, six-month residency."

"Couldn't you talk to someone?"

"Yeah. I could. But permits are a big deal. It wouldn't make a difference." He hesitated. "Is there any reason to think you're in danger? That you'd need to conceal your weapon?"

"Some people in town think Joe Greene shot my mother. Some people don't. I'm in the middle, and I've been asking questions. If you ask around, you'll find I've been making a nuisance of myself. Some people might not be happy about that."

He shrugged. "So they're not happy. People in Haven Harbor, though, don't go around shooting people they're pissed at."

Of course, Mama was that exception.

So if I wanted to carry my gun, I would. But it would be nice if it were legal.

"I'll make a few calls, but don't count on getting the permit early. Now, what was it you wanted to tell me?"

"It's about Joe Greene. I wanted to ask if anyone'd checked whether he'd ever been in legal trouble for any reason." I reached out and touched

Pete's hand. "I know you weren't with the department most of the time he was alive. But there
might have been talk. Especially after my mother's
body was found."

He moved his hand away and straightened up.
"I haven't heard he was ever in any trouble. But I
can check it out. Anything in particular?"

Wide nets caught more fish. "No. I was just
wondering if you could check to see if there were
any closed files. It would make me feel better."

He nodded as the waitress put our food on the
table in front of us. "I'll do that. I will. Maybe it'll
help solve the case."

"That's what I'm hoping for," I said. "I know
murders are officially under the jurisdiction of the
state police, but you work with them, right?"

He nodded.

"And it would be good for your record if you
were to come up with evidence that would help
them."

He nodded as he chewed. "Couldn't hurt." He
leaned toward me. "Tell you the truth, I've always
wanted to be a state trooper. Finding key evidence
might be a step in that direction."

"Good!" I smiled. "I hope it'll help."

Sergeant Lambert covered his French fries with
ketchup.

My stomach lurched. It looked like blood.

Chapter Twenty-eight

Perhaps there is no single influence which has had more salutary effect in promoting the comforts of home and the respectability of family life throughout the length and breadth of our land than the attention given in our Magazine to illustrations and directions which make needlework and fancyworks in all their varieties known and accessible. Home is the place for such pursuits; by encouraging these, we make women happier and men better.

—Editorial of *Godey's Magazine and Lady's Book*, January 1864

After lunch I headed to see the next needle-pointer on my list.

Dave Percy's house was a small canary yellow Cape, with green shutters and a small dooryard surrounded by a picket fence. If you'd asked me a month ago whether there were any picket fences in Maine, I would have said, "Only in the movies." Dave proved me wrong.

I opened the gate, walked up the sea stone walk to his green door, and dropped the brass knocker shaped like a lobster. People really did buy such things.

Dave answered promptly, smiling, with a mug of

coffee in hand. "Angie! How nice to see you! Come on in."

Dave was about three inches taller than I was. I wondered how old he was. Maybe forty-five? His thick hair and neatly trimmed beard were gray. He walked with a slight limp. I hadn't noticed that when I'd seen him at the gathering after the funeral.

He showed me into his living room. I'll admit, I'd assumed a man living alone would accept a little dust and clutter as part of life. Dave's house belied that stereotype; it was immaculate. There was a large flat-screen TV in the corner, but the rest of the furniture was comfortable and covered in fabric. Not a leather recliner in sight. A standing embroidery frame, the kind needlepointers used to hold their canvases straight when they're working on large projects, was next to one of the chairs. Dave was working on a detailed floral design, maybe fifteen by fifteen inches. The background was black, but the shaded pink and red roses and green leaves, which filled the center, incorporated many shades of floss and a bit of gold.

"This is gorgeous!" I said, walking closer to look at it. "Will it be a framed wall hanging?"

"No," he answered. "It's one of the last commissions Lattimore got for us. It's a cover for a chair seat cushion." He pulled out a photograph of a large armchair with a cushion embroidered with the same rose design. "Your grandmother has software than can translate an original design, like the one on this chair, into a pattern. The customer bought a pair of chairs at an auction last summer, and only one still had a cushion. This is for the second chair."

"Will it match exactly?" I said, looking from the needlepoint to the photograph.

"Not absolutely. The earlier embroidery is faded, and has one small worn spot." He pointed that out in the photo. "But when Jacques stopped in to check the colors for the client, he said the customer planned to put the chairs near windows on opposite sides of the room. He understood they wouldn't match exactly, but thought the differences wouldn't be noticed since they wouldn't be next to each other. Your grandmother and I intentionally chose slightly faded versions of the necessary colors."

"You've been working on this for a while, then."

"A couple of months. I started it late last fall, but then had other assignments with shorter deadlines, so I put this project aside. The client was going to Florida for the winter and wouldn't need the seat cover until she got back in June. I'll have it finished before then."

I nodded.

"Can I get you some coffee?" he asked.

"That would be great. Black, please."

"Coming up. Make yourself at home."

I walked around the room, admiring Dave's

collection of old framed maps and a framed needlepoint of breaking waves. Dave Percy had good taste. And was an expert needlepointer. A bay window looked out into his backyard, where his garden was already tilled and weeded. I couldn't see what was growing, but green was returning and he'd left a large space for new plants or seeds. Another needlepoint project—a simpler one, a skiff with the name *Peace* on its stern—lay on the window seat.

Returning, Dave handed me a steaming mug. Strong, the way I liked it. I took the mug and sat on the couch. "You make good coffee. And needle-point. Gram said you learned it when you were in the navy?"

"Sounds a little strange, but, yes, I was assigned to submarine service. When you're off duty, there's not a lot to do on a sub, and not much space to do it in. One of the guys got a lot of hazing from the others because he was doing needlepoint. But he did beautiful work. Pillows, wall hangings, you name it. He usually worked from a kit. He got me and one other fellow interested, and he taught us." Dave shrugged. "A good way to pass long hours." He pointed at the wave on the wall. "That's one I did at sea."

"I'm impressed. How long were you in the navy?"

"Ten years. I'd planned to be career navy. But when I was home on leave, I had a bad fall on the ice." He had a crooked smile. "Leg broke in several places, so I went on medical leave. While I was in the VA hospital having physical therapy, I had time to think about my life. I decided I wanted to change direction. I left the navy, went back to school on the GI Bill, and became a high-school science teacher."

"Have you always taught here?"

"Taught in Williamstown, Massachusetts, for a couple of years, but missed the sea. So when I heard of an opening at Haven Harbor High, I applied. I've been teaching biology here for several years now."

"And you're happy?" I asked.

"I am."

"Not married?"

"That's a personal question," he said. "But, of course, everyone in town knows the answer. Nope. Guess I haven't found the right person yet. But I keep my eyes open. You?"

"I've given that same answer to too-curious people maybe a million times."

We exchanged smiles.

"What brings you here today? You didn't know until you got here how good my coffee was."

"This," I said, pulling his envelope out of my pocketbook. "I brought your share of the money we got from Jacques Lattimore. Sorry it's not more."

He took the envelope without looking. "You did

your best. I'm appreciative. And I'll be looking forward to working with you from now on." He glanced over at the project he was working on. "I have to finish the cushion cover, and then I'll be into final projects and exams at school. I can't take on any more work until the end of June. But by then, I'll be ready. No school in summer means more time for needlepoint. It really is addicting."

"And more time for your garden," I said. "I saw you have one out back. Vegetables or flowers?"

He grinned. "Better stay friends with me, Angie. That's my poison garden."

"What?" He couldn't have said what I thought I'd heard.

"I grow poisonous plants. I'd read about people doing that, and it sounded like fun. Plus, I can take examples of the plants into my classes and make sure my students know them. Believe it or not, a lot of those kids spend days outdoors, camping, hunting . . . and they don't even recognize poison ivy or poison oak. One September a student brought me a fistful of flowers he thought were a different variety of Queen Anne's lace. Turned out he'd picked water hemlock, one of the deadliest plants there is. If he'd put them in water, and, say, a pet had drunk the water, or a child, it would have killed them. Same with lilies of the valley. 'Don't drink the water,' as the song says." He paused and sipped his coffee. "That's why I have my yard fenced in. I don't want any pet dogs or cats checking out my garden. My neighbors know what's in it, and they keep their children away."

"I didn't know there were poisonous plants in Maine," I said. "Except poison ivy. I learned about that as a child once. The hard way." I looked down at my hands. "My hands and arms were covered." Lattimore had been poisoned. I hadn't thought about poisoned plants. But the state police might be even more interested in Dave's garden than I was. Although I couldn't imagine Dave walking around with a vial of poison just in case he ran into someone he wanted to kill.

"A lot of plants in Maine can do damage," Dave was saying. "Some to people, and some to animals. Some poisonous plants are wild, like bittersweet nightshade and sumac. Yellow dock, which is safe for some uses when prepared properly, can also have serious side effects and be a skin irritant. Others, like the white lilies you see at Easter, grow here, but later in the season. They're toxic to cats. And another Queen Anne's look-alike, giant hogweed, can grow up to fourteen feet tall. It's new to Maine, and I don't grow it. Its sap can cause blistering and even blindness. I tend my garden with gloves on."

"I'm going to beware of any Queen Anne's lace after this," I said. "I used to pick bouquets of it when I was little and was always disappointed it wilted so quickly inside. Now I'll be afraid to pick any at all."

"You do need to be careful," he said, "although the Queen Anne's lace you picked was probably fine. The Maine Department of Agriculture has found that giant hogweed in Sebago, Northport, Lisbon Falls, and a few other places so far. Not in Haven Harbor, at least not yet. The state is trying to eradicate it. And water hemlock is usually found around freshwater, not salt."

"Now I know who to go to if I have any questions about plants," I said. "Your students must think it's very cool to learn about plants like that."

"They do." He grinned. "And who knows? What they learn might someday save their lives. Or at least save them a lot of discomfort."

I finished my coffee, said good-bye, and looked at the next name on my list: *Ruth Hopkins.*

Ruth lived farther up the hill, in a small white house in the shade of the church steeple.

After I rang the doorbell, I heard the sound of her walker clomping toward the door before it opened. "Welcome, Angie. Come on in."

I moved past her into her little living room. The chair with the high seat was for her, I figured. Easier to get up and down.

"Sit down, sit down. Tea?"

"No, thanks, Ruth. I just came from Dave Percy's house and had coffee there. I'm caffeined-out for the moment."

"I understand, dear. If I have too many cups of either of them, I tax my kidneys. Such a nuisance. Part of old age, I'm afraid."

"Speaking of which . . . could I use your bathroom?"

"Down the hall on your right. You'll find it."

It was a small half bath. The medicine cabinet door was partially open. I couldn't resist peeking. A large bottle of low-dose aspirin. Arthritis-strength Tylenol. High-blood-pressure medicine. Bandages. Antibiotic cream. Anti-itch cream. (It was almost blackfly season—one part of Maine that I hadn't missed.) Small cakes of soap in the shapes of flower blossoms. Your basic half bath. I closed the cabinet door, then did what I'd come in for.

On my way back to the living room, I noticed that Ruth's dining room included several large, filled bookcases, and a computer with a large screen on a wide desk covered with papers. Why did Ruth need an office?

"Gram sent me to give you your share of the money Jacques Lattimore owed the Mainely Needlepointers." I handed the envelope to her.

"Thank you, dear. My share won't be a lot." She held up her gnarled, swollen hands. "The arthritis got me bad this past winter. Couldn't hold a needle to save my soul. I'm hoping my hands get better when temperatures are warmer and I can sit out in the sun a bit."

"I'm sorry," I said, looking at her distended hands and swollen knuckles. "Your hands must hurt."

"I have pills to take for the pain and inflammation." She nodded. "Sometimes they help. Sometimes they don't. I have salves, too. But when my hands get as bad as this, my doctor tells me I shouldn't hope they'll get a lot better. It's the way arthritis progresses." She shook her head. "It's no fun, I can tell you."

"I happened to look in the dining room when I was in the hall. I saw all the papers on your desk. Are you still able to use your computer?"

"Oh, yes. That I do." Ruth looked down at her hands. "I've been using a keyboard for so many years, my fingers know where to go without my telling them, swollen or not."

"Were you a secretary?" I asked.

Ruth's smile was quick and her words firm. "That's a stereotype, young woman. Just because I could type didn't mean I was someone's secretary."

"I'm sorry. I wasn't thinking."

"No, you weren't."

"But then, why did you do so much typing?"

"Your grandmother has never told you, then? About me?"

I quickly thought through everything I'd ever heard about Ruth Hopkins, recently or in the past. She was a widow. She lived alone. My thoughts ended. "No, she's never said anything about you," I said. "Nothing about typing."

"Well, then, if you can keep it under your hat. . . ." Ruth looked at me slyly. "Your grandma is one of the few people who know."

"Of course," I answered, curious to know her secret. "I won't tell anyone."

"I'm a writer. That's what I do at my computer. I write."

Why should writing be a secret? Maybe she doesn't want anyone laughing at her work? "What do you write?" Maybe she wrote a journal. Or was working on a memoir.

"Books, dear. Books."

Now I was confused. "You're published?"

"Oh, my, yes. Have been for over forty years now. Forty-seven books and counting. Only one out this year, though. I'm slowing down."

"Forty-seven books! I had no idea. I'd like to read one of them someday, Ruth."

There was a definite glint in her eye. "Well, nowadays, best way to read 'em would be as an e-book. My early ones are out of print in paper, but I made sure they were up electronically."

How had Gram never mentioned Ruth's writing?

"I'll look, then. I will."

"Well, then, I should tell you. Don't look for the name Ruth Hopkins on 'em. Oh, no. I started writing years ago, when my husband was still alive, and he said he'd be dead and buried before he wanted anyone to know what I was writing. So I used other names." She almost giggled. "Of course, now he *is* dead and buried, so it probably doesn't make a difference. But I do have a reputation to uphold here in town, and my fans know me by the other names. It seemed easier to just keep using 'em."

"What names do you write under, then?"

"The two I use most frequently are 'S.M. Bond' and 'Chastity Falls.'"

I wasn't sure. Had I heard those names correctly?

"Dear, I write erotica."

I shook my head. "Really?" I'd never thought about who might write erotica. But I certainly never visualized a little old lady who used a walker. Someone who wrote erotica should be tall and blond and leggy. And young. Gram had certainly created an interesting group of needlepointers.

"Really. And my books sell quite well, especially now that no one has to hide the book covers when they use an e-reader. Now, aren't you going to ask me whether I poisoned those cookies I brought to the needlepointers' meeting?"

It might be worth buying an e-reader to check up on Ruth. Or maybe I'd download one of her books to a computer, once I had one of my own. I couldn't see using Gram's for that. Had Gram read any of Ruth's books? That possibility was vaguely horrifying.

But Ruth was now talking cookies. "Right. You

brought a plate of molasses cookies to the last needlepointers' meeting. The one with Jacques Lattimore."

"I did. But I mixed those up way last fall, and just had to take them out of the freezer. I don't have the energy to make cookies now. It's good I can still read. I've gone through just about every large-print book at the library. The librarian says she'll try to get me more on interlibrary loan."

"That's good," I said, being careful not to ask what books she read. I didn't think I wanted to know. "Do you watch much television?"

"I can't take those reality shows they have on now. I do watch the horse races, though, when they're on. And I don't miss a Sox game." She raised her hand and I realized she was trying to make a fist, but her fingers wouldn't touch her palm. "Go Sox!"

"If I get in any more orders for needlepoint, I'll check with you to see if your hands will let you do any more," I said, standing up.

"You do that, Angie. But don't count on me." She started to get up. "I've got my writing to do. At this point in life typing's about all I can do with these hands."

"That's all right. You sit. I can see myself to the door," I said.

"Thank you for coming by. Anytime you're nearby, you stop in. You can tell me all about your time out west. It'd be more interesting than watching that CNN all day."

"I will. Thank you." I closed the door and headed to the next house on my list. How would it feel to live alone, and not be able to control what your body could do? Ruth Hopkins's mind was fine, but how long would she be able to live in her house safely? I resolved to stop in to see her often for as long as I was in Haven Harbor.

The Titicombs lived on Elm Street, the street where ships' owners and bankers and other well-to-do nineteenth-century Haven Harbor residents had built homes. Houses there were three stories tall instead of two. The earlier ones were Colonial or Federal styles built in the early nineteenth century; the later ones were rambling Victorians built after the Civil War.

The Titicombs' wide yard was littered with sturdy plastic toddler-sized bicycles, a Hula-hoop, two balls, and one small pink rubber boot. As I walked up the granite walk to the front door, a small child dressed only in Pampers zoomed around the house. I ran to catch her before she reached the street and almost collided with her mother, who was also in pursuit.

"Cindy!" I said, recognizing my old grammar-school friend as she scooped up the giggling red-haired runaway. She'd put on a bit of weight, most of it concealed by her loose sweatpants and long-sleeved T-shirt, but her hair was still curly and her smile was more relaxed than I'd remembered.

It took a moment before she connected.

"Angie! How are you? I was looking forward to seeing you for lunch. Clem told me you were back in town. And I'd heard about your mother. Sorry. How are you coping?"

"I'm all right." Not really, but you couldn't say exactly how you felt to anyone except a close friend. Since I hadn't seen Cindy in more than fifteen years, she didn't qualify. "I heard you have children."

"Guilty!" she answered. "The others are in the backyard. Come around!"

I walked with her. "You live in Blue Hill now?"

She nodded. "We came for a little visit with Grampa and Gramma. Didn't we, April?" She tickled that young lady's tummy and put her down. April grinned and started back for the front yard. This time she didn't escape.

"I actually came to see your mother. But I'm glad to see you! You look good."

Cindy shrugged and grinned. "I know I'm no fashion plate. My husband says I look maternal. Three kids in five years? I'd better look maternal. I'd feel better if I got to the gym more often. Chasing the little ones is exhausting, but doesn't usually get your heart rate up. But how could I miss being with this angel?" She switched April to her other hip. "Mom's back here."

We'd reached the backyard, where Katie Titicomb was sitting in one of four Adirondack chairs, holding a baby on her lap. Near her a boy of maybe five was playing in a plastic sandbox.

"You'd better get some clothes on that one, Cindy. She'll catch her death of cold," said Katie.

"We have company, Mom," said Cindy. "It's Angie Curtis."

"So it is," said Mrs. Titicomb. "Good to see you, Angie."

"Thank you, Mrs. Titicomb. I came by to give you your share of the money we got from Lattimore." I handed her the envelope. She slipped it into the diaper bag next to her chair.

"Thank you for bringing it over. Truth be told, I haven't missed the money or the work as much as the others. The doctor and I took a cruise this spring, and I've been redoing our living room. I haven't had much time for needlework recently."

"She also worked four beautiful pillows for me," said Cindy. "And a piece to reupholster a footstool I loved, but it had been feeling its age."

"Falling apart, you might even say," agreed Mrs. Titicomb. "But I'm out of projects at the moment. If you get in any more orders, I'm ready."

"Thank you," I said. "I haven't contacted any of our customers yet. That's next on my list."

After I'm sure who killed Mama, I thought.

"You'll be staying in Haven Harbor for a while then?" Cindy asked.

"Six months, anyway," I said. "Maybe more. I haven't decided." How ever long it would take to get the needlework business back on a schedule and making money for these people. "I'd love to sit and get caught up, but I have two other people to visit this afternoon."

"Clem suggested we all have lunch Monday at noon in Bath. It should be fun! So we can talk then. I'm here for ten days. Hubby went to a medical conference in San Diego."

I smiled. "You married a doctor, like your dad?"

"Not quite. But in the same business. Clive's a pharmaceutical rep. Doctors are his customers."

"Sounds interesting."

Not really, I thought. *But lucrative.*

"Actually, it's fascinating. He's on the cutting edge of all the new medical technologies. It's an important field, especially with baby boomers aging. Drugs are critically important," she stated.

"Lunch Monday then?"

"I was about to check with Mom," she said, looking over at her mother.

"No problem for me," said Katie Titicomb. "Take time with your friends, Cindy. I'll keep an eye on the kids. I don't get to see them often enough."

"It's a deal, then," Clem said. "See you Monday, when we have more time to catch up."

Chapter Twenty-nine

While beauty and pleasure are now in their
  prime
And folly and fashion expect our whole time.
Ah, let not these phantoms our wishes engage
Let us live so in youth that we blush not in age.
> —Part of verse embroidered by
> Mary Ann McLellan, four years old,
> Portland, Maine, 1807

Lauren was at her camp. How large a camp would her parents have been able to afford? In Maine, the term "camp" was used for any structure a Mainer used as a vacation home. Lauren was lucky to have inherited both an in-town home and a camp. I felt a twinge of jealousy. Although I didn't envy her the storage facility she'd also been left by her father.

Two more needlepointers on Gram's list: Sarah Byrne and Ob Winslow. Ob's home was on the outskirts of town. I decided to visit Sarah first.

The lilies of the valley were still part of her store window display. After visiting with Dave and hearing about the dangers of those delicate May flowers, I hoped Sarah didn't have a cat.

She waved from behind her counter, where she continued wrapping two teacups and saucers for a woman wearing yoga pants and a Maine T-shirt. Out-of-stater, for sure.

Her store smelled comfortably of old, beloved things. I wondered when Beatles posters had become antiques, and how many people collected flowered teacups. Sarah had three shelves of them. She also had shelves of old leather-bound books. Did anyone read books like those anymore? Maybe people bought them as investments. Or, most likely, as decorative accessories.

I didn't know much about antiques, but I knew about tourists. They shopped. And almost all of them wanted to take a piece of their holiday home with them. Something tangible to remind them of their favorite vacation spot. For some that meant a T-shirt or baseball cap embroidered with the word "Maine." For others it was an antique, a painting, or a piece of sea glass. Or even a rounded stone from their favorite beach that would find new life as a paperweight. People who bought antiques from Sarah might be looking for links to the past, or they might want a souvenir of Haven Harbor.

I valued the dishes and paintings in our house precisely because they were in our house. I'd grown up with them, and, in some cases, so had Gram. And so had her mother. And maybe back further. I had no idea what their market value was, and I didn't care. I did know old furniture was often better made than a piece you'd buy at Ikea. But I'd never been attracted to the miscellaneous bits of china and glass that Sarah displayed in her shop.

I stopped at two small rectangular framed pictures. Then I looked closer. They looked a little like embroidery, but they were incredibly delicate. One showed a coach being pulled by six horses; the other was of a horse race.

A few minutes later the woman buying the teacups left and Sarah joined me. "Like something?"

"Just curious. What are those?" Then I looked at their price tags. They were marked $350 and $400. Whatever they were, I hoped Sarah found a customer who really liked them.

"They're Stevengraphs. Very popular in the 1860s and 1870s in England, and to a lesser degree in this country."

"But what are they? At first I thought they were delicate needlepoint. But up close they look more like fabrics."

"They're woven silk ribbons. About 1860, Thomas Stevens, a weaver in Coventry, England, started making woven silk bookmarks showing scenes of various sorts. They were sold in bookstores and stationery stores, as you'd expect. They were so popular that about ten years later he started to make matted pictures, like the ones you're looking at. He wove over two hundred different pictures and over five hundred different bookmarks."

"Are they all as small as these?" I bent over to examine one of the intricate scenes.

"Pretty much. The largest pictures are about seven by thirteen inches. Most are smaller. They're all silk, and many have faded over the years, or the silk has deteriorated. Since they were matted and framed, though, quite a few are still around. Their prices vary. Scenes of carriages and horses and sporting events are popular."

"Are they still being made?"

Sarah shook her head. "The Stevens factory was bombed in 1940. That was the end of the Stevengraphs."

"Interesting," I said, quickly surveying the room. "Does everything in here have a story like that?"

"Probably," Sarah agreed. "Trouble is, we don't always know what the stories are." She gestured at a group of iron banks and mechanical toys. "But you could make up your own stories. You could imagine who first bought these toys, for instance, and who played with them. And who must have treasured them, or they wouldn't have lasted as long."

"I can see I'd better clean our attic out more carefully," I said, looking at the price tag on one mechanical bank.

"You should. If you find any antiques that look interesting, let me know and I'll give you an estimate. Maybe even make you an offer."

"Here," I said, handing Sarah her envelope. "I

brought your share of the money we got back from Jacques Lattimore."

"I can use that," she said. "Have you any new orders yet?"

"I haven't started going through the customer lists," I admitted. "I need a little time, but I will."

"I'm ready and willing, any time you do get an order. Now that I've opened the store for the summer, I sit here and read or do needlepoint between customers. I like to read. After all, as Emily wrote, 'There is no frigate like a book.' But the needlepoint brings in money."

"I understand. I liked those Christmas sachets you brought to our house the other day. Maybe you could make up more of those. Lobsters and lighthouses always sell," I said, remembering what Gram had stitched when I was growing up.

"I'm tired of lobsters and lighthouses. But you're right. They sell. Maybe I'll try a boat. Or a crab. Or moose. So not all the sachets look the same."

"Fine with me," I agreed. "I'll try to get all your work placed in a gift or craft shop."

"And I've been meaning to call you. I've been researching that old piece of needlework I brought to your house the other day. I agree with Charlotte. I think the design is one from Maine. Possibly late eighteenth century."

I nodded.

"I don't think that little piece was originally meant to be displayed. I think it was a practice piece, for someone learning her stitches. That's why it wasn't signed. But I'm still learning. Your grandmother loaned me one book on nineteenth-century needlecrafts, and I've put in an inter-library loan for several books the library listed on traditional New England needlecrafts."

"Great! Gram has a whole shelf of them. I'm sure she'd lend you more if you need them. I'm going to start reading, too. I'm guessing you aren't the only one in Maine who has a piece of embroidery she'd like to save and know more about."

"If we learn enough, we could advertise in the antique trade journals," Sarah added. "I think that's a wonderful idea."

"And, of course, you'd get the profits from any customers you brought in," I told her. "If they came to the business and we referred them to you, we'd take a percentage."

"It's too early to plan that," she said. "But I'll let you know when I've learned more, and keep my eyes out for other pieces of old stitchery."

"Good," I said. I glanced at an old clock hanging on the wall. "I have to get going. I still have to deliver Ob's envelope."

"On your way, then," Sarah said. "I'm glad you stopped in. You know where to find me."

I borrowed Gram's car to get to Ob's house. He lived in a farmhouse, complete with a barn and an ell that attached the barn to the house. The house "next door" was a couple of acres away. And much more modern. Ob had probably sold off part of the farmland connected with his home to someone who wanted to build. Across the street was a nineteenth-century mansion that had been empty for years. The old Gardener place, Haven Harbor's ghost house.

I parked by Ob's barn. Within a few minutes he appeared, dusting sawdust off his apron. "Angie Curtis! What brings you out here?"

"Brought you your share of the Lattimore money," I said, handing him the envelope. "How's your back? Gram said you were having problems with it."

"Oh, your grandmother talks too much," he said with a smile. "I'm pretty good today. Chopping wood, as you can see."

"What for?"

"What for? Girl, you've been out of Maine too long. For the woodstove next winter. If I split the wood now and stack it so it dries over the summer, it won't smoke much next winter. Got to do it now, 'cause next week I'm putting the *Anna Mae* back in the water, and I'll be polishing her up and getting the gear ready for summer. Already got my first reservation in, for Memorial Day weekend."

"You planning on doing any more needlepoint soon?"

He shook his head. "Not 'til fall, if the fishing's good this season. My druthers are to spend time on the water. Course, a long spell of fog or rain might change my mind. My wife, though, she's been watching what I've been doing, and she might be interested in learning, if your grandmother would take her as another student. I know she taught Lauren Decker a while back."

"I'll ask her," I said.

"I'd appreciate that. I haven't the patience to teach anyone. And I'm on the water so much in summer, the wife gets bored. By August she'll be canning and freezing up a storm, but before that, it'd be good for her to have a new hobby to fill her hours." He leaned over. "Tell Charlotte my Anna wants to learn. I don't know as she wants to learn well enough to be a full-fledged needle-pointer. Just well enough to make a Christmas ornament for the grandkids or a little pillow for the guest room. You know what I mean."

"I'm learning, Ob," I said. A carved sign hung above his workbench in the back of the barn: OBADIAH WINSLOW, MASTER CARVER.

His eyes followed mine. "Yup. I did that. Did it to impress the customers when I was carving decoys and such. Some folks wanted carved letters or numbers to put on their houses. That was to show I could handle that work. Don't do much of the carving anymore, between my back and the *Anna Mae* and the work Charlotte's been getting for me. Working with a needle is like working with a tiny chisel . . . making something from nothing. I like that part of it."

"You do beautiful work," I agreed. "Don't strain your back chopping."

He shrugged. "It's got to be done, and looks like I'm the man with the axe. You say hello to your grandmother for me. And have her call Anna about those lessons."

"I will," I said, climbing back into the car.

Needlepoint lessons? Maybe that's another sideline that could work for Mainely Needlepoint.

I drove back downtown, feeling as though I was working my way back into the community.

Chapter Thirty

Let virtue prove your never fading bloom
For mental beauty will survive the tomb.
                    —Text from a sampler stitched by
            Mary Chase, age eleven, Augusta, Maine

"I'm home!" I called.

"In the kitchen," Gram called back. "Did you get all those envelopes delivered?"

"I did. I'm glad you suggested I go in person. It gave me a chance to get to know everyone better."

She nodded. "A good group."

"Seemed so. Although I gathered they work more at certain times of the year, most are free to work in the winter. If we got in several large orders during the summer, we might be hard-pressed to get them done."

"True," said Gram, who was stuffing haddock for supper. "Sometimes we need to juggle assignments a little."

I stepped over Juno, who was keeping a close watch on Gram. I wondered if Gram was making enough for three for dinner. "Oh, and Ob Winslow's wife would like to learn needlepoint. She wondered if you'd teach her."

"I could do that." Gram put the haddock in a deep casserole dish, covered it with bread crumbs

248

and onion and garlic, and squeezed fresh lemon juice over the crumbs and seasonings.

"I was thinking, maybe we could advertise that you'd teach needlepoint classes. It might be a sideline for the business, and you might end up training people to work at Mainely Needlepoint in the future." I poured myself a glass of ice water. "I should learn, although I'd still rather stick to the business end rather than the creative side of the business."

"Classes might be a good idea." Gram nodded. "A year or so back the local adult school wanted me to teach a course for them, but at the time I wasn't free when they needed me. If we could decide when the classes were held, I'd be able to do it." She paused. "Of course, after I'm married, I don't know what my schedule will be." She shrugged, smiling. "The downside of falling in love with a minister." She took a mess of fiddle-heads out of the refrigerator and rinsed them off.

"You've been single a long time, Gram, since before I was born. Are you sure you want to lose that independence?"

"Every woman needs to know she can survive without a partner. I've proved I can. After your grandfather died, God bless him and his life insurance, I raised one daughter and one grand-daughter, kept this house going, and started a business. I've done my bit. Got nothing to prove to myself or the world about independence."

"Being on your own has advantages," I suggested. "Deciding what you're going to do, and where you'll go, and who you'll take time to see. Even just choosing what you'll have for dinner and what time you go to bed and get up in the morning. No one to tell you your chicken was too dry or yell at you because you forgot to pick up clothes at the cleaners." I surprised myself by being so adamant.

Gram raised her eyebrows. "An interesting perspective. I won't ask you where you came up with those examples. I remember being young, centuries ago as it might seem to you. Marrying then meant choosing who was going to be the father of your children, and who'd share your dreams with you."

I nodded.

"When I married your grandfather, we planned our future together. . . ." She paused, remembering. "It was a wonderful time. As the saying goes, we didn't have much money, but love and joy made up for it." She put the haddock in the oven, the fiddleheads in a steamer, and sat down at the kitchen table. "But at my age, the 'till death us do part' aspect of marriage is what's important. I'm looking forward to sharing my life with someone. And then, when the time comes, we'll take care of each other." She looked at me. "Couples in their twenties don't usually think about that. When you're older, you know that's part of your future.

Tom and I've talked about it. We're both ready to make that commitment to each other."

"Gram! If you were sick, I'd take care of you!"

Doesn't she trust me to do that? Is that the reason she's getting married?

"That's all well and good. You might want to. But you have your life ahead of you. You'll have a job, maybe a husband and children. Although I'd love to have you settle nearby, I don't want you ever to feel obligated to take care of me. I want you to live your life the way you want to, not the way you have to."

I was silent for a few minutes. "You don't have to worry about that, Gram. I wouldn't take care of you because I felt obligated. I'd take care of you because I love you."

"Thank you for that, Angel. But don't you worry! I'm not planning on being disabled immediately." She shook her head, smiling. "Tom and I hope we'll have a lot of years ahead to enjoy life together. So you liked the needlepointers?"

Conversation change. "I did. Ob is a bit of a character, and Ruth seemed lonely. I'm going to try to stop and see her every week or two."

"Good call."

"I still have Lauren's envelope. Her neighbor said she and her family went up to their camp for a few days."

"Caleb must have calmed down a bit," Gram said dryly. "They didn't wait for Lauren's money,

251

and he didn't insist she work today. He's been pushing her to work as many hours as possible."

"And Cindy was visiting her parents. She confirmed we're going to have lunch with Clem on Monday."

"Good. I'm glad that worked out."

"I liked Dave Percy, although his poison garden is a little strange. And I loved the needlepoint he was working on . . . a matching cushion for an old chair?"

"Yes. He's had that for a while."

"He's been working on other pieces, too. I saw a half-finished canvas of a skiff in his living room."

Gram stopped. "What did it look like?"

"I didn't look closely. A red skiff, in water, with a lighthouse in the background. About a twelve-inch square canvas."

"That's not one of Dave's projects," Gram said. "It's one I assigned to Lauren."

"Maybe he's helping her," I suggested. "It was lying on the window seat."

"Maybe," said Gram. "But what was it doing at his house when she's out of town?"

Chapter Thirty-one

We had a busy summer. . . . There were webs of cotton to be made up; delicate embroideries to fashion; shining silks and misty muslins to be submitted to the skillful hands of the city dressmaker. I was to lay aside my mourning on my wedding day.
—"A Wife's Story," by Louise Chandler Moulton, *Harper's New Monthly Magazine*, December 1861

Sunday morning dawned, and I realized Gram expected me to attend church with her. After all, I was now the almost-stepgranddaughter of the minister.

I knew she'd be upset if I told her the truth—I hadn't attended a church service in years, and hadn't intended to change that pattern. So, instead, I found an appropriate skirt and a light sweater. Not elegant, but I was in Maine, after all. Women were expected to dress up a little for church, but anyone who wore *Vogue* fashions would be as out of place as someone wearing L.L.Bean boots in Phoenix. What I was wearing was okay for a Haven Harbor Sunday. I even put on lipstick.

I cleaned up all right.

The sanctuary was half full. Not bad for a

non-holiday Sunday. I wondered if Reverend Tom got paid by the head. Would he be rewarded (in this world) if his church was full every Sunday? I suspected the total of the day's collection plates was critical. I contributed five dollars. I wasn't exactly a regular there.

Gram chose seats for us close to the front, on the aisle. She wanted to make sure Reverend Tom knew we were there. His fan club, if not yet his family.

His sermon was focused on forgiveness—a classic theme. Although I listened, I didn't totally buy in. I didn't think I'd ever forgive whoever killed Mama. She'd had a hard life, and her death had messed up mine, and Gram's, too. How could that be forgiven?

After the service ended, we joined other parishioners for coffee and sweets in the same room used for Mama's funeral reception almost a week before. This time I recognized more people. I picked up a homemade doughnut as Gram went to speak to Reverend Tom.

Ruth Hopkins was standing by herself, one hand on her walker and one on her paper cup of coffee.

"Why don't I get a chair for you?" I asked.

"Thanks, Angie, but I'm fine. If I start sitting all the time, someday I won't be able to get up. Got to keep active." She took a final sip of coffee. "But you can throw out this cup and get me one of those big white-chocolate cookies on the table? I have coffee at home. I don't have cookies."

I did so, and got one for myself. They were much too good. Maybe I'd found a reason to come to church. I wondered if Reverend Tom ever preached about gluttony.

"Tom told me you and he had a session with one of his boards the other day," Ruth commented. "How'd you like contacting the spirit world?"

"I'm not sure. It was my first time. We did get at least one answer. But I kept thinking one of us was pushing that planchette, and I knew it wasn't me." Reverend Tom must have told her about our Ouija experiment. I certainly hadn't told anyone.

She nodded. "Logical. You're very logical. Not unusual. Most folks are. I don't know anyone who's tried Ouija only a few times who doesn't think that. But I believe there's some truth to the answers Ouija gives."

"Have you used a board?" I asked. I would never have thought little old Ruth Hopkins had a penchant for spiritualism. But, then, I never would have thought she was secretly S.M. Bond and Chastity Falls.

"Not on a regular basis, you understand," she confided happily. "But I live alone. Sometimes I'm just in the mood to talk with someone. So I get out my board and see if any spirits are interested' in conversing." She expertly brushed cookie crumbs off her chest.

"Has anything the board told you come true?"

"That would be telling the future, dear. The spirits I speak to are more interested in the past. Oh, occasionally they'll tell me something about today. For instance, about three weeks ago they told me you'd be coming home."

I looked at her. "Three weeks ago! That was before Lauren found my mother's body!"

She nodded. "It was. But, see . . . you're here. The board knew."

It was unbelievable. "Do many people in Haven Harbor use boards?' I asked, beginning to wonder if I'd discovered an underground coven.

"I have no idea. I don't talk about mine much. I consider it a private hobby. Reverend Tom knows, though. Sometimes he joins me." She looked around the room. "I suspect most of these folks wouldn't be interested. Might even be frightened. Or decide I'm a witch, or some other nonsense. I'm just curious. I keep my mind open to possibilities."

"Spiritualism is totally new to me," I said. "But it is intriguing."

"If you ever want to experiment a little, you give me a call and come on over. We can see if my spirits visit when you're present. Or perhaps you'll find a spirit of your own."

"I'd like that," I said. "Using the board with you, I mean." Why not? I didn't really believe those in the spirit world could contact people here. But, then, the whole concept was fascinating. And might be fun.

So long as I don't take it seriously, I reminded myself.

"Then you're invited. For now, I have to get myself to home. I've stood long enough. The Kentucky Derby was yesterday. I missed some of the prerace hoopla then. I'm looking forward to the rerun this afternoon of the stories they tell about the horses and jockeys and owners before the race." She took a few steps toward the door. "Don't forget. You're welcome anytime. Except when the races are on!"

I joined Gram and Ob Winslow. "Angie, this is Anna, Ob's wife," Gram said, introducing me to a dark-haired woman about Ob's age.

"Pleased to meet you," I said. "Ob said you might want to learn how to do needlepoint."

"That's right," she said. "Your grandmother and I were talking about that. This is a busy month, with getting the boat ready for summer. I'm the official brass polisher in the family." She smiled at Ob. "But by the end of May I'll be free. By then, Ob'll be out on the water most of the time. Some days I go with him, but I'd rather cook fish than catch them. We're a good pair, aren't we, Ob?"

"That we are," he said, putting his arm around her. "And looks like this year I've found a couple of young men who'll be home from college by then and agree to crew for me. That way I can spend my time figuring out where the fish are and taking the tourists there, and you can get in a little needle practice."

"I'll call you to set a time, Anna," said Gram. "Angie here may join us, and I'll advertise and ask around to see if anyone else is interested."

"I'm looking forward to it," Anna Winslow said. "Thank goodness that Jacques Lattimore is gone and we can all get on with our lives. This past winter was a nightmare. I don't think I ever hated anyone as much as I hated that Lattimore." She lowered her voice. "I never want to be in a situation that I have to go to the food bank again. Ob and I work too hard to have to do that."

Ob patted Anna on her shoulders.

"How's your boy, Josh?" asked Gram, changing the subject.

"He's back and forth. I always figured he'd grow out of that ADHD he has, but now he's twenty-two. Even when he takes his meds, he can't focus on any one thing for very long."

"You'll be seeing him this summer," Ob added. "He'll be home in a few days. He left his job in Lewiston—"

"He was fired again," Anna broke in. "Didn't take his meds and missed deadlines, and his attendance wasn't great."

"This summer he'll be helping me on the *Anna Mae*," said Ob. "Sea air may keep him straight."

"I hope so," said Anna. "I love that boy to death,

but he's a constant challenge." She shook her head. "It's not easy for Josh, and not easy for Ob and me. But you can't turn around in life. You've got to keep going."

Gram nodded. "Very true. And Angie and I are going to go now. I soaked beans last night, and want to get them baking."

"Charlotte Curtis! Baked beans are a Saturday-night dish! Not Sunday dinner!"

Gram nodded. "Don't I know it! But the past week has been crazy, and I'm a bit behind. So we have to be off."

"It was lovely meeting you, Anna," I said as we headed for the door.

Ob and Anna's son was on meds for ADHD. I'd had high-school classmates who took Ritalin for ADHD. At least one boy sold his pills, instead of taking them. And even those with ADHD skipped pills when they were partying because of what my friend Tim Sanborn once called, "serious side effects." Would those side effects include vomiting and convulsions? I didn't know. Ob and Anna clearly weren't happy with Lattimore. But did one of them hate him enough to kill him?

How fast would Ritalin dissolve in tea?

Chapter Thirty-two

Little Dorrit let herself out to do needlework. At so much a day—or at so little—from eight to eight, Little Dorrit was to be hired. Punctual to the moment, Little Dorrit appeared; punctual to the moment, Little Dorrit vanished. What became of Little Dorrit between the two eights was a mystery.

—Charles Dickens, *Little Dorrit*, 1857

Monday morning I headed back to Brunswick. It had only been five days since I'd been there looking for Lattimore, but it seemed a long time. A lot had happened since then.

Dropping off the cartons at Goodwill made me feel I'd taken a major step toward putting the past to rest.

And buying a laptop turned out to be simpler than I'd thought. I even found the accounting software I wanted, and the store personnel loaded everything for me. Now I had no excuses for not starting to input Mainely Needlepoint's account information.

By the time I got to Bath for lunch, I felt as though I'd accomplished enough for a day. Time for a beer and barbeque.

Clem had gotten there first and saved us a table.

She was wearing three-inch heels and a sea blue silk dress, which wrapped her in all the right places. She could have stepped out of a *Business Week* article about the youngest woman named CEO of a major banking chain.

"Wow," I said. "You look great. Do you look this elegant every day at work?"

" 'Dress for the job you want, not the job you have,' " she answered. "That's my mantra. Plus, clothes are my downfall. I've got charges at most of the Freeport outlets."

Investigating new boyfriends and adulterous wives hadn't required an elegant wardrobe. I might have to do some shopping if I was going to be "the face of Mainely Needlepoint," as Gram had put it. I'd already bought a laptop. I'd have to get Wi-Fi for Gram's house, so I could use her printer. And I had to invest in my wardrobe, too? This business would definitely have to make money.

"If I decide to upgrade my style, I'll know who to call," I said.

"I can't believe you're both here!" While Clem had honed her image from the one she'd had in high school, Cindy, as I'd seen on Saturday, had put on weight. Today she was wearing mom jeans and a Pats sweatshirt. Someone had spit up on her shoulder. They'd made very different choices for their lives, but they both seemed comfortable. I wondered if I'd ever feel as content with mine.

We all hugged and sat down, picked up the

menus, and ordered the same lunch: pulled pork on a bun, with a side of roasted sweet potatoes. Exactly what we'd always ordered.

I turned to Cindy. "I met your three children yesterday, and you mentioned your husband. Now catch me up. Where did you meet him?"

She blushed. "Clive's a dear. I met him through a friend of a friend when I was going to massage school. I needed to practice on people, and he volunteered!"

"So that's what they call a happy ending." I grinned. They both groaned. "I'm guessing you've heard that before?"

"Only a few million times," she answered, nodding. "But you have an exciting job! Mom told me you're a private investigator in Arizona. No blizzards, and hot guys in shorts!"

"Not exactly," I answered. "Hot temperatures, for sure. Sizzling. But, believe me, not all hot guys. And I'm not officially a private investigator. I worked for one. But for the moment, that's in the past. I'm going to stay around awhile and get Mainely Needlepoint, Gram's business, back on track."

Cindy's mother had told her about our business problems; we filled Clem in.

"Mainely Needlepoint sounds like a cool niche business. Once you get it back up and running, maybe I could pitch a story about it to one of my bosses at Channel 7," Clem suggested. "This summer we're planning to run a series on unique small businesses in Maine."

"That would be great! But first we have to settle the little question of whether one of the needle-pointers murdered the guy I'm replacing," I explained.

"What?" Turned out neither of them knew about Lattimore's death or the investigation. I didn't want to say much. After all, Cindy's mother had been at our house when Lattimore was poisoned. She was on the suspect list. Their friend Lauren had been there, too.

"How is Lauren?" Cindy asked. "Is she still having problems with Caleb?"

I wasn't exactly surprised at that question. He'd seemed crazy enough to be dangerous when he'd stopped in earlier in the week. I wanted to know more about him. "I've only seen Lauren a few times. She came to the funeral, and I saw her at the needlepoint meeting and once at Harbor Haunts. We didn't talk much. She told me she was back waitressing full-time because of the mess with Mainely Needlepoint. She didn't mention her husband."

"Well," Cindy said, lowering her voice, "Caleb had a pretty nasty reputation before they got married. Drank too much. Had friends who ended up with records. Considered trouble. But Lauren couldn't see that. Maybe she thought she'd reform him. Or maybe love was blind. I will say when I went to her wedding, they looked great. They'd put a down payment on a lobster boat, and Caleb was real excited about that. But making a living from lobstering's been rough the past couple of years."

"Gram mentioned that," I said. "What is it? Global warming?" Lobsters needed deep, cold water to spawn.

"Partially. But mostly it's competition from Canada. A lot of lobstermen here used to send their lobsters to Canadian canneries. Then a few years ago Canada decided to protect its own lobstermen by putting major tariffs on imported lobsters. A lot of our guys lost their contracts with Canadian firms," Clem explained.

"Tourists, of course, have loved it," Cindy added. "Lobsters have come down in price because now more of them are available for local markets."

"But lobstermen aren't making the livings they're used to." I caught on right away.

"Exactly," Clem put in. "Some of them have even stopped lobstering. Lauren's working her rear off, but I heard Caleb's started hanging around with his old friends; guys who never bothered to stay in school long enough or get decent jobs. Some of them are dealing."

"Drugs? You're saying he's involved with drugs?" If Lauren was coping with a husband doing that, no wonder she hadn't checked out a locker key in Union more quickly. She had other issues to cope with.

"There's a growing meth business in Maine," Clem shared. "It's an open secret in a lot of towns. Not so much on the coast as inland, where the shoe factories have gone out of business and the paper industry isn't hiring as many anymore."

Cindy shrugged. "I don't know if he's dealing. But the word around is that he's using, for sure. And when Caleb was drinking, he'd get violent. On alcohol and drugs . . . it can't be pretty. Or easy to deal with. And Lauren's never been quite the same since her little girl died."

"I heard she had a child. What happened?" I'd forgotten to ask Gram.

"Robin was only two. She drowned. Fell off the rocks near the lighthouse into the surf. Story was Lauren had only let go of her hand for a minute."

Now I was definitely more sympathetic to Lauren.

"It was awful when Lauren found your mom's body. She was all over the news." Clem shook her head. "I tried to get in touch with her then. I thought maybe I'd help her at least get her hair done and give her a few tips on how to handle the press, but she never returned my calls."

"Maybe she thought since you worked for a television station, you were going to interview her yourself. Or try to get an inside story," suggested Cindy.

"Maybe. But at least that story's not a lead anymore. I'm sorry about your mother, Angie."

I nodded. "Now the town seems divided about whether Joe Greene killed her, or someone else was involved."

"I thought all the evidence pointed to him."

"It does. But many of his friends in town don't want to believe he's guilty."

"Remember, Angie, when you and I and Lauren were in Brownies, with Mrs. Greene as our leader?" Cindy said. "Life was so simple then. And we had so much fun. Remember our first camping trip?"

I rolled my eyes. "I've tried to forget it."

"You peed in your sleeping bag because you heard noises in the bushes!"

"That was your fault! You shouldn't have been wandering around after we were all supposed to be asleep," I said.

"I was trying to hide behind those bushes so I could pee!" Cindy laughed. "We were in, what? Third grade then?" She shook her head in disbelief. "My son's in kindergarten already. It all seems impossible."

"Like it or not, we're the grown-ups now," said Clem.

"That's just a rumor," I added.

"I wasn't in Haven Harbor for Brownies, but what I loved best about Girl Scouts," Clem admitted, "was that Mr. Greene sent all the second-day cookies and tarts and muffins over to our meetings for our refreshments. *Yum!*"

"I didn't like Mr. Greene," Cindy said quietly. "Mr. Greene was a pervert."

The table was silent. A long-locked door had opened. "He tried to touch you, too?" I asked.

Chapter Thirty-three

My heart exults while to the attentive eye
The curious needle spreads the enameled dye.
While varying shades the Pleasing task beguile
My friends applaud me and my Parents smile.
　　—From sampler stitched by Dolly Abbot,
aged fourteen, most likely at the Pinkerton
Academy in Londonderry, New Hampshire,
　　1817. At the bottom of the sampler is a
memorial to one of Dolly's sisters. Dolly and
one of her sisters survived to adulthood. Their
　　six brothers and sisters all died young.

None of us spoke for a minute or two. We all concentrated on our barbeque. I took a long drink of beer.

Then Clem said, "What? He never tried anything with me."

"You were lucky. I was scared to go into that shop of his. He was always finding an excuse for me to walk in back of the display case." Cindy's voice was steady.

"To choose your favorite cookie?" I said.

She nodded. "Exactly. I'd go behind the counter with him, and sometimes he'd just touch my rear, like it was by accident. If I had a skirt on, it was worse. His hand would reach under it. . . . I tried to make up reasons why I wouldn't go near him. But my mother thought it was cute that I was so shy. She'd push me toward him."

"You never told her?"

She shook her head. "I was too embarrassed. My mother didn't even want to talk about buying me a bra when my boobs were bouncing all over the kickball field. How about you?"

"The first time I thought it was an accident. That he was just being a little too friendly, you know? But every time it got worse. I was . . . developed . . . pretty early, and he used to grab my breasts. The counter would cover it all. No one would see. And he'd just keep talking about the price of doughnuts and sliced whole wheat bread to whoever was in the store." I swallowed. I'd never talked about Mr. Greene before. He was still in my nightmares. "I was too embarrassed. I thought it was just me." I'd thought he'd done it to me because Mama flirted with him and I'd been singled out. I hated to admit it, but Cindy's admission was a relief. It hadn't just been me. I hadn't done anything to encourage him.

"Lauren used to ask me to spend the night at her house. I never would go," Cindy continued.

"Me either! I came up with excuses every time." I nodded.

"No wonder she got angry with us and said nasty things."

Clem looked from one of us to the other. "I can't

believe that. How awful! Now I'm wondering why he didn't do the same to me."

"You were lucky," said Cindy. "And you didn't come to Haven Harbor until you were older."

"I wonder how many other girls he touched?" I asked. "We can't have been the only two."

"He could have been doing it for years," Clem said. "If no one ever told."

"I once started to tell my mother what happened, but she said I must have misunderstood," Cindy said. "She said that Mr. Greene was a nice man who just liked to tease little girls. That some men were like that. I should smile and move away."

"Today they teach that 'places not to touch' stuff in school. Back then, nobody warned us." Clem shook her head.

"I wonder if he ever did anything to Lauren," I thought out loud.

"His own daughter?"

Clem and Cindy looked at each other.

"Do you think he would have?" Cindy asked. "That's even more seriously creepy."

"She never hinted that her father was a problem," Clem said. "And she took care of her mom, and then her dad when they were sick. How could she have done that if . . ."

Lauren's neighbor had said Lauren stopped coming to see her dad after her mom had died. Maybe she'd only taken care of her mom.

"I was so angry and depressed. I had trouble

making friends. I never wanted to leave my house because I was afraid I'd see him. Finally I convinced my parents to send me away to private school, but the rest of you were in town. You couldn't avoid him all the time. That must have been nightmarish," Cindy said.

"It was," I agreed. "I dreaded when Mama sent me to the bakery on an errand. She thought I should love going there all by myself, because it showed how grown-up I was, and because Mr. Greene always gave me an extra cookie. She didn't know how I was paying for those cookies." I shook my head. "I hate sugar cookies. Every time I see one or smell one, I feel sick."

"But it's over. He's gone. We survived. And, let me tell you, my kids are being taught to tell me if anyone tries that with them," Cindy declared.

"Good. And I hope there's no one like Mr. Greene in your neighborhood," stated Clem, nodding.

The three of us finished our lunches and parted, with hugs and promises to stay in touch.

I drove back to Haven Harbor and set up my new laptop on the old desk in my bedroom.

First I ran a search on the telephone number Mama had written down.

Until a few years ago, that had been the number for Greene's Bakery.

Why had Joe Greene's telephone number been in Mama's pocket?

And I hadn't told Clem and Cindy everything. I hadn't kept silent about Joe Greene. I'd told Mama about him.

I hadn't planned it. But when she'd asked me why I was so happy and excited about flying up from being a Brownie to being a Junior Girl Scout, I'd told her it was because when I was a Junior, Mrs. Greene wouldn't be my leader. I wouldn't have to go to her house anymore, and I hated Mr. Greene. When she asked me why, I'd told her about the touching. Mama had hugged me and told me that I wouldn't have to worry about that anymore. I'd thought she meant I wouldn't have to worry because I wouldn't be a Brownie much longer.

Maybe she'd meant something else.

Chapter Thirty-four

It may be much, or it may be little, but hand-work of some kind must embellish every gown which has any pretention to smartness. The kind of work and its elaborateness being pretty sure indications of the taste and purse of the woman who wears it.

—*The Modern Priscilla*, November 1905

Maybe Mama had Joe Greene's telephone number because she'd called to order a birthday cake or a tray of cookies. True, I didn't remember her ever doing that, but, despite the fact that I'd felt pretty grown-up then, I'd only been nine when she had left that Sunday afternoon.

The bakery wouldn't have been open on a Sunday. That number could have been in her pocket for months.

I kept thinking about what Cindy had said at lunch. All these years I'd thought it was just me. However awful it had been, Mr. Greene had picked only me. At first I'd thought I was special. Then I thought I must have done something to encourage him—or Mama had.

Now I knew Joe Greene had been a lecher and a toucher, at minimum—a pedophile, at worst. The more I thought about it the angrier I got.

How did that fit into the picture? And if he was interested in young girls, why would he have gotten involved with Mama?

She'd been involved with men, sometimes married men. But she was definitely a grown woman.

The longer I stayed in Haven Harbor, the more questions I had.

I looked at my new computer. It had answered my question about the telephone number. Could it help with the murder Gram and I were suspects in?

I Googled, **poison causing vomiting and convulsions.**

No wonder the police were depending on the results of the toxicology reports. Even an overdose of aspirin could cause those symptoms. So could a list of poisonous plants. Too much alcohol. Or the alcohol could have interacted with another substance to cause the vomiting and convulsions. Alcohol combined with antidepressants or amphetamines would have caused reactions stronger than any one of those alone.

But where to begin, unless someone left a vial labeled *Poison* on the coffee table in our living room? So many substances could be poisons.

I turned off the laptop and got into bed. I lay there, remembering being small, and hearing the lighthouse bell or foghorn. On hot summer days I'd opened my windows to catch sea breezes. The laughing and talking from people walking home from a day at sea or a night at one of the restaurants would drift through my windows. I'd pretended I was floating, safe in my room, away from what was happening in the world.

Gram'd put me to bed every night and tucked me in. She'd read to me, until I'd said I was too old to be read to.

Mama was usually out, working or with friends, when I went to bed. But I'd known—for almost ten years I'd known—that she'd be home soon. I would hear the front door open and her footsteps on the stairs. If I were still awake, I'd listen. The ninth step from the bottom creaked. It was a kind of goodnight message.

When I'd needed socks or underwear or a warm hat, Gram had been the one to see the need and find the money. Mama'd bought me hair ribbons and party dresses and dolls. I'd taken Gram's gifts for granted. I'd cherished the gifts from Mama, because they were special. They'd come from her.

Remembering, I looked up at the line of elegant dolls, with immaculately curled hair and old-fashioned dresses that still stood in their stands on the top shelf of my bookcase.

I'd never played with them. They were too good, too fancy, too special. Instead, I'd collected sea stones and jars of green and blue and orange sea glass. Once I'd found a tiny pocket-sized naked porcelain doll on the beach, smoothed like the pieces of glass. I'd put her carefully in one of

Gram's mason jars, so she could look out, and surrounded her with pieces of sea glass.

Now I saw I'd trapped her in the jar. The sea glass was pretty, but it kept her from escaping.

I got out of bed, poured the jar full of glass pieces onto my comforter, and gently picked up the tiny doll. She had a chip on one of her feet and another on the back of her head, but otherwise, amazingly, she was intact. She'd ridden the waves and survived. I stood her up on the shelf and put the sea glass back in the jar.

Then I took all the fancy dolls down from the top shelf and put them in a carton for Goodwill. Another little girl might love them. I didn't.

I couldn't think about Mama anymore.

I'd think about Lattimore.

Somehow the murderer had poisoned Lattimore's tea. They must have done it by sleight of hand, or in a moment no one noticed. Yes, Gram had made the tea, but she wouldn't have killed him. I didn't kill him. So . . . what did I know about the others who'd been in our living room? The other needlepointers, who'd been cheated by the man with whom they were sharing afternoon tea?

Ruth Hopkins. Gram would call her a "tough old bird." She was the oldest of the group and partially disabled. But she'd been able-bodied enough to bake the molasses cookies she'd brought, and to get to the meeting. Ruth had gotten very little of Lattimore's money. She hadn't been working much recently. Working at needlepoint, that is. S.M. Bond and Chastity Falls had been publishing!

She didn't sound like the most logical person to have brought poison, as well as cookies, to the meeting. But, then, it wouldn't take much strength to grind up her medications and dissolve them, would it? Although her arthritic hands would have made it harder for her to poison a teacup quickly, without anyone's noticing.

Dave Percy. He'd been in the navy, but he wasn't as macho as some ex-military types I'd met. But he was no wimp. To have done needlepoint onboard submarines would have taken strength of character. I couldn't believe he hadn't been razzed about that, at minimum. He was working, as a teacher—a steady job, although not highly paid in Haven Harbor—and Lattimore owed him quite a bit. How much had his small house and immaculate furnishings cost him? Did he have any vices I didn't know about? Traditionally, poison was a woman's weapon. But Dave Percy's poison garden put him definitely on my list.

The other man in the group, Ob Winslow, was a wood-carver—as good with a knife as with a needle. He also was owed a lot by Lattimore, and he'd given up his carving business to do needlepoint. He still did fishing charters in the summer, but this year's season hadn't started yet. From what his wife, Anna, had said after church, they were hurting for money. And he had a bad back.

Maybe he had prescription pain pills that, mixed with alcohol, could be lethal. Or he'd borrowed some of his son Josh's Ritalin.

Ob was still on the list.

Katie Titicomb. Her husband was a doctor, so she wouldn't have any serious money worries. But, since he was a doctor, she also might have access to various types of medications. She was able-bodied and, like the others, Lattimore owed her money. She was Cindy's mom. I hoped she wasn't the killer. But I couldn't cross her off the list.

That left Lauren and Sarah, the two youngest of the group. Lauren, whose husband was rumored to have alcohol, and maybe drug, problems. Caleb definitely had a temper. And he still owed money on his lobster boat. Lobster boats cost more than the small houses or the trailers many young Maine couples started out in. Would Lauren have killed? Or Sarah, who, Gram said, seemed to be coping financially, but who was on her own?

I couldn't see the logic in any of them killing Lattimore. True, they were all angry at him. But killing him wouldn't get them the money they were owed. What other possible reason would they have for killing? I didn't know. But they'd all had the same opportunity. And most had some means of poisoning.

I turned off my light. It didn't make sense. None of it made sense.

Chapter Thirty-five

Her needlework both plain and ornamental was excellent, and she might have put a sewing machine to shame. . . . She was considered especially great in satin stitch.

—James Edward Austen-Leigh,
writing about his aunt, Jane Austen,
in his 1869 biography (published in 1870)

Ethan took Gram in for questioning early the next morning. When I objected, he frowned. "We're not arresting her. Yet." He wouldn't share any details, but he did say he hadn't heard the results from the toxicology tests.

I suspected he'd come to the same conclusion I had. Whatever killed Lattimore had been in the tea. And, of course, Gram had made the tea.

Ethan didn't seem to wonder why, if the tea'd been poisoned, no one but Lattimore was affected. I was convinced whatever killed Lattimore hadn't been in the teapot.

I called Pete Lambert again. "Pete, I've got new information for you about my mother's case." Talking to him reminded me I still didn't have that carry permit. I felt vulnerable without it.

"Wasn't Ethan Trask just at your house, to pick

up your grandmother?" Pete didn't sound thrilled to speak to me.

"They've left."

"So, why didn't you tell him whatever information you have?"

"Because you're helping me get my carry permit." I stopped. "And because we had lunch together the other day."

"What's the information?"

"Did you look to see if Joe Greene had a record of any kind?"

"I looked. No record that I could find. Why?"

"Because he was a sexual predator. I know two grown women who'll swear that he touched them when they were about seven, eight, nine years old."

Long pause.

I tried again. "He touched little girls, Pete. And tried to do more. Are you sure there weren't any reports of that over the years? Complaints the local department might have hushed up?"

"Angie, even if there were reports, what would they have to do with your mother's death?"

"I'm not sure. But it's important." I tried again. "It would have been before you were with the department. But maybe you heard talk. Rumors. Especially after my mother's body was found."

"I'll check it out. Ask around. But, Angie, Joe Greene's dead. Nothing could be done about it now, even if you could prove he was a child molester."

"I know," I said. "But I keep thinking it might have had something to do with my mother's murder. She wasn't a little girl when she was killed, but he'd known her all her life. Maybe he expected more from her than . . . from other women."

Could he have touched Mama when she was a child? I suddenly wondered. It was possible.

"Even if that's true, Angie, it's not a motive for murder."

"People around town said nasty things about my mother after she disappeared."

"I've heard that, Angie. I'd be plenty angry if people talked that way about my mother."

"Please check. And let me know what you find out." I hung up. Maybe he wouldn't find anything. Few little girls might have talked, if they were like Cindy and me. But maybe sometime, somewhere, an adult had seen or heard something suspicious. And been listened to.

Gram was being questioned by the state police. So far as I knew, her only secret was her engagement to Reverend Tom. Nothing to be condemned for, although some might find it worthy of gossip.

I glanced through Gram's collection of books on early-American and European needlepoint and picked out a few to read, but I couldn't concentrate. The words blurred.

Our house was silent except when every so

often Juno jumped up and streaked through, as though pursued by an invisible force. Some people in Haven Harbor, with a strange pride, talked of sharing their homes with its former inhabitants. Souls that hadn't moved on, and only begrudgingly shared the spaces their bodies once inhabited.

My ancestors must have been accepting of their fates. They didn't come back to relive their own lives, or concern themselves with those who'd come after them. Unless Juno saw or heard things I didn't.

Today I could have used their company. I understood why Ruth Hopkins and Reverend Tom, two people who lived alone, found comfort in talking with spirits. Real or imaginary.

I was worried about Gram—not for what she might say, but for assumptions that might be made. Like the assumption she might be a murderer, despite there being no proof. But I had faith the police wouldn't hold her long. Despite all that was happening, at heart I was a glass—or teacup —half-full person.

In the meantime sitting and worrying accomplished nothing. Gram and I'd already separated the bills and statements Lattimore gave us, so we could correlate them with Gram's notes as to what work Jacques had gotten for the group, to whom it had been assigned, and what had been completed. Gram had two cartons of finished needlepoint that Jacques should have picked up and delivered.

Now that we'd divided the money from Jacques, my next priority was contacting those customers, asking their understanding for what had happened, and, hopefully, delivering the needlework and picking up checks.

I sat on the couch and sorted through the papers Jacques had brought that we hadn't looked at yet, picking out orders that hadn't been completed. I found the one for the chair seat I'd seen at Dave's house. A work in progress. And there were several orders for specific wall hangings or pillow covers: a geometric design in pinks and reds, a harbor scene including a sailboat owned by the man who ordered it, a pair of pillow covers with teddy bears on them, and children's names. I hoped most of those orders had been completed.

I was almost through sorting the last of Lattimore's papers when I came to several computer printouts of e-mails clipped together. I assumed they were notes between Jacques and customers. Then I looked again.

Every one of the notes was between Lattimore and Katie Titicomb. Had she been working on a project so complicated she needed to stay directly in touch with him? I'd thought Gram did that coordinating after orders came in.

Curious, I sorted the e-mails by message dates and began reading.

From Lattimore:

The Olsons were thrilled with those tiebacks you did for their drapes.
They said your work was beautiful, and the pattern and colors were perfect matches to the painting over their fire-place, exactly as they'd hoped. Thank you!

From Katie:

So glad the Olsons are happy! It was a fun project. I'm now working on the cushions Malcolm McIntyre wanted for the media room he's building. Monograms are simple work. I'll be ready for another assignment in a week or so. I hope Charlotte has one for me! I get bored without needlepoint to do.

From Lattimore:

I'll make sure Charlotte assigns you a new project as soon as the cushions are finished. You're the best stitcher in the group; I never worry when Charlotte entrusts our most challenging work to you.

From Katie:

I appreciate your trust! And thank you for talking to Charlotte. Sometimes she assigns work to the next person on her list, not to the most appropriate needle-pointer. I hate having time between projects.

From Lattimore:

Charlotte's a lovely person, of course, but she is getting on a bit in years. Have any of the other needlepointers had problems with her? Questioned her judgment?

From Katie:

She's sometimes slow to assign work. And we don't always get our floss and canvas supplies at the same time we're given a project. She says the supply houses are back-ordered. Maybe she should keep a larger supply of the threads and canvases we use most often.

From Lattimore:

Excellent idea, to keep a larger stock of supplies. An organized manager should have thought of that. You're practical as well as creative! (And lovely, I might add, if your husband doesn't mind my saying so.)

From Katie:

Thanks. But I'm not a manager. I just see what needs to be done.

From Lattimore:

That's what a good manager does. It's too bad Charlotte's organizing the needlepointers. You'd do a great job.

From Katie:

Sweet of you to say. But Charlotte started the business. Without her, there wouldn't be a Mainely Needlepoint.

From Lattimore:

If there were to be a major screwup— say, if people weren't getting paid on time—do you think the other needlepointers could be encouraged to vote her out? To vote in another person—you, for instance?

From Katie:

Not getting paid on time would be a major problem for everyone except maybe me. My earnings are for pin money, not groceries. Mainely Needlepoint would fall apart if people weren't paid.

From Lattimore:

Maybe paid some. Enough to keep people stitching, but angry.

From Katie:

What are you suggesting?

From Lattimore:

I'd love to see you head up Mainely Needlepoint. Maybe I could hold back on payments due. If anyone contacted me directly, I could say Charlotte got the orders mixed up.

From Katie:

That wouldn't be fair to the needleworkers or to Charlotte.

From Lattimore:

It wouldn't be for long. I'd suggest to the
others that you'd do a great job
replacing her. You'd like that, wouldn't
you?

From Katie:

Assuming I'd go along with that . . . what
would you get out of a change in
management?

From Lattimore:

Besides working with a lovely lady who
could run the business better than
Charlotte . . . I'd want a change in my
contract. Fifty percent of the profits
instead of forty.

From Katie:

If we can do it without Charlotte's
knowing we've been contacting each
other.

From Lattimore:

Leave that to me.

That was the end. I went back and re-read the messages.

Had Lattimore followed through with his plan? Had he intentionally withheld payments to make Gram look bad, so he could push Katie Titicomb into replacing her?

But so far as I could tell, no one had blamed Gram for the lack of money. They'd blamed Lattimore. And Katie hadn't replaced Gram. The group had decided I'd replace Lattimore, and would take on some of Gram's responsibilities as well.

So . . . when he died, did Lattimore have more of the money he owed people? Was he waiting to get Katie installed as the new head of Mainely Needlepoint before he paid it?

I'd assumed he'd gambled it away.

Or maybe, knowing the plan wasn't working as she'd hoped, Katie had decided to get rid of Lattimore so he couldn't blame her if anyone discovered she'd conspired with him. She could have gotten medications relatively easily. And if she knew Lattimore drank, she could have made sure she had pills that would interact with alcohol.

I called Ethan Trask; as part of his investigation

he should have checked Lattimore's assets. If there was any chance Jacques still had the money he owed the needleworkers, we could put in a claim on his estate. It was a small chance. . . . If Lattimore had any money, why hadn't he paid his rent? But if there was any chance at all, I wanted it checked out.

I waited as Ethan's phone rang. He didn't pick up. But, of course, he was busy. He was questioning Gram.

How would she feel if she found out one of her needlepointers had been plotting against her?

I folded the incriminating e-mails and hid them in my room. I wouldn't tell Gram about them until I was sure.

In the meantime I needed to talk to Katie Titicomb.

Chapter Thirty-six

Behold o'er deaths bewildering wave
The rainbow hope arise
A bridge of glory o'er the grave
That bears beyond the skies.
Sure if one blessing Heaven on man bestows
Tis the pure peace that conscious virtue knows.
—Sampler worked by Betsy Nason Googins,
age nine, in Saco, Maine, 1808

Someone once told me the rhythm of a small town is like a child's heartbeat, regular and steady.

That person didn't remember that both towns and children change. Residents change. Ideologies change. Economies change. Perceptions change. Children don't always sit with hands folded. Sometimes they run and skip and fear ghosts under their beds. Hearts' rhythms change. Become erratic. Undependable.

Murder was a beat out of order. It was discordant. It distracted from the normal rhythm of life.

Or towns.

The Titicombs were one of the most respected families in Haven Harbor: the surgeon and his gracious wife and my friend Cindy, their private-schooled daughter. Could Katie have fallen into Lattimore's plot because she wanted a larger role in town? Or because she really thought she could do a better job managing Mainely Needlepoint than Gram could?

I hoped Cindy and her kids had returned home. I didn't want her overhearing my conversation with her mother.

Katie answered the door quickly. "Good morning, Angie. Cindy's gone back to Blue Hill, if you were looking for her."

I shook my head. "No. I came to see you."

She opened the door wider and gestured that I should come in. I didn't have to ask what I'd interrupted. A pile of toys on one of the living-room chairs and a vacuum cleaner in the hall said Katie'd been cleaning up after her daughter and grandchildren had left.

She gestured toward the living room.

"So. Congratulations on your new job. Welcome to Mainely Needlepoint!" she said. She didn't act as though she resented my being the new director—the job that Lattimore had tried to wrangle for her.

"Thank you," I said. "I came to ask you about something."

"Yes?" Katie and I sat on chairs facing each other across a coffee table covered with Legos.

"I've been sorting through the files Jacques Lattimore gave my grandmother right before he died. Most of them are lists of customers and orders. But among the papers I found a series of e-mails—messages between you and Lattimore."

She sat back. "You must think I'm a horrible woman. I never dreamed he'd print those out. Has Charlotte seen them?"

"No. Just me."

"Thank goodness." Katie's voice was soft and hesitant. "I hoped he'd deleted those. I deleted my copies."

I didn't tell her that a good computer technician would still be able to find the messages, even if she'd pressed the delete key.

"Last fall, right before Thanksgiving, Jacques started contacting me directly about orders. He'd never done that before. At first I thought he was checking up on me, that maybe he was getting complaints from customers about my work. But he never said that. In fact, he kept praising my work. It made me very uncomfortable."

"Your notes back to him didn't sound that way."

"Good. You see, at first I thought he was interested in me. Personally. And let me assure you, I wasn't interested in him at all. I was interested in the orders he brought in. But I thought if I played along a little—after all, it was online, not in person—then maybe he'd get me more orders. Challenging designs. Ones that would be fun to work on."

I listened and watched her face. "Then his

messages got more personal, and, finally, he offered you a deal."

She nodded and leaned forward. "By the time he'd done that, I'd talked to Ob Winslow. Ob did a carving for my husband's office a few years back. He and my husband got to know each other pretty well. They had more than just a doctor–patient relationship. Ob and Anna, his wife, are our friends. In fact, Ob took up needlepoint because my husband recommended it. So when I realized what direction Jacques' notes were taking, and I panicked, I needed to talk with someone. I trusted Ob to be straight with me."

"And?"

"First I asked him if he was having any problems with Charlotte. And can you guess what he said?"

I shook my head.

"He asked me if I'd been talking with Jacques Lattimore."

"Really!" That I hadn't expected.

She nodded. "Turned out Lattimore had been telling him the same story he'd been telling me. He even told Ob to document every time he talked to Charlotte to prove she wasn't doing a good job. And that maybe Ob should replace her."

"The same line he'd given you."

"Exactly. So then Ob and I checked with Sarah. He'd contacted her, too. I don't know if he'd gotten in touch with Lauren or Dave. At that point we knew enough. Together, the three of us called Lattimore and told him to stop. That we were all happy with Charlotte, and this wasn't the way to change his contract. We told him he had to pay us the money he'd withheld."

"What did he say?"

"It wasn't good. By that time it was January. He easily owed us a full month's money, but he denied it. He denied everything he'd written in the e-mails. He said he'd pay us when he had the money, and not before—that we weren't to be trusted." Katie shook her head. "Can you believe that man? *We* couldn't be trusted! He hung up, and that was the end of it. People like Ob and Lauren were hurting. And you know what happened after that. A few more dollars came in after our call in January, and that was the end."

"Did you ever tell Gram what Lattimore tried to do?"

"No. And I don't think Ob or Sarah did, either. We didn't think it would make a difference. It wouldn't get our money, which we figured Jacques had already spent, and Charlotte would have been more upset than she already was."

"What do you think was really happening, Katie? Was Lattimore just looking for a better contract, as he said?"

"Ob and I've talked about that. We think Lattimore was in trouble. Most likely, as you've confirmed, he had a gambling problem. He probably collected the money when he delivered completed work in early November, but for some reason—addiction, habit, or chance—he took more than his share of the receipts and lost all of it at the casino. After that, the situation got worse. He'd be paid a little, and hoped he could win it all back by gambling."

"And, of course, that didn't work," I agreed. "So he tried to cover himself by dividing the group. Sorry to say, that makes sense."

"When your grandmother called last week and said you were bringing Jacques to her home, I was worried he'd pull out those old e-mails and make it look as though I'd been complaining about Charlotte or conspiring against her. Or bring Ob and Sarah into it. Luckily, although from what you've said he still had the e-mails, he didn't bring them up at the meeting." She hesitated. "Or he was poisoned before he had a chance."

"Did you see anyone add anything to the tea-pot? Or to his cup?"

She shook her head. "No. Honestly, I wasn't paying any attention to what people were eating or drinking. I didn't even have tea myself. I was crossing my fingers that Charlotte wouldn't find out that, even for a few days, I'd complained about her management of the business. I was furious with Jacques for what he'd done. And with myself for allowing myself to betray Charlotte, even briefly. I didn't kill him, Angie, but that man deserved to die. I'm just sorry he didn't come up with more of our money first. I'm guessing it's long gone."

I sat for a few minutes, trying to digest all Katie was saying. "I haven't been here, Katie, so I don't know exactly what Gram was doing or not doing. But as I read the e-mails, I thought you made good points. Since you've all entrusted me with Mainely Needlepoint now, I'm going to try to do what you suggested. As soon as we get the financial situation straightened out, I'm going to take some of our earnings and invest more in basic materials."

"Good," Katie said. "But maybe I shouldn't have complained. It wouldn't pay to order a great deal. We're not a needlework shop. And special supplies, like gold and silver thread, or beads or unusual colors, would still have to be ordered as they were needed. Keeping a few more backup canvases and basic flosses does make sense."

"I agree," I said. "And I'll try to ensure that the turnaround on orders is quick."

She nodded.

"But I'm new at this. Totally new. So if you have any other ideas you think would make it easier for those of you filling orders, or would save Mainely Needlepoint money, please let me know. I'll need all the help I can get to put the business back on track and keep it there."

"I'm glad you're taking over, Angie. We all are. The business needs a new start. I don't know why Charlotte decided to resign, but I'm excited about working with you."

"Thank you. I'm excited, too." I couldn't tell her why Gram had decided to back away from the business. That was Gram's secret to tell.

I headed toward home. I needed to destroy those incriminating e-mails. Katie was right. Gram didn't need to know what had happened last fall.

Two murders in one small town. My investigative skills weren't helping me. I hadn't made progress on either case today.

My mind was swirling with fragments of information. Vignettes from the past. Snapshots of the present. Hopes for the future. Nothing I'd learned seemed related to anything else.

And then, suddenly, as I walked through Haven Harbor's streets lined with newly green maple trees and dark pines, pieces of the puzzle started to come together.

If I was right, at least one person was in danger.

Getting home, I picked Gram's car keys up from the dish in the kitchen, where she always left them, and retrieved my gun from under the gloves in the hall sideboard. I might not be legal, but I'd be safe.

Then I drove to Dave Percy's house.

Chapter Thirty-seven

It was then that I began to look into the seams of your doctrine. I wanted only to pick at a single knot, but when I had got that undone, the whole thing raveled out. And then I understood that it was all machine-sewn.

—Henrik Ibsen (1828–1906),
Ghosts, Act 2 (1881)

I dropped the brass lobster knocker on Dave Percy's door. Hard. Several times.

He was buttoning his shirt when he finally answered.

"Angie! What are you doing here? I just got home from school."

"You have to tell me," I said, moving past him into his house. "Tell me about Lauren Decker. You're having an affair with her, right?"

He shook his head, as if to clear it. "What are you talking about? Where did you hear that?"

"It's true, isn't it? Dave, this is an emergency. I think Lauren murdered Lattimore, and I think she's going to kill Caleb."

"No! She wouldn't do that," he said.

"But you were having an affair."

"We weren't sleeping together, if that's what you mean. It started about six months ago. But it wasn't serious," he said. "I was lonely, and she needed someone to talk to. We've become . . . close friends, yes. But not lovers. You think she poisoned Lattimore? I can't believe that. And why do you think she'd poison Caleb?" Dave shook his head. "Lauren's been upset and depressed. But she's never sounded as though she was close to considering murder. Divorce, yes. Murder? Never."

"I understand Lauren's had problems with Caleb for years."

"I've only heard details in the past six months." Dave paused. "Caleb hasn't made it easy for her. He's troubled. She's tried to convince him to get help for his addictions, but he refuses to admit he has a problem."

"He hurts her sometimes, doesn't he?" I asked.

Dave nodded. "But she always excuses his behavior. Says she'd done something to deserve it."

"When her father died, he left Lauren his house and his camp, right?"

"He left her all he had," Dave confirmed. "Caleb wants her to put the property she inherited in both their names, but Lauren's holding out. That's one of the reasons their relationship has been . . . volatile . . . during the past few weeks."

"But if Caleb were gone, there'd be no questions. She'd have the property she inherited, and everything that's now in Caleb's name, too. She'd be independent."

"That's true, I guess. But I'd never thought of it that way."

"But it makes sense."

Dave slowly nodded.

"And you told her about water hemlock, right?"

The color in Dave's face vanished. "I warned her about it, the way I warned you. I warn dozens of people. I showed her my garden, of course, but it was winter, and there wasn't much to see. She *was* curious about poisonous plants that might be here in Maine. I told her water hemlock was the most dangerous. It might look like Queen Anne's lace, but the sap inside the stems was potent, especially in the spring. If someone ingested it, that would be fatal." His face changed as he realized what he'd said. "I warned her about it, the way I warn all my students. I never thought she'd . . . use . . . it."

"Did you know Lauren's family had a camp on a lake?" I asked.

"Sure. She said it was a peaceful place where you could hear loons at daybreak." His eyes widened slightly. "Water hemlock grows in freshwater swamps. Most lakes in Maine have swampy areas."

"Lauren and Caleb are there, at their camp, right now," I said quickly. "Do you know what lake the camp is on?"

He hesitated. "It's north of here. Northwest, I think."

I shifted my weight impatiently. "The name of the lake. I need to get there."

"I don't remember it." He shook his head. "But . . . wait. Once she showed me where it was on a map. Maybe I'd recognize the name."

"We don't have much time."

"I'm sorry. She only mentioned it once, months ago. She always called it 'our family camp.' "

I followed him into his kitchen. A large framed map of Maine hung on one of the walls. As I waited, he looked at it closely. My pulse raced. Caleb Decker wasn't my favorite resident of Haven Harbor, but I'd seen Jacques Lattimore suffer after he'd been poisoned. No one deserved to die that way.

"I'm sorry this is taking so long." Dave was peering carefully at the map. "I remember Lauren's saying it was south of Moosehead Lake. Just give me a few more minutes."

Caleb might not have a few minutes. Or maybe he was already dead. He and Lauren had been out of town since Saturday.

"Here it is!" He pointed at a spot on the map. "I remember now. Their place is on Fisher Lake." He turned to me. "I commented that it must have been named that because it was a good place to fish. And she'd said no, it was named after all the fisher cats in the area."

Fishers. A member of the weasel family. Not the largest animals in Maine, but one of the meanest.

If a cat or small dog had been out at night and was missing, chances are you blamed the fishers. And you'd be right. Fishers were one of the things the Maine tourist bureau didn't advertise. Their territories weren't far from many towns, and they were common in rural and forested areas. I looked at where Dave had pointed on the map. Prime fisher territory.

I pulled out my cell and entered *Fisher Lake.* My GPS said it would take about eighty minutes to get there. And then I'd have to find the right camp.

I headed for the door.

"I'm coming with you," said Dave, pulling his fleece jacket off a hook in his front hall. "Lauren trusts me. If we're not too late, maybe she'll listen to me."

I hesitated, but I wasn't stupid. I could probably use some help. And I didn't know the law enforcement people at Fisher Lake, and there wasn't time to reach Pete or Ethan to explain and ask them to find out.

As we drove, I filled Dave in on what I knew. He said very little.

But I was glad for the company. Lauren had picked a good listener for a friend.

Driving in Maine isn't complicated if you want to go north or south. Along the coast you can follow Route 1 from Kittery to Eastport. It'll be a long drive, but a scenic one, and you'll be in no danger of getting lost. If you want to go north from Kittery to New Brunswick, you follow the Maine Turnpike (also known as Interstate 95). Its last exit after Houlton is a border stop.

But if you want to drive from east to west, or east to northwest, you have a challenge. My GPS routed us as best it could, taking us on country roads that curved around hills and connected small towns. Roads built for oxen, and then for horses, and then for horses and wagons. Designed to connect farms and centers of small villages—not to draw straight lines or make fast time.

Finally we reached a sign that said, FISHER LAKE, TWO MILES. We stopped at a small general store a little farther along the road.

"The Greene place? That would be about three miles ahead, on Lake Road." The woman giving us the information also gave us a good look. "It'll be on your left side. Red mailbox, just past where the Clifford family used to live."

Dave and I glanced at each other. We could watch for a red mailbox. Neither of us knew the Cliffords, past or present.

We headed out again. I watched the mileage indicator. Dave watched for red mailboxes.

The woman at the store had been right. We'd driven about three miles when we saw the mailbox. I turned into a rough narrow road through a heavily wooded area. Mud season might have ended on Maine's coast, but here it was still in full force. As were frost heaves. I feared for the axles on Gram's old car as we jounced our way down the drive. I swerved around the largest holes, but the road was narrow. Not much swerving space.

Finally the driveway opened up on a turnaround. I parked and Dave got out. I tucked my gun into the back of my belt and joined him.

"Their truck isn't here," Dave noted. "And ours is the only car."

"Maybe there's another parking area?" I wondered. "But I don't see any connecting roads or drives." We were both speaking softly. We were far from civilization, but that didn't mean we were alone.

"One of them could have gone out for groceries. Or beer," Dave pointed out.

I nodded. "Let's find the camp."

We chose the path headed toward the lake. A crow overhead cawed a warning that humans were invading his territory, and two other crows answered in the distance. A murder of crows. Other than that, the woods were silent.

I stumbled once, then felt for my gun. It was still safely available.

The camp was small and fronted on the lake. Likely, it was a large room that served as kitchen, dining room, and living room on the first floor, and maybe two bedrooms. From the placement of the windows one bedroom was on the first floor, off the main room, and another bedroom was in the loft overhead. That one might have been Lauren's when she was a child.

I knocked on the door. No one answered. Then I turned the knob. It opened. Dave and I looked at each other, questioningly, but we went inside. Not all Mainers locked their doors, but that didn't mean they were inviting you in.

"Lauren? Caleb? Anyone home?"

No one answered.

We'd come looking for someone we thought was a killer . . . and her victim. The place smelled like a mixture of cat piss and rotten eggs. Maybe they weren't the best housekeepers. And any house closed all winter smelled until it was aired out. I checked closets and cabinets. When I came down from the loft, Dave was still standing in the kitchen area.

"Angie, we need to get out of here," he said much too calmly. "Now."

"There's no one here," I said. "I'm not sure what to do next."

"I do," he said. "As soon as we get somewhere my cell phone works, I'm calling the local police." He shoved my back a little, herding me toward the door we'd come in. "Don't ask. Move."

When we were outdoors again, and back up the hill to where we'd parked the car, Dave took out his cell phone. "I don't know where Lauren or

Caleb are, but we have to tell the police what we found."

"What?" I asked, trying to think of where we should go next to find Lauren.

He was dialing. "911? I have an emergency. I've found a meth lab in a camp on Fisher Lake."

Chapter Thirty-eight

Give me o Lord thy early Grace
To Guide me in the paths of life
And fit me for celestial scenes
Where Peace and Joy forever reign.
—Stitched by Jane Elizabeth Bunting,
aged seven, in 1818

"How did you know?" I asked as we waited for the police to arrive. "How did you know it was a meth lab? And why did you wait until we were out here to tell me?"

"I may teach biology, but I know a little about chemistry," Dave answered. "And as soon as I figured out what they'd used that place for, I knew we had to get out of there. Meth is dangerous, even if you're just breathing it. Not to speak of the fact that it can explode. I wasn't hiding it from you. I was getting both of us as far away as possible, as fast as possible."

I shivered. And not from the cold. "It must be Caleb's doing. I don't think Lauren would have gotten involved with meth."

Dave nodded. "Caleb may have been lending the place to friends. Lauren's told me about some of them. Not exactly upright citizens."

We didn't have to wait long, by Maine

wilderness 911 standards. Ten minutes later a car pulled in and parked next to Gram's.

"You called about a possible meth lab?"

I stared. It was the same woman we'd asked for directions—the one who'd been behind the counter at the country store.

"We're the ones. The camp's down that path." Dave pointed. "The place stinks of it. There's no one there now, unless they've come by boat."

"I didn't think so," said the woman. "Sergeant Marge Windham. Fisher Lake's in my territory. We've had a problem with people breaking into places closed for the winter. Used to be youngsters broke in to have sex, or drink, or steal valuables. Recently people have been using the places for meth labs."

"Aren't you going to go down to see?" Dave asked.

"Nope. I've called in the experts. You won't catch me hanging out somewhere used to manufacture meth. I haven't got a suicide wish."

"You said you didn't think anyone was in the camp? How did you know?"

"Lauren and Caleb stopped at the store to pick up cigarettes and beer about an hour before you two were there. Lauren said it was too cold in the camp, and they couldn't light a fire." Sergeant Windham shook her head. "At the time I figured she meant they didn't have any wood for the fireplace or didn't have matches. But now I suspect they couldn't light the fire because if they did, the whole dang place might blow up on them."

"Why didn't you tell us they were gone when we asked for directions?" I asked.

"You didn't ask," answered Sergeant Windham.

For a moment I'd forgotten I was back in Maine. "Did Lauren and Caleb both seem okay?"

She shrugged. "If 'okay' includes arguing and practically spitting at each other, then, yeah, they were fine. Couldn't even agree on what brand of cigarette to buy."

"We need to find them," I told her. "The camp's open. Could we leave you our reach information and get going? We're two hours behind them already." I looked at Dave. "They probably headed back home."

"Haven Harbor, right?" asked Sergeant Windham. I nodded.

"You folks live there, too?"

"Yes," said Dave.

"Didn't think I'd seen either of you in these parts before." She looked us over, as if deciding whether we were worth paying heed to. "All right. Names, addresses, phone numbers. And any identification that proves you are who you say you are."

We dug out our licenses. Dave's, she didn't question. Mine, she took a second look at. "Says here you live in Mesa, Arizona, and you're Angela Curtis."

"I just moved back to Maine."

"When would that have been? That you moved to Maine?"

"About two weeks ago. But I grew up here."

"You'll need to get a new license, you know," she said, writing down the information about my current one. "State says you have to turn in your Arizona license and get a Maine one within thirty days of changing your residence."

"I will." I felt as though my hand had been slapped.

"And, welcome back to Vacationland."

Chapter Thirty-nine

[Rose Tremaine] . . . was intently busy with an elaborate slipper, which she was embroidering, while by her side a high, open basket glowed with the vivid tints of her many-colored wools.

—"Mademoiselle," by D. R. Castleton,
Harper's Monthly Magazine,
February 1862

My biggest immediate worry was that we'd run into the backup team Sergeant Windham had called and have to back down that narrow drive. Luckily, we got out before anyone else arrived. I hoped the sergeant had her gun with her, in case some of Caleb's buddies showed up.

And I was sure glad she hadn't questioned me more closely. Or seen what was under my jacket. If she'd found I was carrying without a Maine permit *and* had an out-of-state driver's license, I suspected I'd be staying in Fisher Lake for a while. Or at least overnight.

Thankfully, Dave hadn't noticed I was armed.

We headed out of Fisher Lake and reversed our drive to get back to Haven Harbor.

"If Lauren's planning to poison Caleb, I'm surprised she didn't do it at the lake. No one might have checked there for weeks. But Lauren must have known about the meth. Maybe she didn't want a body to be found there," I thought out loud. How long had the Greenes owned that place? Could Joe have taken Mama there? It might have been her last stop before the freezer in Union. Someone could scream for hours and no one up there would hear them, especially at this time of year. Sounds carried over water, but I suspected most residents of Fisher Lake were seasonal visitors.

"What's our plan?" Dave asked. "We have a little time to think. I don't like the idea of just barging in on them and asking Lauren whether she's poisoned her husband."

I hadn't figured that part out myself. I thought a few minutes. "I have a reason to visit Lauren. I still have her needlework money. She wasn't home the other day when I delivered it to every-one else."

"That's a start, then," said Dave.

"Right. One step at a time."

The light was fading over the harbor by the time we got back and the pewter gray sky was streaked with pink and orange. I pulled the car up in front of the Deckers' home. Their pickup was in the drive.

"Okay. Here we go."

Dave rang the doorbell. Lauren came to the door a few minutes later. Seeing us, she came out to the porch, closing the door behind her. Not an inviting gesture.

She folded her arms over her chest and looked from one of us to the other. "So? Why are you here?" She was tapping one of her feet, and her words tumbled out on top of each other. "Why are you both here? Together? What do you want?"

"You were anxious to get your share of the needlepoint money," I said. "I brought it."

"Good." Lauren held out her hand.

"Why don't we come inside? Talk a little." I held the envelope out, but I didn't hand it to her.

"We don't need to talk. Give me my money."

"Lauren, it's all right. You can trust us." Dave's voice was calm and reassuring, like he might have been talking her down off a bridge. I was glad he was with me.

"So, what are you doing with her?" she asked him.

"Visiting you. That's all. We've been looking for you. We even drove all the way up to your camp, thinking you were there."

Lauren grew pale. "You went to Fisher Lake?"

"We just got back," I said. I wasn't entirely comfortable with sharing that information with Lauren, but Dave knew her better than I did. I trusted him to say the right thing.

"Did you go inside the camp?"

"We did," said Dave.

"Shoot," she said. "Why'd you have to go and do that?"

"We were worried about you," Dave continued, his voice steady. "Lauren, I know you. What was in that camp had nothing to do with you. It was Caleb's doing, am I right?"

She nodded slowly. "He said it was a way we could make some money. No one would ever know." She turned to me. "When a man wants to do something, you can't just say 'no' and have him stop. He wouldn't listen to me. I told him it was against the law, and it was dangerous. I didn't want him blowing up my family's camp."

"Of course, you didn't," I said. "No one would want that. Or want to be married to someone who would."

"Exactly," Lauren said. "You do understand." She smiled, seeming to relax a little. But she didn't move.

"Where's Caleb now?" I asked. "In the house?"

She nodded.

"Can we see him?"

"This isn't a good time," she said, glancing behind her at the closed door. "Caleb's resting." She looked from Dave to me and then back again. "He gets awful angry if someone wakes him when he's taking a nap."

Dave and I exchanged glances. We had to get inside.

I took a risk. "Did he have a drink before he fell

asleep, Lauren? We stopped for directions up in Fisher Lake, and a woman at the store there said you'd been by to get beer."

"She had no right to tell you that," said Lauren. "That was private business. I'm over twenty-one. I'm allowed to buy beer."

"You are," said Dave. "But, Lauren, you don't drink beer. You always told me beer was too bitter for you. You drink wine, instead."

"Maybe I've changed," she said defiantly. "Or maybe the beer wasn't for me. You don't know as much as you think you do, Dave Percy, even if you do have those college degrees."

"So you gave Caleb the beer," I said.

She nodded. "He's sleeping now. He always gets sleepy after he drinks beer."

"Lauren, remember when we talked about water hemlock? The pretty weed that grows in swampy water?" Dave asked quietly.

Her eyes opened wide and she stared past us.

"Did you put any of the hemlock sap in Caleb's beer?" Dave was insistent. "Tell me."

"Why would you even ask such a thing?" she demanded.

"Because Caleb was messing up your life. You and I've talked about that lots of times."

"That doesn't mean I'd poison him."

Then Dave gambled. "But you poisoned Jacques Lattimore."

316

Lauren didn't blink. "I didn't know if that hemlock you told me about would work. I put a little in that man's tea. Just to see what would happen." She turned to me. "It was so easy. I was experimenting. I didn't know he'd die."

Dave took a deep breath. "Lauren, unless you show us Caleb's alive and well, I'm going to call an ambulance. I think he's inside, and that you put some of that hemlock in his beer. If I'm right, Caleb needs to go to the hospital right now. Maybe they can still help him."

Lauren's arms went limp. "Go ahead and call. Someone would have, anyway. But I don't think they can help him. I gave him a lot more than I gave that Lattimore."

Dave stayed out on the porch and called while I followed Lauren inside. Caleb was on the floor of the living room, as though he'd fallen off the old blue flowered couch I remembered from my Brownie days. A can of beer lay on the table next to him.

Lauren was right. No one could help him. Caleb was dead.

I didn't say anything. I looked from Lauren to Caleb and back again.

"You don't understand. He's been rotten to me. You don't know what that's like."

"I do, actually," I told her.

"And I'm in trouble, anyway, so you might as well know about your mother."

Lauren sat down on a love seat only a few feet from Caleb's body.

I sat next to her. "What about my mother?" I reached up and touched my angel. The police and ambulance would arrive any minute. Whatever Lauren had to say, I wanted her to say it now.

And she did.

Chapter Forty

Behold our days how fast they spend
How vain they are how soon they end.
> —Words on a sampler,
> "wrought by Rebekah Peabody,"
> age twelve, Bridgton, Maine, 1810

Lauren told me a story.

"That Sunday afternoon I was ten years old and bored. The minister's sermon had been long, dinner had been ham when I'd wanted chicken, and I was tired of playing with my dolls. Mom was having trouble with the pattern of the sweater she was knitting. 'Go and play. Find something to do,' she'd said. 'Go bother your father.'

"So I went looking for him.

"I didn't see Dad most days. He left our home early every morning, before Mom or I were awake, and went to the bakery to cook the bread and cookies and pies and cakes he sold during the day. While I was in school, Mom would join him behind the counter. After school she'd meet me at home. By the time Dad got home, he was tired and grumpy. Mom would say, 'Don't bother your father. He's had a hard day.'

"But sometimes, very early in the morning, before he went into the bakery, he'd come into my bedroom. Sometimes he just looked at me. But sometimes he pulled down the covers and touched me. Touched my chest. And other places. It was scary, but exciting, too. I always pretended to be asleep, and Dad never said a word. When I was sure it wasn't a dream, I thought of it as our secret. I never told anyone.

"That Sunday I looked for him, and I decided he'd gone to the bakery. Often on Sunday afternoons he worked on bills and accounts in his office there.

"So I went to find him. I knew Mom wouldn't have let me go if I'd asked, so I didn't tell her. I just left.

"I felt very brave, crossing streets by myself, and saying hello to grown-ups I knew who were out walking. I was a little scared Dad would be angry I'd come all the way alone, but then I remembered his early-morning visits to my bedroom and somehow knew he wouldn't tell on me.

"The front door of the bakery was closed and locked. No lights were on inside. That didn't surprise me. I knew the bakery was closed on Sunday. I went through the narrow alley, where Dad always parked his white van—the one with the words 'Greene's Bakery' and a picture of a big loaf of bread. He kept that van sparkling. The back door to the bakery led to the kitchen, and to Dad's office, where I figured he was working.

"The heavy metal security door was unlocked. I

decided to surprise him, so I opened it slowly and slipped inside. The ceiling lights were on, and it smelled the way it always did—of yeast and vanilla and baking bread.

"I tiptoed to the door leading to Dad's office. I tried to keep my shoes from making any noise on the hard linoleum floor. I planned to jump out and yell, 'Surprise!'

"But when I got near the door, I heard voices.

"I peeked around the door frame. Your mom was there. She was talking. Talking real fast. She sounded mad. I didn't understand all the words, because she was too far away. But I heard her tell my dad to stay away from you and your friends. She said he was sick, and she'd tell the police if he didn't stop. Then Dad moved closer to her, and she pushed him away, hard. He pushed her back, against the wall.

"I got scared. I didn't want her to call the police about my dad. So I ran into the store and got the gun Dad kept there. It was always in the same place, in the second drawer in back of the counter. I wasn't allowed to touch it, but Dad always said it was there in case of an emergency, and this was an emergency.

"By the time I got back to the office door, your mom was away from the wall. She was backing toward the door. Toward me. My dad was following her, shouting bad names and saying she wasn't fit to be a mother. If she went to the police, he was going to tell them so. Then they'd take you away and give you to a decent family.

"I wanted to help. I wanted them to stop. I held the gun out and I fired." Lauren looked down. "Your mom fell toward my dad. There was blood all over him and her, and even on the ceiling."

"What happened then?" I asked. I heard sirens outside. Lauren didn't seem to notice them.

"It all happened so fast. I don't remember it all. I started crying, and Dad put your mom down on the floor. He took the gun away from me. He kept saying, 'This didn't happen. It didn't happen.'

"He made me promise not to tell anyone. Not even Mom. Not you. He stood there, with your mother's blood dripping down his face, telling me I should go home. 'And don't tell your mother you were here. I'll take care of it. Just promise never to tell anyone.'

"And I didn't, until now. I was too scared. When I got home, Mom was still knitting. She told me to go read a book or color, and she'd heat up some soup in a while. And I went and read *Little Women* and tried to forget what had happened.

"Dad never mentioned it again. Neither did I. After a while I wondered whether it had actually happened, although I knew your mom had disappeared. People said nasty things about her then, and I thought maybe it was all right, what I'd done. I'd hurt a bad person. But most of the time I didn't think about it. I wanted my memories of that afternoon to go away.

"But they didn't. And Dad didn't come into my room again, ever. So I knew then I'd done something really bad. Because I knew he didn't love me anymore."

As though on cue Pete Lambert and the local ambulance squad burst in.

I pointed to Caleb's body.

And Lauren started crying. "Caleb was a bad person. He was."

Chapter Forty-one

The time draws near that I must go.
And bid adieu to things below.
And if these lines you chance to see
When I am dead remember me.
> —Words on a sampler
> "wrought by Mary Bradbury," age thirteen,
> Biddeford, Maine, 1806

By midmorning all the needlepointers had gathered. Except Lauren, of course. Even Dave Percy had taken the day off. It was the first time I'd convened the group, and I was a little nervous, but Gram wasn't letting me off the hook.

"Our new director has something to tell us," she said, turning the meeting over to me. She sat down and Juno jumped into her lap and started purring.

"I'm sure you've all noticed Lauren Decker isn't with us this morning," I said. Several people nodded. "I wanted you to hear the news from me before you heard it on the street, or even on the TV. Lauren's been arrested."

Ruth Hopkins gasped.

"For what?" Sarah asked.

"For murdering her husband, Caleb. And poisoning Jacques Lattimore and," I answered, pausing as Dave Percy sat a little farther back in his chair, "for killing my mother."

The room was silent.

"But why?" asked Sarah.

"And how?" added Ob. "I don't know about Caleb or about your mother. But we were all right here that afternoon with Jacques. We were together. How could we not know?"

I swallowed. "Joe Greene wasn't the friendly baker and neighbor most people here thought. He was a sexual predator. He particularly liked young girls. Really young girls. Ones who hadn't reached puberty yet."

Ruth put her hand over her mouth for a moment and then said, "And no one knew?"

I shook my head. This wasn't easy. "I don't know how many victims he had. But I was one. Lauren was one, too."

"Her own father?" asked Sarah, almost whispering. "And she didn't tell anyone?"

"No, but I did. I told my mother." I paused. "Mama confronted Joe Greene in his office at the bakery. She threatened to tell the police. They argued. Lauren was ten, then, and she overheard them. She heard her father being threatened. She was scared, and she panicked. So she got the gun she knew he kept behind the counter in the bakery, and she pulled the trigger." I paused. "I don't know exactly what happened then. But my mother was dead. Joe told Lauren to go home. To forget what had happened. To never tell anyone what she'd seen."

"So to hide what she'd done, Joe must have taken your mother's body and hidden it in that freezer," Ob said slowly. "It's ironic that Lauren was the one who found it there."

I nodded. "And Lauren says he never molested her again. He never touched me, either, although I avoided the bakery as much as I could for the rest of the time I lived in Haven Harbor."

"So your mother—your daughter, Charlotte—was brave enough to confront him," said Katie.

Gram shook her head. "Brave enough. Or stupid enough. Maybe if she'd gone directly to the police, she'd still be alive."

"But would the police have listened to one child's story?" I said. "Mama wasn't known to have the highest moral standards in town. She might have thought no one would believe her, that she could solve the problem herself." I glanced up at the picture of Mama and me on the mantel. "She did what she thought was right. How could she have guessed it would turn out the way it did?"

"What about Lattimore? I know we were all furious with him for gambling away money that should have come to us. But what made Lauren go further?" asked Katie Titicomb. "We've all been angry with people in our lives at times, but we didn't kill them."

"I've thought a lot about that," I said. "Anger's the other side of depression. Lauren had lost her mother. Her daughter had died. She and Caleb were struggling financially, and Caleb's way of dealing with that was to drink, use drugs, and be abusive. He even ran a meth lab out of what had been Lauren's family's camp. Since Lauren was close at hand, she got the brunt of his anger and frustration. And then last winter, because of Lattimore, they lost more of their income. That hit hard. And while they were still dealing with that, Lauren's father died."

I had a rapt audience. Dave nodded at me, confirming.

"At first the death of her father offered Lauren and Caleb some relief. They were able to sell their trailer and move into the house where Lauren had grown up. They had a little money. But for Lauren, moving into her childhood home brought back memories of what had happened to her as a child. She didn't tell anyone, but in her mind she relived the abuse she'd suffered. The great secret she'd kept. And you all know Caleb. The way he treated her convinced Lauren she was always fated to be a victim. She needed to feel in control of her life. And then she met a man who seemed to value her as a person, as a woman. She was relieved and excited. But, of course, that was one more part of her life she had to hide."

Sarah shook her head. "Seems to me having an affair would only complicate her life."

"It did. And she didn't go as far as having an affair, although I suspect she thought about it. But the relationship added excitement to the life she felt was hopelessly dreary and fated to remain so. And then she opened that freezer. She hadn't known my mother was in it. She'd almost, but not quite, forgotten that Sunday in May, nineteen years ago. She called the police, never thinking they'd be able to connect her to the killing. The body was in her father's freezer. People would assume he'd put it there." I paused. "Which, of course, he did. And, in a way, it made her a heroine. She was interviewed on television and radio and by the press, as well as by the police."

"That's true," said Ruth. "The media coverage was sympathetic to her. The innocent daughter who didn't know what her father had done, and yet he'd left it to her to clean up his mess."

I nodded. "All that attention focused on Lauren made Caleb even angrier. And Lauren, perhaps for the first time in years, felt empowered. Although it was serendipitous, nineteen years before she'd solved one problem—her father's abuse—by killing someone. I think she decided to do it again."

"She decided to kill Lattimore?" said Ob, who'd been quiet up until then. "Killing him wouldn't get her money back."

"No," I agreed. "But she didn't plan to kill Lattimore. She planned to kill Caleb. With him gone, she'd be free to start again. She'd own a house and a camp. She'd have a little money. Best of all, she wouldn't be Caleb's victim any longer. And she'd still have that relationship she had hopes for. And then her friend, without knowing it, provided her with the means to get rid of her husband."

"I didn't give her poison—or anything else that would help her kill Caleb!" Dave looked beseechingly around the room. "Yes, I'm the one Lauren was spending time with. I didn't think it was serious. I felt sorry for her." He turned to me. "I had no idea she was planning to kill Caleb. Or anyone else! I would never have helped her do that!"

"I'm sure you never thought she'd try to kill anyone. But you told her about poisons. You showed her your garden. She was interested, so you told her what you told your students. One of the plants you told her about was water hemlock."

"I warned her about dangerous plants. I didn't tell her how to kill people with them!" He looked around the room. "Especially not water hemlock! She'd told me her family's camp was on a lake, and there was swampy land nearby. I figured it was the right environment for water hemlock. I remember telling her it looked like Queen Anne's lace, but she should be careful not to pick it. Or dig it up, for that matter. The roots are its most poisonous part."

"And she found it. Maybe she did her own research, after you'd warned her. She made a solution from the sap in the roots. She filled one of the old pill bottles she'd cleaned out of her parents' house, and she waited for a good time. A time she could poison her husband."

"She was carrying a bottle of poison around with her?" Sarah asked incredulously.

I nodded. "She didn't want Caleb to find it until she was ready. So she hid it in her purse. And when you were all meeting with Lattimore, she decided to test it. See if it would make him sick. So when you were all focused on what Lattimore had done, and what you were going to do next, Lauren poured a little of the solution into his teacup." I sat back. "You all know what happened then."

Dave kept shaking his head. "I never, never thought she'd kill anyone. *Never.*"

"I believe you," said Ruth, patting Dave's hand. "Life works out in strange ways, doesn't it?"

"In any case, that's what happened. Caleb's dead and Lauren's in jail, but Mainely Needlepoint will go on. Between Gram and me we've computerized all the files. Next I'm going to contact all of our former customers to ask them what we can do for them. Those of you who still have jobs out-standing, make sure you finish them up, because I'm hoping to have new work for us soon."

Smiles around the room.

"I'm also going to design a brochure advertising our services that we can leave with designers and decorators and gift shops, and hand out with our products. On it we're going to include two new services. There are going to be lessons in needle-point, which Gram has agreed to schedule, and identification, conservation, and preservation of old textiles, especially embroideries of various sorts. Sarah's going to head up that effort. But we'll all have the opportunity to help out with the classes, if they become as popular as I hope, and to learn about the needlework our ancestors did, here in Maine and, I hope, in other places." I looked around the room. "Thank you all for trusting me. For giving me a purpose. And a reason for staying in Haven Harbor." I paused. "Any questions?"

"Only one," said Sarah. "Why don't you offer us some tea?"

Later that afternoon, after everyone had left, I found a package on our porch wrapped in pink floral gift paper. An envelope with my name on it was attached.

"Do you know what this is, Gram?" I asked as I brought it into the living room, where we'd been sitting, enjoying a little wine. We had a lot to think about and talk over: what had happened during the last week, the future of the business, Gram's wedding.

"I have no idea," she answered. "What does the note say?"

I opened the envelope. Inside was a piece of creamy thick stationery:

Dear Angie,

This, I think, was meant to be for you. Unlike the twig, you struggled with your past, and grew straight and tall. I'm proud to know you, and look forward to working with you. I've done the best I can with this, but, together, I hope we'll be able to discover and conserve many other pieces of the past.

Your fellow Needlepointer,
Sarah Byrne

Inside the package was the small piece of needlework Sarah had shown Gram and me a week ago, cleaned and lined and framed.

I read the verse again: *Just as the twig is bent, the tree's inclined.* Perhaps. But now I knew Mama hadn't left me. She'd tried to save me. And a twig could also grow toward the sun.

Acknowledgments

With thanks to everyone who contributed, knowingly or unknowingly, to the writing of *Twisted Threads:*

John Talbot and John Scognamiglio and Barbara Ross, who suggested I write a book centered on needlepoint. Robin Cook and Stephanie Finnegan, for their close reading and copyedits and keeping all the details of Haven Harbor life straight.

Mary Anne Tomlinson Sullivan, who suggested the poison my killer used. The real Sarah Byrne, a charming young woman who still lives in Australia, and who won a Bouchercon auction to name a character in Haven Harbor. Elayne Star, Kennebunk, Maine, antique dealer extraordinaire, who shared her collection of Ouija boards with me. Kathy Lynn and Sandy Emerson for their knowledge of the world of crime fighting in Maine.

My fellow bloggers at www.MaineCrime Writers.com, past and present, for their advice, support and enthusiasm: Kate Flora, Kathy Lynn Emerson, Barbara Ross, Dorothy Cannell, John Clark, Paul Doiron, Gerry Boyle, Vicki Doudura, Sarah Graves, James Hayman, Julia Spencer-Fleming, Susan Vaughan, Al Lamonda, and Jayne Hitchcock.

Pamela Parmal and Meredith Montague of the Boston Museum of Fine Art's Textile and Fashion Arts division, who spent time with me explaining conservation concerns related to antique needle-point. Janet Palen, owner of Stitcher's Corner in Wiscasset, Maine, who introduced me to needle-point. And Barbara Hepburn, president of the Maine Chapter of the Embroiderers Guild of America, for correcting my errors.

Any remaining mistakes, in any area, are solely my responsibility.

And, as always, to my husband, Bob Thomas, for listening, loving, and giving me time and space to live in my fictional worlds.

Center Point Large Print
600 Brooks Road / PO Box 1
Thorndike, ME 04986-0001 USA

(207) 568-3717

US & Canada:
1 800 929-9108
www.centerpointlargeprint.com